Things Get Funnier

Okwudiri Gabriel Job

*For being the most precious person in my life, and for always saying to me each time **'things get funnier'** in my life: I gave birth to greatness, I dedicate this novel to Mercy Job.*

Things Get Funnier

Text copyright © 2025 **Okwudiri Gabriel Job**

Edited by Lisa Diane Kastner

Published in North America, Australia, and Europe by RIZE.
Visit Running Wild Press at www.runningwildpublishing.com/rize,
Educators, librarians, book clubs (as well as the eternally curious),
go to www.runningwildpublishing.com/rize.

Paperback ISBN: 978-1-963869-25-5

CONTENTS

CHAPTER ONE
A Pinch-sting Affliction..7

CHAPTER TWO
Manna in Mama's House 23

CHAPTER THREE
Pickings from 'Froglings'...33

CHAPTER FOUR
As It Was In Baruru 45

CHAPTER FIVE
The Strayed Dog Is Traced 53

CHAPTER SIX
Leaving for Merogwu..61

CHAPTER SEVEN
The Waylay...65

CHAPTER EIGHT
Nancy's Pregnancy...69

CHAPTER NINE
A Triplet 81

CHAPTER TEN
Igwe Dimanochie Is Dead..89

CHAPTER ELEVEN
Nancy's Dowry Paid 97

CHAPTER TWELVE
The Run Man Now a Yeoman..113

CHAPTER THIRTEEN
Fun Turns Folly..*125*

CHAPTER FOURTEEN
A Series of Silly Crises..*135*

CHAPTER FIFTEEN
Different Waters in One Pumpkin...................................*145*

CHAPTER SIXTEEN
A Verdict of Deficits...*155*

CHAPTER SEVENTEEN
A Day of Fest and Fate...*167*

CHAPTER EIGHTEEN
The Conspiracy; Returning to Baruru............................*177*

CHAPTER NINETEEN
Coup De Grace..*191*

CHAPTER ONE

A Pinch-sting Affliction

W henever a dog begins to bark at its owner, it tells us that he has misplaced its bone. But what bone has a dog got other than the very one its owner gave it? So the man is both owner of the dog and bone. Put differently, the dog and bone both belong to the man.

Mazi Ikenga had just lost his appeal for Igwe Dimanochie to overturn a sentence handed him by Igwe's legal advisory committee, which ruled that he should neither cultivate nor harvest from his many farmlands for twelve planting seasons.

What was his offence?

He leased out a portion of his land to a stranger, a non-indigene from Alaqur, Boreal Gnishere. In Nsogbubaruru Kingdom, it was forbidden for anyone to lease out land, or sell a property, to Alaquri bonafides, who were stereotyped dominion-crazy. They were avoided because they easily dominated and outgrew natives of host communities when they migrated and settled among

But he didn't purposely do that. He didn't. He knew not that Ndukuba was a Boreal Gnisherean, so he leased out his land to him. Ndukuba bore a typical Orient Gnisherean name, had no birth marks or speckles, and he spoke Ajum dialect fluently. Insight only made Ikenga to think that Uba was from Mununu people, who were well welcomed in Baruru. And the people of Baruru weren't going to forgive him. Not after they somehow survived what was globally acknowledged as the scariest internecine war of all time, an apocalypse-like inter-kingdom war, which greatly de-peopled Nsogbubaruru kingdom, which was one of the boles of Orient Gnishere, commerce-wise. They weren't going to take it easy with a matter as sensitive as this.

So, when Ojemba saw Ndukuba on Ikenga's land twice, he suspected him, because Ikenga had neither son nor slave. And although Uba tried so much to act natively, his air and gesture gave him away. Alaquri people were known for smarmy greetings and readiness to give help. Ojemba began investigations forthwith. He, once more, confirmed that the land in question actually belonged to Ikenga, and that he wasn't the one who put up a shelter on it. He continued to collect intelligence on the situation and it yielded a great result the day he met Ndukuba and his brothers at a local restaurant. Uba had a felt hat on his head. One of his brothers was holding about five bidets, while another had a sheathed dagger on his waist. They had been speaking pure Ajum ever since they arrived in Baruru. But that day, Uba's tongue slipped and he spoke their native language. Although he said in a low tone, Ojemba heard it and knew what it meant. He was familiar with almost all the tongues spoken across Super Gnishere, having travelled to all parts of it, doing business. His real name was Ndimele. It was for his avid business adventures, which translated into chrematistic fortune that fetched him the nick-name Ojembaenweilo, meaning that a traveler had no enmity. He made friends everywhere he went, and they gave him their daughters liberally as wives. At only 27, he had eleven wives already and his harem increased by 1.5 odalisques every two years.

One could say that it was his first wife's terrible attitude that made him start seeking love more. A marriage of happenstance, it never showed any promise or future up to its cotton year. Obuteaku was imposed on Ojemba by her visceral parents when he accidentally hit her with a wheelbarrow. She feigned a broken waist and, dowry or none, her parents told him to take her home for treatment. A year later, they had a daughter together. That was when she agreed the waist problem had stopped. Obuteaku chose to lack peace on purpose, and she ensured there were some storms in her husband's cup of water. She was the most abrasive woman on earth then, and she had the harshest of hearts across Sahara Desert. In fact, her heart was an orchard of pepper, ginger, and garlic. Her air was repulsive and her countenance dismissive. She was simply an implacable, impossible woman.

When Ojemba confirmed that "a harsh-hearted woman will

never be a sweetheart," according to his late father, when he saw her beyond redemptive condition, he took in another wife. This happened the day Obuteaku broke the head of their daughter with a wooden spatula, for accidentally stamping on her. "You broke your own daughter's head!" her mother-in-law petitioned. "Where has *obinwa* gone...? Mothers of these days, the only thing they know is just to get pregnant. But whether they give birth or not, whether the child survives or not is none of their business." She just couldn't come to terms with what pain or offence there was in a child stamping her own mother with a harmless, soft foot.

"You and who are mothers of these days?" the harridan retorted. "Let the child not survive now. That one doesn't concern me. Do I still carry her in the womb?" That same day, Ojemba's mother went to her village and returned with a second wife for her son. The people of Baruru believed that the best way to punish a badly behaved wife was to hand her a matrimonial opposition. "I'm your mother, in whose womb you slept, and on whose laps you sat," his mother had said. "I know what is good for you, and I have done just that."

However, until a man paid a woman's lobola, she wouldn't be recognized as his wife, in Baruru. So, Ojemba, seeing his mother's will, went and did the needful on the lady's head. That was how his polygamy started. Every part of Gnishere he went to, he found a new love for himself. One of them was Titi from Alaqur. Therefore, when he heard that language at the bar, which Uba had spoken in respect to the land Mazi Ikenga rented him, he readily reconciled it with its variant, which Titi, his wife, spoke each time he bought her jewelries. The words meant: "With what you've given me, I shall settle down well and dominate deeply." And while Titi hoped to have dominion over the other wives of Ojemba, Ndukuba and his brothers hoped to dominate Baruru denizens for Boreal Gnishere.

"*Na* them oo ...!" Ojemba had said. "*Na* them be this." The unease with which he turned when he heard those words made Uba to suspect that their mission might have been uncovered. And they were certainly on a mission, a subdue-and-rule mission of century-long initiation and brooding, and with insidious stratagem of One United Gnishere. Over the decades, Orient Gnishere was known for one agricultural produce of commercial value, palm fruits. So, when the Borealers learnt that palm oil was soon to become a product of international export, they began to plan a maneuver and monopoly of oil palm plantation and palm oil production, and sales. This was during a regional overspill in 1982. The best way, they thought, they could drive this idée fixe was to send and establish their children across Nsogbubaruru, the capital borough of the Orient Kingdom. That was Ndukuba's mission. He was adequately sponsored and well cared for.

Ojemba went to Igwe Dimanochie and told him everything. Dimanochie was alarmed. After their tête-á-tête, Igwe wrote to High Chief Utarandu, chairman of a local committee which oversaw internal land disputes. Utarandu was called thane of Baruru because of the vast area of land allotted to him on a basis of permanence by Igwe Dimanochie's predecessor. He fought injustice with his wealth. This got him love, and he continued to assist indigent indigenes greatly. A toff, he co-owned a multinational clothing company with one Ferd Gerusht from Oslo. In spite of his class and status, he was humble to the point of serving in Igwe's cabinet. He was based abroad but came home once or twice a year to do charity for people of restrained resourcefulness, who were politely called "the less privileged". However, a few people were against his cabinet position. They said it was improper for him to head a local department from an international base. They called it greed. Others called it craze. Yet, others called it zeal.

Utarandu was going to come home at an unusual time in the year, because the letter sent him had a tone of emergency and a clause of danger. His every resource was needed. The Borealers weren't a snake one could kill with a blunt machete. They were ferocious cutthroats. Following the ensued conclave between Igwe Dimanochie and High Chief Utarandu and, of course, other key figures in the kingdom, they unanimously decided to deport Uba and every other Borealer. Only three of them initially came, but in less than three weeks, they were over a hundred in Baruru.

When Ojemba divulged everything to his Alaquri wife, she forewarned her brothers to mobilize themselves and resist any such eviction move. The same Ojemba who reported the Borealers to Igwe, went and told Uba and his brothers to go report Nsogbubaruru to the central government, which represented the Super- Kingdom. And a Borealer was central governor then. "He will call Orient Gnishere to order, and if they don't shelve this plot, he will sanction them greatly..." Ojemba had suggested to Uba and his brothers. They knew he had a strong point because Gnishere Charter of Co-existence authorized every Gnisherean to settle and live in any part of the Super Kingdom and to enjoy any sort of association, trade, and religion. But the Charter wasn't really for everybody, because people from Austral Gnishere were conditioned on how to live, when they went to settle in other parts of the domain.

Baruru preemptively withdrew the eviction order, and Uba and his brothers stayed on. But when the three years rent of Ikenga's land expired, the legal advisory committee, which had taken over the land pending the twelve year confiscation period, refused to renew it. Therefore, the Borealers took an inevitable natural exodus. Ojemba's complicity was exposed when he refused to refund the money he took from Uba and his brothers to fight along with them. People wondered how it was possible that same man who once declared: "We shall kill them and nothing will happen" could take bribes from the same people to be killed. This made the people of Baruru to see Ojemba as a proven protean fellow, and he continued to chop all the days of his life. "What else did you expect from a man who excels in cross-kingdom trade?" a local wheelwright said of Ojemba. "All he wants is money." However, they did not charge him with treason. They only told him to mind his world and his god.

When Ikenga could not access his crops, hunger and hardship untold took its toll on him and his grandson, Nwabunna, whose father was Ikenga's only survivor of the Inter-Kingdom war, which claimed the lives of the rest of his family, including his wife, Madam Nsisong, who hailed from Littoral Gnishere. He died half a decade later from a stray bullet. That day, Ikenga attempted suicide but his ancestors refused to welcome him to the netherworld. He had thrown himself into River Omimi, but a current of it launched him back ashore immediately. His survival of it proved that he had never nurtured evil against anybody since birth, because River Omimi didn't spare evil doers or plotters of it, and such people avoided it completely. Therefore, it became an item of oath in Baruru. People began to call him a river reject and a 30-seconds mad man. And yet a few people called him an unsuccessful suicider—a suicide 'attemptee'.

Later that year, his crops were harvested and shared among members of the advisory committee, and three years after that, the worst happened to him; his grandson, Nwabunna, the only thing life left for him, ran away. An apprentice with Mr. Obiuwa, a general goods trader, Nwabunna returned from work one evening, exactly 5:38 pm. Having nothing to eat, he decided to 'drink' garri. Over in their empty barn was a jute bagful of palm kernel. He picked some of it, which he cracked with a stone for the nuts. Unfortunately for him, Chief Okwubungbo was passing along a path in their backyard, on his way to a caucus of Igwe Dimanochie and all red-cap men at the palace. Identifying the sound for what it was, he hurried to Ikenga's compound to know who the hell the 'tabooist' was. Throughout Baruru, it was forbidden for anyone to crack kernel between 6 am and 6 pm. It caused pests to ravage food crops across farmlands and gardens. This noumenon necessitated the law which was held sacrosanct. Busted, Nwabunna fled the kingdom, fully aware of the nature of penalty that awaited him – lapidation.

Okwubungbo reported the news to Igwe Dimanochie, news that made him cancel their meeting. Before the crack of dawn, a kingdom-wide wail was heard, as all farmlands had been destroyed by pests; crops of harvestable sizes and inestimable value had perished. There was just no need to cast lot on the cause. Okwubungbo caught Nwabunna on the very act. Had he not run away, he would have been stoned to death by a kill-ready mob. Lapidation was the ultimate penalty. Gods of Baruru didn't entertain pleas when abomination of that weight was committed, and had Okwubungbo not reported Nwabunna to Igwe, the gods would have struck him dead. In Baruru, whoever saw evil and sealed his lips was considered a doer of it as much.

How the law came about could be traced to Nze Ututu Umedi, first path-breaking immigrant to settle in the territory, after its aborigines were completely decimated by fleeing guerilla, during the

Scramble for Africa in the 1880's. Ututu died the day he forgot to offer ambrosia to a deity he had carried from Ndalandara Ancient Kingdom in Liberia which protected him from European explorers who turned human merchants. He promised the deity that if it kept him from being sold into slavery, he would worship him all the days of his life, wherever he dwelled. The two parties kept to the covenant until that fateful day, when Ututu forgot to feed his goddess with goat blood and its bowels, because he was very busy cracking kernels which he bartered for other items of his needs. The goddess, whom he called Birthmother, was terribly pissed off. He remembered it late on and rushed to her shrine. It was 6 pm according to a sundial. The thurible was already in his hand when she struck him with blue blotches and winding. He pratfell and later vomited blood. Somehow, his oldest son noticed the scene in the shrine and ran to help his father. But nobody and nothing was going to be able to save a man whose god had chosen to kill him. When the young man confirmed that his father had breathed his last, he pleaded with the deity to withdraw her hovering anger, which carried in a gust and cloud-like appearance. A pertinent thing he learnt from his father was that the gods were attracted by offerings and vows. So, he swore an oath to Birthmother that if she withdrew the eclipse, which would go on to last for ten market days, and brighten up the sky, he and his three brothers would serve her their whole lives. That was when the goddess ordered him that nobody should crack kernel in the land until 6 pm, the very hour his father remembered to feed her that day. "If you or your descendants disobey this order, pests shall devour all the crops in your farmlands, and all the foods in your houses shall be diseased, and you shall starve the way your father starved me today," she pronounced, her voice came from a tenebrous image within the shrine, which housed a wooden art work of a woman with a baby in her hands, depicting the goddess.

This order was what later became known as "Past-six-post-meridian kernel crack law." To enforce it, lapidation was adopted as penalty for defaulters. Secondly, Birthmother rejected palm kernel as a fruit of libation. As a result, they began to offer her kola nut which was the only other fruit in the territory at the time. The land had been completely burned by a guerilla, and this destroyed plant life. As at the time Umedi arrived, plants were still undergoing primary succession. The people came to love kola nut even more than palm kernel, especially because of its having lobes, and it became an important item in their culture. This all happened in the Nineteenth Century.

Some years later, however, the other sons of Umedi rebelled against his oldest son, accusing him of using the goddess' injunction to strengthen his primogeniture and denying them of their share of the bequest. They withdrew from the oath and declared themselves independent, claiming that their mother was different from his, whom they called a slattern their father never wanted to marry. They said that their father only wanted to have a fling with her and then ditch her, only to get her pregnant, and eventually having him. The secession automatically split Baruru into four different but inherent subkingdoms, each having control over the resources and revenues of the land he inhabited. To distinguish themselves from one another, one allowed his teeth to decay. Another allowed his hair to grow into a mane. The other guy chose to never wear clothes again. Only Ututu's first son remained normal, and he and his lineal generations continued to observe the law.

However, later in early twentieth century when petroleum was discovered in Littoral Gnishere, the brothers collapsed back into one entity, because of the nature of resource control and redistribution introduced by the central government.

The law was still extant when Nwabunna cracked the kernel. That was why he was said to have committed a taboo. So he scooted Baruru. He fled because he feared the people. Ikenga really ate a dinner of depression because of the dispossession of his land and disappearance of his son's son. He couldn't access his farmlands and now he didn't know Nwabunna's whereabouts.

Before 9 ' o clock that day, what happened in Baruru had burgeoned like a wildfire across sister kingdoms, and Mazi Ikenga was a popular figure, famous for his "Your Rule Makes me Rude" speech which he delivered in response to a British viceroy, who had earlier said of Gnishere, "Britain chose to colonize you because you couldn't make riches out of your resources on your own." That was in 1956, four years before Independences of Madagascar, Senegal, Somalia, Togo, Burkina Faso, Ivory Coast, Republic of Niger, Gnishere, and others.

An epic speech, it fueled pro-Independence movements and crusades across Africa. In his verbal derring-do, Ikenga accused London of perching on a springboard of colonial rule to have a picnic of smorgasbord on the "synthetic" country they created, leaving it wide open, like snapdragon, for international exploitation. He dared the viceroy, saying of Britain and of Europe at large: "You easily find faults with Africa but hardly have faith in her, and you fill your vaults with proceeds from the continent's resources." Of his entire tantrum, what got to the viceroy's bone were the words: "I shall fight your cruelty to a stop!" And he did.

A docker in the capital city's port then, he began to attach tags to briefcases and portmanteaus of diplomats and other sailors, with the help of stevedores. "London has killed Gnishere. Help us get them to leave now," the tags read. It worked. People began to have bad perceptions about Britain's handling of Gnishere's administrative affairs. The Governor-General was disturbed. He wondered how an ordinary docker was able to pour gravel into his garri, and he vowed to punish Ikenga's stricture. "What the little black boy doesn't know is that sticks and stones can't break my bones," the louche Governor-General had said. Ikenga lost his job at the port the next day, and when clairsentience told him they were after his life, he left the capital district for Baruru, where his younger brother, bought over by the Governor-General, accused him of pillage and defrauding sea travelers. After being tried, he was jailed in a borstal for five years. He was twenty-three then, and he found his wife, Nsisong, there. One of the prison cooks, she always treated him better than she treated others.

However, the movements he sparked continued strongly. What did the younger brother get in return for the inside job? A job in England. He was employed to head a postal agency in London. And he was happy. This whole thing got their older brother angry. "You got your brother in prison and you're happy!" he had rebuked him. And that was the undoing of an African son − self-selling. He sold his brother for a stranger's broth which bore a strength-sapping hole in his stomach eventually. As a result, he kept eating but it wouldn't show in his body. The food passed through the holes in his stomach back into the stranger's bowl, and he wouldn't realize it.

Ikenga was freed a year after Independence, in 1961, during the first Indigenous Governor-General's prisoners' pardon, an amnesty initiative which saw thousands of agent provocateurs absolved and released. It was when Ikenga couldn't get any compensation for the pathetic treatment done to him or recognition for his pro-Independence heroics from the central government that he retired to the village and fell back on farming. A man who had previously lost his first three children to present-at-birth diseases, and later lost two others to an internecine war, before finally losing the sole survivor to a hunter's stray bullet, Ikenga couldn't help being a happy-less man when Nwabunna fled. "That boy is my sole solace," he cried. The heat of his sadness was further fanned to flames of fury by his younger brother who was later disgraced and relieved of his London job. One of the beneficiaries of the colonial government who were opposed to home rule, he taunted Ikenga everyday with meioses like: "Next time, before you choose to be a freedom fight-man, ensure you'll be a free man, whatever the outcome."

"Don't break the hedge if the cost of mending it is greater than your 'head worth'. By asking the viceroy to leave, you already chose to live without joy, and here you are a sad soul. Enjoy your joylessness, my brother."

He was the happiest man in Baruru when Ikenga's lands were seized for twelve years. "What he wished against innocent Europeans has found ingress into his own life," he gleed. A day was lived when Ikenga went to his younger brother's house to see if he could have some food. He was told to go home and enjoy the moth in his mouth and the worms in his stomach. That was the day he agreed that the moon of his suffering had reached its perigee. It was that day that he told Nwabunna to go learn trade or craft. The next day, after apprenticeship arrangements were made and its conditions met, an agreement was struck between them and Obiuwa. So, Nwabunna began to learn trade in Obiuwa's hands.

A tough, strict master, Obiuwa's heart was at his back and his hands on his mouth. He made sure none of his 'learnees' got anything from him, either by gift or stealth. He settled none of them financially upon completion of their training. He always found a fault for which he should not fulfill his part of the agreement. "A servant can never be innocent before his master," he always said to defend himself. One of his protégés pursued a case against him but found himself behind bars, and his relatives had to spend hugely to get him out, because a battery of impossible charges was laid on him by Obiuwa. If the young man had walked away gently, the money which the case 'ate' would have been enough to establish his own enterprise. But then, would those relatives of his have been that willing to give him the money as a take-off grant? In this part of Gnishere, people withheld assistance from a struggling man, but offered largesse to a carcass just to sell their inflated ego balloon. They would see a man in suffering and tell him to struggle some more that a breakthrough lied in his next round of pain. After spending seventeen weeks in cell, the young man was released on bail. He moved elsewhere, a place far and remote. There, he started his own business humbly. Initially, there weren't any successes, but it later went from bust to boom.

When people saw all that he suffered in Obiuwa's hands, they stopped sending their boys to him. They were really surprised when they saw Nwabunna with him. The name Obiuwaajoka – the heart of the world is wicked –was given him by his disheartened mother, Uju, whose previous pregnancies aborted spontaneously. And when she finally had her first child, her husband's wife smothered the baby. The heartless woman, however, was caught by a door-to-door advanced pap seller, who had come around to see if anybody in the hamlet would buy from her. Strangest thing about the whole incident was that, of all her sixteen husband's wives, that Egonne, his most recent wife who was always face-smiling and belly-laughing did such a hell-sponsored and Satan- supervised thing. She was always looking happy that people began to call her Anurika, never knowing that it was just an ordinary *ochieze*.

The hawker granny, who beat Egonne's watchfulness, thank goodness, saw her right hand on the baby's neck and her left hand on his mouth. She knew it was something harmful and not playful. So, she made a gong out of her shrill frail voice box, which alarmed the baby's mother, who was bathing in a makeshift bamboo bathroom, singing some ditties which countered whatever faint guttural sound the baby might have made in his unsuccessful struggle for breath. Greatly petrified, she rushed out of the bathroom, wrapper-less and speechless. Meanwhile, the harpy had suddenly lifted the baby from his cot, placed him on her bosom, and pretended to be petting him to sleep.

"What's happening here?" his mother managed to ask.

"I don't know oo!" the evil doer lied. "Ask this witch of an old woman. She just appeared from the firmament and started shouting," she lied on. "I insist that someone should tell me what's happening here," Uju pursued, taking over her baby's corpse from the hands that just cut life out of it.

"Your baby is dead," the old woman said with a certainty as absolute as autumn cold. "I'm just afraid," she continued, shaking her head in sadness. It was when she felt no life in her sprog that Uju began to weep. Her ears-splitting screaming of *"Ewoo!"* drew a crowd which was larger than that which collected during President Ronald Reagan's inauguration. The few women amongst the first set of people to arrive took care of her nakedness, but could do nothing about her helplessness, because her baby, the very first child she ever bore, after many miscarriages, was now dead. So her unhappy childless days returned upon her.

The custom of the land demanded that when a woman wronged another, she should go to her with a pullet and ask for forgiveness, because by way of mutual respect a woman begot another. Egonne, however, refused to toe that line. She steadfastly denied the witness' testimony, claiming strongly that the baby was arrested by seizures and that she had placed her hands over his face to stabilize him. In Baruru, hair suite women were deemed to be wicked, and Obiuwa's mother was one, with many strands of rubbles on her chin. Stories had it that she kept a goatee in her pre-marriage days. So, she swore that she would stop at nothing to find out who actually killed her baby.

And she invited Onumuo over for divination, against her husband's will. The gods confirmed that Egonne actually killed the baby and the *dibia*, consequently, asked her to go ask for Uju's forgiveness. Secondly, he ordered her to not 'meet her husband' until her husband's wife had had another baby. Again, she refused to apologize. She called the oracle daft and flounced away. The gods must have been on a mercy spree that day to not have struck her dead. It was at this point that Okeahialam took his heart-rent wife into their hut and told her to leave the case for the gods. He believed that the surest way to give closure to malevolence was to throw out a bone and allow a dog to fight it out with ghosts. If it beat spooks to the bone, it was innocent. If it got beaten by them, it was guilty. "You shall forever be childless if you don't heed to these words," the *dibia* had pronounced on Egonne.

Egonne later got gone, and her husband dragged Okeahialam, his older brother, to their *umunna*, asking them to punish him for allowing his wife to accuse his own wife falsely. Egonne began to disparage the other woman, mocking her thus: The gods have just justified me from this evil woman, a witch that gave birth to children who don't survive, children that die in harmless hands.

The more her stomach protruded with the pregnancy, the more people doubted the power in the curse laid on her. But it was still in order. The spell said she would be childless, not barren. And, in any case, a tree, they say, doesn't wither same day it is felled and *aturu* usually says that nothing beats observation. Finally, Egonne had a son and named him Anaebom, meaning "While they accuse me, my god justifies me."

Two weeks later, seizures took over Anaebom. The same thing Egonne lied with befell her own son. Interesting. "The gods are honest beings," the *dibia* said to Egonne. "They don't take sides with lies or injustice, and when a mortal tries to embroil them in a wrongdoing, they quickly exonerate themselves, implicating the mortal same time." She continued to deny her crime. She resorted to a sibyl afar, seeking for healing for her son. Death actually came to kill this particular puppy, so it wouldn't let it perceive feces. Her son died in the hands of the sibyl, same age as the boy she had killed.

The other woman took in and later gave birth to Obiuwa. She was initially going to call him Dibuikenwannyi, in appreciation of her husband for sticking by her while the child-bearing prickle lasted. She only changed her mind when she remembered how an evil-hearted harpy had killed her first child. As for the women of Baruru, returning scorn was some savory sport. It was an interesting and rewarding sport. So she began to sing-mock Egonne:

The fruitful woman is yet childless

To men she lied

The gods she disobeyed

How funny that is.

Children of the innocent woman

Seizures don't have

Happy she always is

How lucky she is.

This bless-curse song got Egonne terribly peeved, but she was long shorn of her thorns. A narration of all that happened to Obiuwa as he grew up must have been what indoctrinated meanness in him. People believed that he was an incarnate of his brother and that he hadn't forgotten and would most likely not forget how he was killed in his previous life. And he sure was a revengeful soul. Nobody found favor or peace with him and only a few asked. They looked at a woman's face before asking her the gender of her baby. Obiuwa's countenance alone kept people at bay.

One afternoon, he refused to give Nwabunna money for lunch because he wasted time in attending to a customer. He told him to go and collect some money from his father's grave. Nwabunna returned home that evening jolly hungry. He went to Ikenga's younger brother's house to see whether he would be given some food. He received some unkind words instead. "Your grandfather traded your future for fame and now you're destiny-less," Ikenga's brother had told him. These words stung Nwabunna down to his yellow marrow, like the fangs of adder. He was also told that the alleged stray bullet which killed his father actually came from a hunter hired by one of the men who lost mega money contracts because of the departure of the colonial leaders. "… because your stupid grandfather was the one who pioneered movements for Independence, they decided to get at him by killing his only surviving child. Spineless father of a destiny-less boy like you." When he couldn't take these words any more, he left, disappointed in a man who had continued to live in affray with his older brothers for decades.

It was when Nwabunna remembered that the man who refused to give him food was the biggest farmer that year, and that his grandfather didn't plant any because his lands were seized, that he chose to punish him by cracking kernel at a wrong hour, so as to have his crops damaged by pests. But he never knew he would be caught. So, he fled Baruru through the same Omimi River which spared no evil doer. The river rather developed an unusual ford, through which he fled. Unbelievable!

CHAPTER TWO

Manna in Mama's House

There is no rest for the breasts of a dog which gave birth to too many puppies. This is due to the fact that wherever she goes they follow her, jostling for her parallel pairs of dangling breasts, the tits of which they hold on to even while lying down. There is no rest for her breasts at all. But then this doesn't stop the mama dog from searching for a bone. She's always ready to grab one when it is thrown.

Nwbunna escaped through an unusual ford in River Omimi to Merogwu, a coterminous kingdom, only separated from Baruru by the river. He was prowling like an animal in the bush when he saw a wiry old woman fetching firewood and he offered to help her. She readily accepted, without minding that he might mean harm for her, being an absolute stranger. Nothing was going to frighten an old woman who had seen and tasted scourges of war before: foodlessness, 'shelterlessness' and breathlessness. Quick with his hands, he soon fetched a sizable bunch, and again, he volunteered to help her carry it home. Quite long and heavy a bunch, Nwabunna stood it on its head, bent low, and lifted it from its base on to his head, to the admiration of the granny, who was only wondering where the heaven such an august angel must have come from. She led the way through a narrow track which was flanked by wet, luxuriant, and spiky grasses, which were athwart on the path.

"But, my son, what were you doing here before you saw me?" she asked him, as they hoofed it home.

"I was hunting bush meat," he lied, afraid she might act funny if told the truth there and then. He was simply being careful, and that was wise of him. He once told the truth in Baruru and got into trouble and telling lies brought him no fewer problems either. "I killed an ediabali yesterday, and I thought I would be as lucky today," he further lied. The whopper got the woman uneasy, because wild dogs had not been seen or killed in Merogwu for over fifty years and were therefore believed to have gone into extinction like the mastodon. However, she didn't react to that. Her family was long dead. That was what she concerned herself with – the distressed misery she had become. If her children were alive, she wouldn't have come to the bush to fetch wood for fire. Her latter life had become suffering-ridden and agony-laden. She had no one to care for and none to care for her. Called Mama lately by villagers, she was probably the Icarus of the Gnisherean War, which created a thorny whorl of a world for Orient Gnishere. Mama, like other families, lost her two children to starvation and her husband to an at-close-quarters bazooka bullet, not from an enemy soldier, but from a saboteur colleague, who had become a soldier of fortune.

After the war, she had hoped one of his brothers-in-law would inherit her, as tradition demanded, but it didn't happen. She wanted to return to her father's house, but some large number of her step-siblings, who all survived the war, discouraged her. Days turned to decades and yet nobody inherited or remarried her. So, she began to think of herself as a bunch of fluted pumpkin which couldn't be sold in the marketplace. She was thirty-one when the war ended, in 1970. Her distress was made worse by the fact that no welfare packages were arranged for living victims of the war. They were abandoned to recover on their own. Mama and Nwabunna were welcomed home by passerine sounds as birds began to fly away from her grains, which she spread outside to avert decay. When her hen began to lead her chickens to their space of sleep, Mama knew it was 6pm – the time when local fowls went to bed – already. The hen initially had eleven chicks, but six of them were taken on an aboreal holiday of no possible return by birds of prey. Mama nearly broke a tarsal bone the day the fifth chick was taken by a lucky lurking hawk, which was covertly perching on a palm tree. She unimaginably jumped up as high as twenty-five metres and pursued the predator, hitting her left foot against a stout stem. But it beat her pace and height, with its talon firmly holding on to the helpless and hapless chick. The attitude of her fowls gave Mama loaves of joy because they never ate from her grains, which she always spread outside to self-defeat mildew. The hen was so motherly that she catered for her young ones and fought hard to keep them from their aboreal beak-butchers of brothers. Her major undoing was the presence of many trees in the surroundings, which gave the predators perch platforms and eventual picking of her chicken.

"Before you leave, I'll like you to eat," Mama said to Nwabunna, as he lent the woody fuel by the inglenook.

"Ok Mama," he replied, asking himself if he had any other place to go. And that was a simple but significant question. Mama placed her pot of dried okro and fried groundnut soup on fire immediately.

"Mama," he drew her attention, "I have something more important than food to ask of you, and eating your food depends on your doing it for me," he besought her.

"Well, tell me what it is. I'll give it to you or do it for you if I have it," she replied with concern.

"Have me stay with you for some time. I have no place to go for now."

Mama was taken aback, and, with a half-laugh, she asked the boy what he really meant.

"I'll tell you my story in the morning. That will be the fifth thing I'll do tomorrow. First thing is to wake from sleep. Second thing is prayer to the gods. Third thing will be to greet you. Breakfast is fourth thing, and then I will tell you the story which I shall call 'Penance of a pariah'. It's not a story a hungry man can tell, that's why breakfast will happen before it."

Mama couldn't remember the last time she was told a story that had a title. So she was interested and expectant. Nwabunna attacked the food with zeal and interest, although very tired, and the soup was delicious. He did not need to ask who made such a delectable soup. An old woman, they say, doesn't age in the dance that she knows how well to dance. It was actually her previous weekend's soup, and although it had lasted six days and turned dark, it still retained its olfactory-lobe-arousing aroma.

"If she had run a restaurant once in her life, she could have made the fortune of a lifetime," the visitor chatted with himself, as he bulldozed down a heap of yellow garri, about four cups of it, in no time. The stodgy food restored strength in him. However, he was so tired that he couldn't bathe that night even when Mama twice asked him to do that.

He drifted off on the spot of eating. Mama woke him up and guided him to an *agada*, a wooden bed in one of the four rooms of the house. He was so dreary-eyed that he didn't know about the displacement from the kitchen to the room, which would later become his personal room. An earthen pot of water was beside the bed, as well as a box of wrapper, which was an echo of infant sarcophagus. Inside it were Mama's assorted clothes, which included wrappers, blouses, and stoles. Also in the house were a few other effects which were in utter disuse. An earthen pot was a refrigerator of a kind those days, and water scooped from it was as revitalizing as the one the Psalmist drank and said, "... He restoreth my soul...."

Under the bed were dust-laced saving boxes which Mama had made for her ill-fated children. She was a thrift who loved saving, one of the habits she and her siblings developed as a result of their parents' teachings. "The real coin is not the one received. It is the one kept. And to make sure the kept coin is safe, to make sure you don't get to spend it, stow it in a box, lock it up and throw the key into the latrine." That was the instruction, the lesson, and the culture they grew up with. And they lived by it, and it shaped their lives well. Irrespective of their polygamous state, characterized by numerous births, Mama and her sibs got established early on in life.

The second value which Mama and her siblings learnt from their parents was honesty. The lesson was given the day Mama's younger brother Eziokwu hid his report card in the bush, because he ate the money which he needed to submit the dossier with—his 'handwork'. Afraid of being scolded and hopeful of getting at least a moiety of the money within a week, he chose to keep the booklet in the bush. Unfortunately for the smart boy, termites feasted on the paper. He knew it wouldn't be easy to get enough money for both 'handwork' and a new dossier, so he opened up to his mother, who was most junior wife. She scolded the boy, and after temporizing, she took the matter to her husband, primarily to get some money for a new report card for her son.

Egwu was angry. He was disappointed with the fact that a product of his seed could behave that unfaithfully at such a tender age. For him, the sin was not just spending the money meant for his 'handwork' on moimoi-*oka*. The actual wrongdoing was that a boy that little chose to hide something of that huge importance from his parents until the damage outweighed him. He battled within himself that for a small boy to have a big skeleton in his thin cupboard, he must be toeing a wrong dark path. The money he 'ate' was an alternative for three bunches of broom, which was a token for 'handwork' or class assessment. Other children made their own brooms by themselves from palm leaves but not Eziokwu, an over-cosseted child, who barely did any work at all, domestic or farm-related. He was only good at plays and foods, and at sleeping on his mother's body, with his waist facing heaven to avoid the tendency that could come from hell. This made his father to fear that he was going to attain puberty prematurely. Egwu was downright discontent that a child he named Eziokwu, or Truth, was already dishonest, though still young. It suggested to him that a bad life was budding and needed to be uprooted from the marl before the seedling would become a great tree. And he was going to do that with a spade and cutlass. He knew that an adult shouldn't stay at home and watch a goat deliver in the tether. So, he summoned all his children, twenty-seven in numeracy, twelve in literacy.

"Whose children are you?" he began, after they had all taken their seats, and he expected a reply from them, yes.

"Your children of course, Papa," they chorused, looking each other in the eyes. "Is anyone out there claiming ownership of us with you? We are all children of Egwu Nweke, and we look exactly like him." He called Eziokwu out, and ocular beams converged on him. "Your brother here has shamed our family name..." he began the admonition proper. "Never has dishonesty been seen or heard of in our lineage before now. So I'm disappointed in him.

"If any of you must do well in life, he must not tell lies. Lies injure men and infuriate the gods. And when a man has offended both mortals and the gods of our land, he's accursed for life already.

"An honest man is rarely applauded, but he gets honored, ultimately. As a boy, there was nothing that I did which I didn't tell my parents about. When I got things wrong, I told them immediately. It saved me unnecessary sufferings. The complication of secrecy warrants difficult situations."

By 5:23 am the next day, Mama was already in with Nwabunna's breakfast. She waited for about thirty minutes before her visitor of circumstance woke up. He went outside, urinated, washed his face, and rejoined her in the room. Mama's mien made him to forget the votive prayer.

"I'm here already, my child," Mama began, removing the stick she chewed from her mouth.

"I did something horrible," Nwabunna began, overlooking the food, "something I'm not proud of right now, and so I ran away."

"Go on, my son. What exactly did you do?"

"I cracked kernel before 6 pm." Those words were still in his mouth when Mama began to scream.

"So you are the taboo boy from Baruru!" This got Nwabunna apprehensive, more than the crime he committed had.

"Yes, I am...I am, Mama. But I regret it all. I was simply overcome with hate for my grandfather's brother for refusing to give me some food, and given that he is the biggest farmer this year, and, also, given that my grandfather has no hope of reaping anything from his farms this year, I chose to do that...I didn't really believe that it was possible that pests would destroy crops across farmlands when someone cracked kernel before 6 pm and after 6 am. I thought the gods were joking."

"How then did you expect your enemy's crops to perish when you didn't believe in the law?"

"Maybe by selective destruction. I thought only his own crops would perish."

"Uh-uh," mama whirred. "A weak miserable child has committed a wicked sacrilege which no sacrifice can cover. I condemn what you have done. It's too bad of your heart. Disbelief in the custom of a land doesn't warrant a man to violate it. You're such a lucky thing to have escaped alive."

"The gods helped me to escape."

"Which gods? The ones you just defied? Leave the gods out of your disobedience. You'll be incurring their wrath more if you try to bring them into it."

"I knew I would be stoned to death if caught and that drowning was a more peaceful way of dying. So, I ran headlong to River Omimi to throw myself into it. But, as I approached it, a portion of it began to get shallow, as though it was parting. That was how I crossed and later found you. The river rejected my grandfather years back and yesterday it respected me. That tells me that the gods are not actually angry with me." Nwabunna said those words with satori.

Mama was disturbed by the tall story, which sounded like a koan in her ears. She knew, deep down, that the boy was going to be scragged by the gods their own way some day. "After all," she had said in her head, "a tree does not wither same day it is felled." "Get up and leave my house," she ordered him.

"Please, Mama!" Nwabunna begged. "You can't do this to me. I can't afford to go back to the bush. I know nobody here."

"So what do you want me to do for you now?"

"Keep me here for a while, please. I'll be killed if I return home. My grandfather has lost everything and everyone but me."

"Sorry, child. I can't keep you here."

"You see, you're already calling me your child, and who knows? I might be your real child after-all."

These last words of his gave Mama a for-thought food, and she laughed lightly, her face skyward. "To keep a fugitive in my house is very dangerous, especially one who neither has regards for laws nor awe for the gods. I know that the gods you offended are coming for you and I don't want to share in your troubles."

"They won't, Mama. They just won't. Their jurisdiction is limited to Baruru kingdom. They know there will be an inter-deity combat between them and the gods of Merogwu if they cross the frontiers, yes."

"I marvel at your wit, my son. But I don't want to witness another blood spill, this time in the hands of the gods. I have seen people die in their numbers before."

"Let me stay with you. If the gods come for me, turn me in. I'll surrender."

"If you must stay with me, you must pledge to abide by the laws of my land."

"I will, Mama, provided none of them forbids a man from breathing." Nwabunna was relieved. He felt like an animal that was just released from a menagerie. Nature had long passed the buck to him since the days his grandfather lost control of his farmlands. Here in exile, he knew he had to fend for himself and for the old woman, who had just granted him asylum, too. He had just become a grandfather and a father to himself. The time for him to put the instructions of Mazi Ikenga to use had come. Like a ruminant, he began to regurgitate and apply them. One of the things his grandfather taught him was self-reliance and independence. "Nobody can fare fine or far in life if he depends on another person for everything. So learn to stand on your own feet always. Know your worth and work hard, and you'll never be among mere men." These were Ikenga's words to his grandson. And they formed a principle for him, a bedrock upon which he built his survival in Merogwu. He chose to pound in the mortar and not on his thigh. At first it wasn't easy, but he coped with time.

Later that day, he began to move around Mama's house, which was covered in algae. She had a very large land space in the compound which lied fallow with many trees.

"I can cultivate the soil so you plant cassava on it," he patronized Mama. "Do it if you can," she replied brusquely. "But I don't just have a hoe."

"I saw a spade somewhere. I can't quite remember where exactly." He cultivated the soil, about four plots, in three weeks. Mama, who tried in futility to stop him from tilling all of it, marveled at his brawn.

"Don't kill yourself with work, my child. The Creator who has kept us alive will surely provide for us. You're very strong and determined. You must have outmuscled the gods of your land to escape. Perhaps they saw your strength and decided to join forces with you against your people," she joshed him.

Her husband's people were lurking like birds of prey, waiting for the day she would die, to take over the lands. Mama had always wished she knew where her family were buried, so that she would have the opportunity to occasionally lay wreathe on their graves in memory of their ill-fated lives. Her husband must have been one of the many people slain and mass-buried in shallow graves, while her children, who were more-or-less sticks of bone before they died, as starvation left them with no muscle or flesh, could not be accounted for. She had always wept and mourned, but sorrow couldn't help the misery she had become.

The ultimate undoing of the grim war was that its outcome was the same as its causes. Nothing improved at all. Same old tales. Same old tellers of the tales. Same old feelings. Same old fears. Same old milieu. Same old malevolence. People didn't become civil. Evil didn't die in the missiles. Ethnic hate didn't die of the measles. People died in the millions, yet problems survived in the myriads. No solace was in sight, so sorrow lived with survivors, making them no better than casualties. The Inter-kingdom War, which oversaw a near absolute genocide of Orient-Gnishere, which comprised 29 sub-kingdoms, took humanity out of its survivors – living victims and victors alike – leaving the entire entity a community of mind monsters, like in the Jurassic times.

CHAPTER THREE
Pickings from 'Froglings'

A dog answers whatever name its owner gives it, but doesn't accept every food it is given. For example, it doesn't eat forage, so doesn't accept grasses from its owner, however fresh it looks, and irrespective of how emotionally the owner caresses it while dropping the leaves.

Nsogbubaruru had called Ikenga a failure and punished him severely by withdrawing all his entitlements as a high chief. But even before they did, he had always preferred being called *mazi*, or mister, to being called *nze* or high chief. He accepted it when they called him a failure, but he refused to accept the food of a failed fate. He was determined to get the best out of his being, by becoming the man whose confidence defied colonial clout once again.

He led pro-Independence cum anti-colonial rule movements and got imprisoned. On the day he went to help a friend somewhere his grandson fled. If he had been at home that evening, Nwabunna wouldn't have broken the law. Ikenga wasn't really exposed academically, but he had a fine sense of civic responsibility. A man of his dignity and standing should have been a liege in Gnishere, or at least, one of its post-Independence notable figures. But he was nowhere near the elites and grandees of his time. Rather, he was somewhere in the village, insulted and accused. And he didn't mind. "A leader is not desperate to rule a country someday. Rather, he is disciplined to abide by her rules every day." That was his response to his detractors who had accused him of indirectly aspiring to become the first indigenous Governor-General of Gnishere, saying that he wasn't the most prominent person or best positioned man. He told them that he led those campaigns simply because he wanted the exploitation of his people by Europeans to end, and nothing more. For fighting for his own people the reward he got was incarceration. For leasing out his land to visitors his lot was dispossession. He was always receiving refuse for giving out his resources to help others. This was a luck he didn't bargain for, and he was ready to turn it around.

But he wasn't interested in illegitimate money, just as he wasn't interested in illegitimate children. Although an African traditionalist, he was sad when he began to see natural laws becoming upended in Baruru in the aftermath of the war. Whatever bastion of humanity, decency, and temperance which existed in Orient-Gnishere, which central district Baruru was, was eroded by blood-like waters of the war. He was greatly distraught that elderly ones were no longer accorded due respect through genuflection; maidens no longer bowed to married women. He was pained that the days were gone when people saw a wounded bush meat and took it to the hunter whose bullet had hit it, or the man from whose trap it had escaped in the bush; the days when young men gifted their seats to older ones in a gathering and stood up till it was dismissed; the days when women didn't talk when their husbands talked; the days when young ladies saw an old woman and offered to help carry her load; when girls knew how to sit, how to talk, and gave a thought to clothes before wearing them. A time when men defended and fought for their families; when they used their organ with restraint, not just for the fear of their wives, but also for the fertility of the soil. The war took away all those values leaving them empty-handed. "The children we give birth to since the war, somehow, feel a vacuity of values in their minds. Something ethereal tells them that something defeating happened to their parents. We don't tell them the stories, yet they find out. Their emotion, their mind, their mental sensitivity learn about it somehow." That was Ikenga complaining to one of his good-old-days friends.

They started life anew in an alien milieu, full of exotic ethos. That was the basis of feckless and divided Orient-Gnishereans, who were once known and respected for cleanness of hands, innovation, and hard work. Theft, greed, and sloth were unheard-of before the war. People only ate their rightful food. No child picked objects along the road. Parents investigated any gifts their children brought home or anything they didn't buy for them. Ikenga would never forget the day a little boy brought home a wounded and weary grass-cutter. Upon seeing it had a gunshot wound, the boy's father paid a town crier to go round the village and look for the hunter whose bullet had hit it. The little boy couldn't believe both his eyes and ears, and the hunter arrived a few minutes later. He thanked the man and left with the meat. After about an hour, the hunter's daughter arrived with a plate of pepper soup which contained the *ukwu anu* for the boy. Propriety and modesty were the norm of pre-war Orient Gnishere, while do-as-you-deem-fit became the order of the post war days. Most of the things that were theretofore upheld became unpopular and invidious, and vice versa; *juju*, land-grabbing, fraud, and leg ulcer became commonplace.

Ikenga was terribly missing Nwabunna. His disappearance gave him frostbite in Spring. He wasn't in any way proud of what the boy did, especially because of the famine it brought upon the land. He could only wish he had been around and that he had rejected the palm kernel which Mrs. Ijeoyibo had given him two days earlier. It was a thank-you gift from her husband, whom he had helped purchase some plots of land at cheaper rates. He accepted everything in positives and wished his grandson well, wherever he might be.

Although he was called a blighter, he knew he still had an even brighter future at 67. And while his own brother wanted to skin him alive, his god decided to equip him with some rare skills. One might choose to say that he learnt left-handedness at old age, or that he became fortunate late in life. What's new with Ikenga? He took to fishing one morning, two months after Nwabunna's disappearance, but didn't make any catch. "Must I fail in everything I do?" he grilled his god. The next day, he returned to the river again, murmuring, "Man will just die if things continue this way." After making a few launches without a catch, he chose to rest for a while and then continue later. As he laid his hook and line aside and draped his head on the embankment, and hoping that he would catch at least a fish when he resumed, he observed a frog voraciously eating a particular leaf. He studied the situation closely for some minutes and decided to take the frog home. It was quick with its limbs, and with high leaps it dribbled the old man around, making him taste some fits of slips and jerks. But he finally caught it and took it home. He fed it intensively with those leaves for two weeks and noticed a marked growth and vitality. Just with leaf and water, the amphibian was well fed.

Meanwhile, frogs were an indispensable item of dowry in one Imukwanya Kingdom, and it was very scarce. So he thought he could rear and market it there and make some cash of obesity from it. He knew his main job was to get a mate for the one he already had, the gender of which he didn't know. He set out the next day looking for another frog but couldn't find any. The animal was just scarce, very hard to come by. The search continued for three days without success. When he returned home after a fourth day search, he saw the surprise of his adult life. Guess what it was? The only one he had had already laid as many eggs as the number of days his grandson had been missing. There was spawn everywhere. He was grateful. He wondered how it became possible for a single frog to form and lay eggs on its own. All along he had been thinking it was male. He never had any inkling it was a hermaphrodite. That was how he switched from fishery to 'frogery', and it soon paid off chrematistically, with subsequent supplies of the animal to Imukwanya.

He did all these secretly, thanks to the fact that most of his friends had abandoned him. They no longer visited or asked after him. He converted his bedroom to a silage store, and he built an out-of-bound semi pond in his backyard. To ensure the water didn't pollute the environment, he drained it into the soil directly. Again, this kept his business from becoming known to people. The eggs hatched after 21 days into numerous 'froglings' which mated one another and multiplied even more. It was when he saw that his frog population had grown terrifically that he began to make supplies. His first sales of six hundred frogs nearly caused trouble in Imukwanya as people fought for them. There was a gezump, and some people bought and resold to others at even higher prices. There were sudden marriages the days that followed, as many young men who had long been preparing for marriage but found no frog, the chief dowry material, having now found it, continued from where they stopped. In Imukwanya, people toiled distances at night with headlights in search of the nocturnal animal to no avail. Because of what they passed through in order to marry, they respected and placed value on their wives and daughters.

CHAPTER THREE

No man dared to beat or put his wife away. Also, nobody dared to leer at another man's wife. Her husband would go for his stranglehold. A story had it that one of those who succeeded in buying the goods from Ikenga that first day was Nkworie, who had impregnated his lover and needed to pay her lobola within eight days, or his lungs would stop working. He was about going to China to go look for frog when his younger sister brought him news that a man brought frogs to their market and that one sold for twenty pounds. He ran headlong, but before he could reach there the stock was finished already. It was another man who had earlier bought ten pieces that resold four to him at one hundred and twenty pounds.

The frog dowry brought honor to Imukwanya maidens before those from other kingdoms. And when their sons went to other kingdoms to marry, they would tell their girls, "I'll give you the frog treatment."

"I'll go to China for your sake."

"I'll pay your dowry with a Chinese frog."

The height of drama happened the day about one hundred and nine suitors came for an Imukwanya princess. Her father looked for a possible elimination strategy without success. They were all wealthy and handsome. Thirteen were educated but it didn't matter a thing to him. In fact, he disqualified them as a result of their being educated, claiming that a man who had allowed a strange culture into his life was not deserving of his daughter. He knew they could all afford to go to Asia for frogs. He equally knew they could flaunt wealth if asked to. Eventually, he asked them to go build a frog aquarium with local species in fourteen market days. This condition got the men of connubial prospect helter-skelter until a man referred them to Ikenga of Baruru. They contracted him for the job, paying him hugely in advance. What was funny was that as one of them was leaving Ikenga's house, another was entering it, and paid him higher than the other guy. At one point, Ikenga feared that his large house was going to be burgled. When some of the suitors saw what restlessness the requirement had continued to bring their way, they quit, even after having spent some fortune in the process. All but one of them did not make those efforts. All he did was to get one frog ready, according to custom, and every day, he went to the Igwe and told him, "My business is doing well and my frog for your daughter's dowry is waiting. I shall embark on a business trip tomorrow." That was how he became the eventual husband of the pretty princess.

When Ikenga finally delivered the job to the men who were still in the race, after he had built them the aquaria, they went to the palace to see whose frog pond Igwe would accept. They were stung when he rejected them. In his weird frame of reference, the ruler asked them, "Who amongst you, gentlemen, neither built an aquarium nor abandoned his business for once because he wants to marry my daughter?" A finger went up and he beckoned the man to come forward, with happy smiles all over his face. Others were greatly disappointed.

"Go bring your people," he said to him. "This day shall you become my worthy son-in-law." There was an apparent chagrin with the rest of the suitors, and an additional cheer-grin with the preferred suitor. And Igwe continued. "A man who stops at nothing just to marry a woman will definitely start with anything to maim her in future. You didn't abandon your business for anything. That tells me that you will never let anything make you poor. And, as a result, you will always have enough resources to take good care of my daughter." To others he said, "I want you to go and resume your businesses which you abandoned for weeks simply because of a woman." Those words gave those men sour frisson and they wanted to walk out on him, but nobody dared a traditional ruler in Orient-Gnishere. A wealthy ruler, he offered to pay them everything they lost in expenses and abandon, but they wouldn't take. They went home very sad, because of the honorable embarrassment.

The huge 'frogling' pickings handed Ikenga his biggest ever financial fortune, as each of the suitors paid him in excess of £400 for the tadpole aquaria. With it he went to Asia and imported exotic breeds and crossed them with his local breeds and the products were wonderful. He established his name as a foremost merchant of frog products: its meat, liquid extract, and 'froglings'. In Imukwanya, frog meat was believed to cure frigidity. Its macerated tongue was believed to enhance necromancy, and its liquid was an important skin smoothener, and the indigenes were always sloughing because their skin cells were always dying as a result of the very intemperate climate they lived in, hence the need for constant exfoliation. All these warranted the liquid's high demand amid its scarcity.

Ikenga was extremely grateful to his god for how he made him an ugly duckling in his late sixties, through a business he initially knew nothing about. It was a testament to the fact that he wasn't a failure after all, and that a man's god always listened to his prayers, provided he kept his hands clean. For never had he seen a grass-eating frog before, and never could anyone have imagined the one he saw would be a 'herm'. The ban on his lands was yet to be lifted, so he bought some plots of land elsewhere and built himself a great house. Also, he bought himself a car, and this brought joy to his heart.

"Why not remarry, Ikenga?" one of his age mates suggested to him. He was Nwani, one of those who had persecuted him and supported the ban on his lands. They reconciled recently when the people saw that they could neither stop his frog business nor start theirs. Many Baruruans including Nwani tried to, seeing how lucrative it was, but the gods did not approve of it. That was when he sold shame and sued for reconciliation with Ikenga.

"A brother's anger doesn't reach to the bone," he had patronized Ikenga Nwoke-ike as all his age mates called him for fun. His other name, Uche, was relegated during the Independence struggles. "It was in the interest of our land and its dignity that I played that role," Nwani continued.

"In life, we intentionally fall to laughter. It's not laughter that pushes us down," Ikenga replied tentatively. "Justice, we all know, lies with the gods, and they have vindicated me their own way. So who am I to hold on to malice? I forgive you, my brother." In response to his remarriage suggestion, he told Nwani that such a thing wasn't in his plans.

"You need a woman to take good care of you when old age will start getting young and strong on you."

"I don't want tears again, not now, not another time. It's possible that if I remarry and remake children, another war will come, and I'll lose them all, like the other time. My destiny doesn't permit me to have a family in this realm of life. Maybe, when I unite with my ancestors, I'll have as many children over there that will live in my presence and not get killed."

"You must not make children when you remarry. All you just need is a woman who will take care of you. You have made huge amounts of money. But money is not sweet in the mouth of a man without the companionship of a woman. Every time children, children. Are they not the ones denying me peace and laughter at home?"

"And here you come again! There's no way I'll bring in a woman and she wouldn't demand children from me. Our married women think of themselves as maidens until their laps have nursed a baby." When he saw that Nwani wasn't losing the case, he told him he would have to turn it over.

"Every dawn comes with four new done deals: energy, ideas, answers, and hope. All a man needs to do is to keep his mind open and to be willing to make choice decisions," Nwani submitted, getting up to leave. The emotional war which Ikenga was fighting because of the loss of his family was more terrible than the war in which they died. He had suffered a lot in his life, both in the hands of humans and those of nature. But he didn't let that harden his heart against people. He had made some money, and was willing to help others, including those who saw him in hiccups and poured away water instead of giving him a cup of it – those who saw him gasping for breath and tightened the rope some more instead of loosening it out – and those who saw him groping for the switch and pulled out the fuse instead of giving him light. "Although they made him a fall guy, he chose to be a Mr. Nice Guy, by paying them back with kindness. He wasn't going to be inured. The chambers of his heart were kindness-cast. If, however, there was one lesson which hardship taught Ikenga, it was that one should not run a charity foundation when he's yet to build a firm foundation for his own future. He learnt that a helper could need some help for himself.

He told Nwani he would think over his remarriage suggestion, but he found himself thinking about how he could help him, a man that once called him "the chief enemy of our land", a signatory to the paper which authenticated seizure of his lands, too. He was not impressed with his friend's family state of sad domesticity. Nwani's children were more lamentable than those of a misery. His first son was difficult. His only earthly usefulness was fight mongery. He was always challenging his father to a fight with projected fists. Nwani's first daughter was a porous pot of ammonia herself, and she was always choking and drying up waters of joy in her mother who lived in her own husband's house on her children's sufferance. His remaining nine children were all grenades of a kind. His house was more or less a beehive or formicary. Only difference was that while bees hummed, his children thudded, and while ants lived in harmony, his self-lost children fostered chaos. Each time their mother cooked, while the food was still on fire, they would devour it like wolves would.

"Is this the kind of family this man wants me to raise?" Ikenga mulled, "Is this what he is trying to get me into? It will not work." He thought it was more precious to be a childless widower at peace than to have a family wheel and yet not have a joyride.

After much thought, he decided to give Nwani some money to start up any business of his liking. He was one man who went to people he was going to help. He liked saving them the stress of coming to his house and the inconvenience of carrying gifts long distances. There was a day an old man whose son Ikenga paid his apprenticeship fee to learn woodwork had brought him seventeen tubers of yam. As he tried to help bring down the load, which was in a basin, the man slumped, like a carelessly dropped dud. Ikenga couldn't keep the situation in proportion. He rebuked the weak man so much. "I didn't do that for you to do this to yourself. So you shouldn't have bothered yourself... you could have simply poured out some drinks on the ground to the gods on my behalf. The gods are the ones who give us children and other things of goodness."

When he got to Nwani's house, he observed that everywhere was quiet for the first time since their family began to expand. Imagine a beehive being so quiet. So, he feared that something might be wrong somewhere. But he was reassured that nobody died, given that there wasn't any gong alarm or cries.

"Kpai! Kpai!! Kpai!" he clapped up on them. "Anybody in the house?" It was at this point that Nwani's first son came out to see who it was that was disturbing his crisis-oriented peace. He didn't greet Ikenga.

"Come here this boy!" he ordered the brat, who was already going back into the house. "Where is your father?"

"My father? I sent him on an errand," he replied with a cheeky tone.

"You sent your own father on an errand?"

"Yes. I asked him to buy cold 'hot drinks' for me."

"Head has spoilt you. It's either you are mad or manipulated. You no longer bully your father...you now send him on errands. Shame on you!"

They were still bandying words when Nwani and his wife appeared from a path which led to their farm. They had left as early as the cock-a-doodle-doo to plant fluted pumpkin.

"Emenike, what is it?" he asked his son, already disappointed in him. It wasn't yet long since he repaired his relationship with Ikenga, he wasn't going to keep quiet and watch his son get it strained again.

"He called me a boy," Emenike replied.

"So? Are you a girl? Must you disrespect your father's mate, the man who single-handedly won us Independence, sending the colonial masters packing in the process? Is that how you talk to a man whose gods kept vigil when his enemies refused to sleep?" This last statement pinched him terribly. He felt that he just shot himself at his foot. He knew he was one of those enemies. By-the-by, his puffery was going to change nothing.

"Continue insulting your elders. You're just a foot from your grave and you don't realize that. If you think you're a man, then do what men are known for."

"What do men do?"

"They marry early enough, and they take good care of their parents, too."

"You're not completely right, old man."

"What truly makes one a man is a secure income source, a business...and you're here worried about my not having married yet."

"Then go and start one or two businesses. Your mates are already established in life."

"You're right here, old man. But you're my life's greatest threat. I can't start a business when you're still alive." Both Nwani and Ikenga were shaken by this assertion, and the young man continued. "You have made me offend so many people that should I start a business now, their cursing me will bring it down."

"Don't mind the stupid boy, Ikenga," the highfalutin man said offhandedly, in defense of himself.

"The gods shall deliver every one of us someday, including all our enemies," the visitor replied. A little-talk-and-all-action man, he told his friend why he came, and handed the money over to him. Nwani and his wife thanked him a lot, and the benefactor left, after eating cocoyam porridge with his friend-turned-enemy-and-later-reconciled age mate.

He hadn't gone about fifteen metres when Nwani's wife told him it was about time he bought her new wrappers. Pointing at her boxes, Nwani told her that she already had enough clothes, and that at her age, she should be bothered about something worthwhile and not wears.

"Your first son is still living with you at 42 and you still feed him. That should be your concern, woman, not clothes."

"If he likes let him continue to live with me till he dies. I don't care. I'm not carrying him in my belly any more. All he knows how to do is drive favors away from me. At my age I still weed people's farms in order to eat. You must buy me new wrappers with some of this money...."

"Have you finished tying all these wrappers I'm seeing in this room? Soldier ants should visit us as soon as possible. We have enough kola nuts to welcome them with. I will make fire with these clothes and kill the ants with them."

"Mind where you keep the money. You know you gave birth to terrible reptiles, especially your last son. That one can burrow into anywhere in search of anything. It's only the gods who can save me from the hands of these things they gave me in the name of children."

"The behavior of our children makes me want to believe that missiles poisoned the wombs of our women during the war. What they give birth to since after it have been far from human beings."

The words of his first son woke him up from sleep by the witching hour. He tried to figure out what he did which he shouldn't have done, or what he didn't do but should have done for that young man. He found none. "The young man has just chosen to be irresponsible," he concluded. However, he decided to give him two-thirds of the money his friend just gave to him. He agreed with his father's saying that "a man who fails to train his children well enough has launched an offensive against the society." With the money Emenike became a successful businessman. "Everybody is possible after all. Just withdraw your doubts and realign your thoughts about them," he rejoiced with his wife, for whom the son had bought some resplendent wrappers.

CHAPTER FOUR

As It Was In Baruru

W hen the fireplace of a kitchen is cool, a dog will sleep in it. Otherwise, it walks out of it, and if need be, it keeps vigil.

Nwabunna had finally settled in Merogwu. He had found his feet in their paths. He had started earning a living, and although it was small, he subsisted on it. It was already six years since his arrival, and a few things about him had changed. He quickly picked up their variant of Ajum language. He had thought, as a little boy, that glutton was a thing of an unusually 'longer throat'. But when he grew up, he realized it was actually a thing of desire – a thing of the heart, not necessarily throat or stomach. He readily reminded himself of his grandfather's words that "a man's stomach accepts whatever he allows to pass through his throat, but his heart sifts all thoughts carefully. Whatever he gives his stomach that it takes, little or sufficient, rich or deficient."

His mother died when he was only three. His father was killed by a stray bullet when he was five. His only guardian was now separated from him. He realized, and very painfully, that he only had himself to direct and scold him. Mama was always there for him, but her persistent knee problems meant the young man couldn't have any 'moderator eyes' on him. At 22, Nwabunna had gotten brawn, brain, and beard. But he lacked bread and brake. His enormous physical strength enabled him to become an effective and reliable farmhand, tilling people's soil for pay. His brain helped him to evaluate the critical nature of his stay in exile. And his beard showed him the challenges that had refused to go away from his life. But, despite the fact that he was working real hard, he couldn't account for his wages. So he couldn't provide enough food for himself. Had it not been for crops from Mama's farms, he would have sold his bowels for a bowl of food. Mama suspected that he was suffering from empty pocket spell and that it was a doing of the gods he had disobeyed.

Another problem which Nwabunna had, earlier on, was lack of brake or self-control. He unnecessarily showed off his strength and till power by always challenging other young men, natives of the land, to see who would have the biggest number of heaps. For always trying to outwit elders of Merogwu, they saw him as an arrogant charlatan and began to look for his parents, for them to explain why they didn't teach him that "a child first has to wash his hands properly before he can qualify to eat with elders." His smugness ended—and this was to his benefit—the day he refused to forgive one of his workmates, Agbani, who had mistakenly caught his foot with a cutlass as they cleared a bush together.

"I'm very sorry, my friend," Agbani had begged Nwabunna. But he refused to let go. Rather, he told him to position his own foot for revenge. Even the owner of the bushland was surprised that none of his four workmates could make him change his mind.

"I have never seen a human with a heart of stone before," the man said, shaking his head, snapping his thumb and middle finger in Nwabunna's direction. Agbani summoned some courage, placed his foot on a bacon, and asked Nwabunna to strike, closing his two eyes. Nwabunna lifted his cutlass and went for the target, but a thorny tendril-like grass diverted his cutlass away. He wanted to repeat it, but the owner of the job refused. "He caught you in his first try. You've had your own chance. It's your business if you didn't succeed. I'll personally deal with you if you ever...who is your father by-the-way?"

"So you had the mind to really attempt it in the first place, Nwabunna!" Agbani charged him. "Now, I want the food you ate in my house last night."

Nwabunna was concussed. He was undone. He had gone to Agbani's house the previous night for he and Mama had nothing to eat. Agbani, whose father sold 'papa put', ladled for him two helpings of jollof rice and *kanda*, which the ungrateful well-welcomed lad delivered to his bowels, after which he stood up, dusted his cheeks, and left, still chewing the tough cow skin.

"I want both the jollof rice and *kanda* now-now-now!" Agbani pressurized the retaliator.

"I can manage to provide jollof rice later this week but not the *kanda*," Nwabunna said faintly. What I have at home is *mbasa*."

"You must provide the meat, not fish," their hirer pursued, but he later changed his mind and asked Agbani to drop the one-count charge. Nwabunna went home very ashamed of himself. That was how his change in attitude came about. It started gradually, increased with time, and continued. He kept improving.

As he continued to adapt in Merogwu, he began to notice that boy-girl relationship was not common as it was in Baruru. He found it both strange and impossible. For instance, he was yet to see a boy going to the river or bush with a girl cheek by jowl. In Baruru, young people enjoyed the open slather for such things. "This is some strange!" his heart complained to his head. "Man is no electric pole. Even electric poles release sparks sometimes."

One evening, as he was returning from work, with his hoe slung on his back, his sheathed cutlass in his right hand, and a container of water in his left hand, he saw a girl that was attempting to lift a basin of cassava onto her head by herself alone. He dropped all he was carrying and ran to help her out. She thanked him for his unsolicited help thereafter and took a path opposite his. She had gone some metres away when Nwabunna raised his voice and asked her: "Excuse me, please. What is your name, in case I have to…"

"Her name is Urudinanwanyi," interrogated a man from another segment of the bush. Nwabunna was disturbed. "Why are you looking at somebody's daughter that way? What do you want with her?"

"I was just looking at her…nothing more," Nwabunna defended. Meanwhile, the girl had gone beyond their sight. "I don't have anything in mind. I was just looking…"

"You don't have anything in mind but tomorrow she will have something in her belly, and you will deny it and she will go and remove it and ..." pursued the man. These words got the young man angry. But then, the man wasn't done yet. So he continued.

"Boys of nowadays, they will see a girl and their body will be doing them *jijijiji*, as though they are epileptic. And some of them, even before they meet a girl, they have already slept with her in their imagination. *Tufiakwa!*"

"What is your business here, old man? Is it your nowadays? Is it your *jijijiji*? Is she your daughter? Old men of 'these-a-days', even before they see a boy with a girl, they conclude that he has already slept with her. Your own *'tufiakwa'* there. In fact, *kwatufia* there!" The man was stunned by Nwabunna's coarse rudeness. Never had it been seen or heard in Merogwu that a young man argued with or spewed invectives at an elderly person. He asked Nwabunna whose son he was, but it fell on deaf ears. At this point, Urudinanwanyi walked past them, returning to carry some tubers of cassava which remained. Nwabunna didn't look at her again – not even a dekko did he give her this time. He was disappointed in the man who just foiled his choice opportunity. The man later left him and went his way.

Nwabunna didn't see any appeal in the body of the lanky lass. So, as he dawdled home, he wondered what on earth made her parents give Urudinanwanyi such a name. He saw no *uru* or flesh in her. All he could see was cherry-like rudimentary bobbies and badly depressed buttocks, typical of a carton of ice fish on which a 1000kg weight had been laid for ten hours. For him, a girl who was to be called Urudinanwanyi ought to have been chubby at least. He was yet to learn that the actual *uru* or benefit in a woman surpassed flesh to fortune. When he got home, he began to fry some worms which he had collected from the pulp of a decaying raffia palm tree. The segmented succulent white insects had a rufous head and tapered tail-ward. It was such a tasty delicacy when fried, and people used to intentionally fell raffia trees for the worms to form, as they decayed. In fact, the worms, like bush meat, were a kind of game. A combination of these worms, mushroom, periwinkle, and snail made their local soup more delicious and nutritious than any earthly dish. There was a boy in Merogwu who rejected an opportunity to study in England because he didn't want to miss these worms. The grig said that depression would take over him if he stayed a week without *utukuru*. He stayed back. The offer was one of many retirement benefits for his father, who had worked with the Brits when they ruled Gnishere. It was originally meant for his daughter, but he passed it over to the boy, alluding that giving such a privilege to a girl meant enriching the family of her eventual husband, ahead of his. He wasn't willing to wash his hands and crack kernel for a fowl. So, it was passed to yet another son of his, who eventually went to Birmingham and studied Engineering.

After Nwabunna brought down his frying pan from fire, he tripped and hit his foot against the gridiron. The heat was so intense that he sustained a third degree burn, which made him to release a loud scary screech that made a threadbare oil palm-cutter to abseil a weak shaky palm tree which he was pruning for a better fruiting. He was originally named Ibe, but was fondly called "Smally," because of his miniature size. There was a day a courier brought a parcel to his house which his older brother had sent him from Ulaanbaatar. The delivery man met his wife at home and told her he was looking for "one Mr. Ibe Eluwa."

"This is Smally's house, not Ibe's house," the ignorant wife replied. They were still trying to reconcile the names when Ibe walked in and took over from his uninformed wife. It was when the courier left that he told his wife his real name was Ibe Eluwa. They courted for three years before marriage yet she didn't find out who and what he was. And her ignorance of a thing as sensitive as name, a spouse's real name, and maybe age, was crude carelessness. Well, stupidity could be interesting sometimes. What if the delivery man had walked away with the parcel?

Ibe always climbed oil palm trees with bitter kola in his mouth and pockets. This, it was believed, scared snakes away and sometimes some of them surrendered to his sharp machete, which could cut grapheme to halves. He was one of Merogwu's favorite top dogs, as far as palm fruit cutting was concerned. Besides, he was yet to experience a fall, unlike every other cutter.

The pain which Nwabunna nurtured far outweighed the taste of the worm, and two days later, a bunion formed on his right foot. Meanwhile, it was only three days prior that Mama had developed a biting whitlow, which left her thumb with blisters. What a week of wounds for them – Mama's thumb and Nwabunna's big toe! What a period of pain! But Mama had kept her pain to herself. She believed that there was a form of joy in nurturing one's pain quietly. Yet that wasn't solecism she was preaching, nor was it masochism she was having. She simply meant that smiling in pain staved off sympathizers' glee. But the pain of whitlow was such a stubborn one that it spread and persisted until biologically walled off. So, when she saw that it was beginning to go beneath her thumbnail cuticle, she sent for Ogwueleka.

Nwabunna got to Ogwueleka's house only to find out that the naturopathy expert, who was known as Ogwonnuoria, was down with severe fever and sore throat. He referred Nwabunna, whereupon, to Oforbuike's house. Imagine a physician telling his client he was sick. Wonders are abstracts being real! Nwabunna pedaled his bicycle with his hurting foot to where he was referred to. Lo, he found out that it was the man he had insulted just the previous day, the man he called an old man of "these-a-days". He suddenly felt grime entering his mouth but couldn't spit it out. He realized that he had hit a man who was now going to heal him if he chose to. He was at his mercy now. He knew, at least, that Oforbuike would accept to go with him to treat Mama. He couldn't even say a meaningless vocable. He expected the man to react, but he didn't. It was actually herbs and roots and leaves that Oforbuike had gone to pluck when he saw Nwabunna trying to woo Urudinanwanyi. With them he made a decoction which served as medicine for various ailments. Oforbuike showed maturity. He didn't say anything about their encounter. He acted as though they just met. What goes around, they say, comes around. They also say that a snake will always climb down a tree same way it climbed up. So the dude of undue demeanor saw that what he threw up had fallen freely.

Oforbuike followed Nwabunna home, treated Mama and the young man, and then he left. But before he did, he asked Nwabunna to visit him by the weekend.

Mama returned to her room to continue her rest, while

Nwabunna prepared to go for the evening job. Mama tried to talk him out of that arrangement, but he discouraged her from encouraging him to stay back. A strong-willed young man, he did things on his own terms. There were times he would agree with certain decisions of Mama's with his head, like lizard the conformist, only to do another thing altogether, like tortoise the rationalist. Ever since he arrived, he had been variously helpful to Mama. He sheared bunches of palm fruits, took them to the mill, and then took the processed oil to the market. He harvested cassava, peeled it, ground it, and fried it. He fetched water and firewood. Hardworking was the word. A thing he never liked doing, however, was dishwashing and kernel cracking. While the former reminded him of his foodless days in Baruru, the latter reminded him of the taboo he committed, which made him flee his homeland. He even preferred washing Mama's clothes to dishes. So, although palm kernels were as a good business as palm oil itself, cracking it was his bête noire. There was a day Mama, trying to turn him on to help her crack some of it, told him that kernel was making people rich. He replied that she had better remain poor. So Mama cracked kernel and washed dishes by herself.

She woke up the next day but couldn't find her on-the-run son. She was alarmed because he had told her he wouldn't be going for morning job that day. She was troubled that the gods he flouted might have flown him back to his homeland to face the wrath he incurred. It was *ugba* seeds he had gone to the forest to pick, meanwhile, which he sold to top up his earnings. Nwabunna wasn't the kind of person who waited for instructions before he did errands. He identified tasks and tackled them by himself, voluntarily and judiciously. As for his toe, he didn't mind. He was back home by 10:32 am, with a wodge of the nut and seed – about half a jute sisal bag. He preferred going to the forests either in the morning or evening to beat snakes, creatures he hated with verve. When cooked and sliced, oil bean seeds made rich proteinous food. Its value was more appreciated during festivals and landmark occasions, like coronation and marriage rites. In fact, it was food for big occasions and for rich men. So, it was costly in the market. Its cassava equivalent was the one reserved for the poor. But *abacha* was really rich in its own right too, especially when jazzed up with garden eggs, onions, and scent leaf. The meal was altogether proteinous and farinaceous; you sure would like to taste it. A story was once told of a man who bought a plate of *abacha* and pleaded with the seller to gift him two spoons of *ugba* as incentive. "Crown me a king with one or two spoons of *ugba*, please," he had pleaded. It was food for kings, for proven men, and, much more, for sons whose souls appreciated the soil which gave birth to them.

Mama was relieved when he saw him. She was excited with what he brought home. She knew that if Nwabunna continued to desire and demand good things from life, he would certainly have his way. She had no doubt that a young man who worked so hard would one day become prosperous. All she prayed for was to be alive and witness the reaping moments of those efforts. She served him his brunch, and she spread the seeds and nuts under the sun, as her fowls watched on. They knew those were not their kind of food. So they walked away afterwards.

CHAPTER FIVE
The Strayed Dog Is Traced

A well trained dog can still stray and a wild dog can be tamed. All a man has got to do is trace his strayed dog and retrain it, and it will stay. If it goes astray again, still retrace it. Never bid your dog bye and buy another one while the old one is still alive. Always recover and retrain it because all dogs have some wild tendencies. It will definitely turn to a good puppy-boy someday. But while training it to stay, teach yourself not to stray, because a dog is always watching its owner, learning a whole lot from him.

Nwabunna went to see Oforbuike, as arranged, two days later. Oforbuike was seeing him for the third time but he was able to tell who and what he could become if guided. Critical yet objective observation told him that Nwabunna was a child of sheer behavior who had a deficient parentage, which contributed to his problems.

A traditional psychologist, he knew that children who were always scolded as infants grew up to be easily apprehensive; children who were always interrupted in public became shy grown-ups; those who were always freely tolerated grew up to be expressive, and those who were appreciated grew up to be confident and composed. He knew about those attitudinal forks. From their conversation, he found out that Nwabunna was an urchin whose attitude was shaped by the things he went through growing up. The fact that his cousins lived in plenty while he starved, the fact that they had toys while he toiled got him bitter, jealous, and woe-be-gone.

"Those things affected you because you attached your heart to them," Oforbuike began the counseling. "You allowed the wrong things to get to your head. Success or failure ought not to live in a man's head. The only thing that should get to a man's head is how to improve on his life and those of others. You're now a man. Be serious with life and be sincere with people.

"Discourtesy, as well as dishonesty, does a child no good. It only scares favors and opportunities away from his life. I can always assist you with anything and in any way. So look up to me whenever you're in need." Nwabunna thought for a while before responding to him. When Oforbuike mentioned discourtesy, he knew the man referred to that incident where he insulted him. But he couldn't quite figure out what exactly Oforbuike dug for when he mentioned dishonesty. He always heard the elderly say that when *Omara* was told a parable, he would know but when *Ofeke* was told one, he would drift into the bush. He never saw himself to be shiftless or dull. He always knew what was what.

"If I had met you three minutes before our first meeting, I would have behaved three times better than I did. All the same, I'm sorry for those words, and I hereby withdraw them. I'm grateful that you're concerned about me —a stranger in your land."

"They say that whenever one wakes from sleep it is his morning. But there's a time you will wake up and you can't greet or be greeted 'good morning'. So, it's always good to wake up early in life because we can never sleep enough, no matter how long. Missing an unusual opportunity is terrible. But more terrible is gaining a fortune through bad character. It won't last and it will destroy you.

"Help me greet mama when you get home."

"I will, *Nna-anyi*. Her bones are troubling her with ambition these days."

"Aging has a way of giving women stories to tell their grandchildren. It knows that men are too busy tying up yams in the barn that's why it gives us less trouble. So it is going to be well with mama with time. Like I said before now, remember to run to me whenever you get into trouble."

"I'll run to you even before I get into trouble," the counselee said and bade his host bye. He mounted his bicycle and headed home. He had bought the bicycle with the first series of money he made from tilling. What he spent decorating it was more than what he bought it for. All kinds of accessories adorned it. He simply wanted to make other boys jealous then. But when hunger flogged him one day, he nearly sold it for a pittance. Hunger so much dealt with him that his buttocks no longer had any muscle to sit on the bicycle. All of it happened during the days of his serial stupidity, when he bought any damn thing that caught his fancy, before he learnt that a swallow doesn't make a summer in life. Mama took her time to teach him one of the invaluable lessons of his life–savings. She told him that, "a man's earnings may not be enough to save him every time, but his careless spending can kill him any time." And hunger is an effective punisher of a wasteful living. It visits the frivolous with 'stomachal' torture and self-taunt. Also, Mama told him that "Poverty is more interested in remaining with a man than the man is willing to step out of it." Finally, she told him that, "We work hard to have a quality life, not to please people or get them envious of us."

As he pedaled home, he wondered what reason there was in Oforbuike's submission that bones were aching an old woman just to give her stories to tell her grandchildren when she hadn't children to start with. He disagreed with him in retrospect. He believed that a woman as kind as Mama should have been given her own stories in a peaceful manner. He empathized with Oforbuike post hoc on the state of his only son. "The gods seem to be quicker to punish wickedness than to reward good deeds," he chose to believe. He wasn't the first person and wasn't going to be the last person to walk in that line of thought. Traditional philosophers in Merogwu taught that one of life's unpredictable pregnancies was a delayed and disguised pattern of reward delivery. One of them, Akwarandu, taught that, "It is evil in the eyes of the gods for mortals to expect the gods to reward them for good deeds. Expect not rewards from mortals too. It makes your next motive evil." He also taught them to, "explain not thyself to the gods, for they know you and your entire lineage." These were the teachings of Akwarandu, one of a few men who had received education from white missionaries but rejected their religion. He refused to call his father's barn tattered, even though he couldn't stop the strangers from dumping their refuse on it.

A father of two, a mentally retarded son, and his beastly burly sister, Oforbuike knew what was obtainable for any child growing up without essential factors of adequate upbringing, especially parental presence and provision. Such a situation gave the child challenges to conquer before he or she could become successful in life. What he thought Nwabunna needed most was courage. His daughter was so strong and mesomorphic that villagers started calling her Lady Unshakable. And true to her fun name, she was unshakable until she caught a beat fever in 1982. She was 29 then. She could roll a mountain uphill. There was a day she went to the river with a fifty-litre capacity container to fetch some water but ended up feeding a woman with water. The woman was sieving breadfruit right inside the river from which people drank. This got the mouth of the river unpleasant. Lady Unshakable told her to take her job to the bush side so as to allow the water to settle and clear out. The woman refused. This made the beast to beat the beauty to pulp. She kicked the woman, her breadfruit, baskets, and buckets into the river, and then she filled her abdominal barrel with the universal solvent. In other words, she fed her with water and wasted the food that roiled the river. When she came out, she emptied people's receptacles of clean water into her container, placed it on her shoulder with a swing of her arm, and she left.

Some people rushed and brought the victim ashore and resuscitated her. Others ran and reported the incident to her family. When the victim's sons accosted Lady Unshakable, she gave them a rebirth of a beating. As a result, they automatically evolved into crying marsupials, with their tear glands terribly torn. As she gave them the beating of the decade, her retard of a brother cheered her on. The children of the water-fed woman, although grown and groomed, wept until they wetted their clothes with tears. You couldn't have beaten that; that a lady took three men out with candy ease, and they cried? Just imagine what hormonal aberration could cause. As they staggered home, they kept sniffing like wild pigs. When the matter which was one of caseloads of urgent weight was looked into by their *igwe*, he asked Lady Unshakable to go apologize to the woman for shaming her in public. He further ordered her to sieve at least ten buckets of *ukwa* for her. She told Igwe that she would do that only if he threw his *ofor* and crown to the ground for her to stamp on them. She walked out on him, and when some palace beaus wanted to stop her, she dished out their own portion of her beating delicacy for them. Igwe's special adviser suggested to him to let the sleeping dog lie. But a dog as stubborn as Lady 'Unshaka,' as a few other people called her, neither laid nor slept. She was just a Talbot which hunted and bit people randomly. She was the only person in Merogwu who saw their *igwe*, a man whose staff determined the fate of the entire kingdom, and didn't bow before him. And no sanctions were given to her, whatsoever. Only a groundswell of grudges, disapproval, rebuke, and threats.

"Papa," she addressed Oforbuike, her father, when she returned home, "I gave Igwe the disrespect of his entire reign today. I walked out on him and his foolish cabinet in majesty."

"Congratulations, my daughter. Your stupidity level has finally reached an all-time high," he mocked her. "What remains is for you to be officially recognized as the rudest living thing on earth. And that will happen the day you disgrace your own father in public. If you have the guts to insult a man of Igwe's person and prestige, who am I? So congratulations, *agu nwanyi*." And he sighed, which was a sign of resignation. "You have the gut to insult Igwe, right? Don't worry. The gods shall soon seal up your lips. They call you Nwada Akwaakwuru and you now think you can withstand the wrath of the gods. Well-done, you hear!" She didn't even give her father any damn attention. All he said entered her right ear and exited the left one.

When he turned and saw his retard of a son habitually slobbering and dipping his index finger into his nostrils, almost chiseling away the roof of his nose, bringing out and licking boogers in the process, Oforbuike wondered which sin of his must have brought him such a poor luck in childbirth. "Whose child did I kill or render useless to deserve this?" he queried his ancestors, facing the sky with supine palms. His palms facing up was a way of suing for vindication and an affirmation of his innocence. There was a day he took a trip down memory lane when he remembered that he used to take out Egedi's hens and chicks with a stick, as well as stole her eggs. In all honesty, he confessed everything to Ezemmuo and pleaded with him to help appease the gods. But incantations revealed that that wasn't the cause of his child-bearing challenges. "I thought as much," said Ezemmuo. "A suitable repercussion would have been incessant deaths of your own fowls, were the gods punishing you for that atrocity."

Egedi was the oldest woman in Merogwu then. She spoke with the soothing grace of a baby and firmness of an adult. She was easy-going, thoughtful, yet outgoing. Altogether, Oforbuike believed that his unhealthy exuberance as a boy was haunting him, somehow. Orient Gnishere, essential parts of which the likes of Baruru and Merowu were, believed that a man would always have returns from all his deeds.

That same day, when fowls began to go to bed, he went to the palace to apologize on his daughter's behalf. He took with him seven tubers of well-fed yam, five bottles of hot drinks, and a fat she-goat. Igwe was humbled by Oforbuike's great sense of responsibility when he saw him with those materials. "Igwe, may you live long, longer than all your ancestors," greeted Oforbuike, genuflecting same time. "I just heard what happened... Don't mind that *akpanjo* of my daughter. I gave birth to her outside will. I honestly don't know how that 'suffer head' entered my wife's womb. She almost killed her mother as she tried to come out with her legs. I've always wanted to send her back to the Creator and re-order for another child."

"Get up Oforbuike," Igwe asked him. "I don't hold your daughter's sins against a responsible man like you. My cabinet and I have chosen to let the matter fade away."

Oforbuike got up from the floor and cleaned off dust from his clothes. Authorities were duly respected those days. People had deference for rulers and awe for the gods.

"Child-birth is like untying *ngwugwu*," reacted Igwe to Oforbuike's remarks about his daughter. "Whatever parents see, they should accept it in positives."

"Excluding my daughter, Igwe. That girl represents one of the undesirable harms the Europeans did to Africa." And they all laughed. A king's kola nut, as they said, was in his hands, but a guest's drink ceased to be his once he stepped into the palace. So, the red cap men, all of whom were excessively ambitious that they wanted to walk on Buckingham's red carpet, took over the hot drinks Oforbuike had brought. Their eyeballs reddened some more, and they cleared their mucus-troubled throat, without hawking up though. Their temperature increased and their stomachs each became a pot. No wonder it was said that the land not being good was a benefit for red-cap men. Each time someone committed an offence and needed to atone for it, he took drinks and other materials to the shrine. They ended up in the bellies of these men, after a fraction of it had been offered to the gods. Meanwhile, they poured out some of the drinks on the ground, asking the gods to drink from it and to bless Oforbuike for always taking side with justice and truth. He was the kind of man who wouldn't mind sentencing his own mother to death if she was found guilty of an offence of commensurate weight. For him, until one presided over a judgment that condemned his own mother, he wasn't a good judge. He believed that the gods owed him normal adorable children in his subsequent lives.

CHAPTER SIX
Leaving for Merogwu

L ove for his dog doesn't make a man sleep in its kennel. It makes him allow it to sleep on his mattress. But then, he is sure the dog is well-trained and won't pee on it.

Ikenga finally found out about Nwabunna's whereabouts. He had missed him greatly, and he had badly wanted a reunion to happen. He was not going to move to Merogwu, however, to pack into an old woman's house, neither was he going to build a house there and live with his grandson. His actual plan was to pay him a visit and return to Baruru afterwards.

News about Nwabunna's exile in Merogwu didn't reach Ikenga exclusively. Baruruans learnt about it too, seven years on. That was after the Oforbuike counseling. Seven years was such a long time during which they were expected to have forgotten about the incident, were it a matter of light weight. But it wasn't, and so they hadn't forgotten it. It was an act that brought plenitude of deaths through famine throughout Baruru. So they vowed to mete out the penalty whenever his feet were seen within their territory. "We must stone him to death," they resolved, calling him an accursed lost cause. And they weren't being wicked. They were simply bent on the dictates of their tradition, which placed authority of the gods over everything else. "It's only proper to definitely fine a man who deliberately broke the law," they held this position dearly. Before the Oforbuike confidence assistance, Merogwu people only thought of Nwabunna as Mama's nephew. Upon his identity disclosure, they tried to force him out, but for their Igwe, who stood in their way. "Our kingdom is liberal to everyone from every earth part. A man is free to stay until he breaks our sacred laws." This official asylum granted to a Baruru expatriate was a second devious thing Igwe Udorji had done, according to his subjects. Before this time, he had been giving one-third of their monthly allocation from the central government to coterminous Umuakaekpe kingdom for a reason they only saw as malarkey. They were undone by the fact that Igwes were untouchable and unchallengeable. They knew they needed an unusual swivel to stop such a drivel. And they chose to bide their time.

Mazi Ikenga decided to wait till one Madam Nnebuihe's burial had passed before going to Merogwu to see Nwabunna. She was his mother's younger sister and both of them were married to the same biological brothers. As one of the rites required of her children, they had to repay her dowry three Nkwo market days to her burial proper. So, they got a huge she-goat which they adorned with wrapper and palm frond and led her on a lively celebratory procession to Madam Nnebuihe's maternal home. That was one ritual for proper burial for women, and it had some phenomenal significance. Without it, the person, even when interred, was deemed to not have been buried.

Midway into their journey, the goat became reluctant to continue, couchant now. And they started pleading with her, with all manner of solemn cultural ditties. It was when the deceased's first son and daughter came up with their mother's most favorite food and started praising her, calling her all the good names they had for her when she was still alive, that the goat resumed the journey. When they got to their point of aim, the people that gave birth to the woman welcomed them well enough. The party that brought the goat told them that they had come to repay their daughter's dowry, as well as officially inform them of her funeral. In that community, dowry at death was as important as the one at marriage. The goat was to be slaughtered on the day of burial and its meat shared among those that gave birth to the woman and her husband's people.

Madam Nnebuihe's only surviving sibling, her younger brother, Ukoh, was grieved by the death of his sister, despite the fact she died a fulfilled old woman, aged 96. That was because Madam Nnebuihe was the only one who believed in him. Overtaken by hardship upon his conception, his parents perceived him to be a terrible baby, a bad-luck bringer. And upon his birth, a shaman administered palmistry to him and told his parents he was going to be a person of empty destiny. This oracular declaration constrained them from training him in anything, school or craft. They chose to only feed him until he would die and waste away naturally. The feeling was also nursed by the entire community, who called him *efulefu*. And why won't they? His own parents despised and almost disowned him. When someone called his barn dilapidated, they said, neighbors would definitely dump refuse in it. And whatever a man called his dog, that others would equally call it. Their derision of him nadired when Ukoh was denied observing *Iwa Akwa* Festival alongside his age mates, to mark their attainment of manhood. They told him that a man who was destiny-less had nothing to do with manhood. In fact, they suggested that he should give himself out to 'boy-boy' work.

But Nnebuihe stepped in. She told a discouraged, devastated, and deserted Ukoh that a man could always re-align the axle of his life's wheel and move to wherever he desires to be in destiny. She helped him find reason for sanity, light, enthusiasm, and ambition. With her guidance, Ukoh went on to become an accomplished man in his lifetime. He went to school, excelled academically, and won a scholarship to study in the university. Most impressive of it all was that his parents, as well as all those who wrote him off, lived and saw what blessing he became to humanity. It was these things he remembered and mourned his sister for; that she held the fort for him and fought people's rejection of him.

Like Ukoh, Madam Nnebuihe did well in school. And upon completion of her secondary education, she got a job with the Ministry of Public Utilities where she met her husband. She was so informed and smart that she rejected marriage while still a little girl, something that was common amongst her equals. And that was against her parents' will and coaxing. She had been so diligent that she rose through the ranks smoothly and earned herself renown far and wide. When she retired, she was massively missed by the civil service. Her 'dropping of hoe' ceremony was full of memory-worthy moments, as people she had helped poured some precious praises on her, for her destiny-defining largesse and kindness to them. Particularly touching was a testimony from a widow she had helped with shelter and sustenance until her children grew and began to earn a living. And she was honored with a title, thus becoming the first woman to be so recognized throughout Baruru. Such was her prestige and personage that Mazi Ikenga would not fail to pay his last respect to a woman whose life weathered storms and cleared fogs in other peoples' lives. She had no foundation for philanthropy, but her acts of mercy made people great and built her society. What a woman she was. What a life she lived. You could say she was a re-maker of men.

Despite different foods that were made available in their abundance to people during Nnebuihe's funeral, a few persons went about complaining that they ate nothing. One of them was a man who went missing when his own mother was buried. He couldn't even afford a casket let alone hearse for us to talk about good food. It was his age grade that went and brought him from where he hid and rallied around the whole place. The only thing the barefaced ingrate of a son contributed to his mother's funeral was his presence and then dropping earth on her remains. Yet, he had the mouth to complain that the plate of rice given him at Nnebuihe's burial contained the legs of chicken instead of thighs. If he had provided the legs or even hands of chickens during his mother's burial, she would have been proud of him in her grave. He had the mouth to say that a family who killed six cows, cooked twenty-three bags of rice, made six bags of garri, eight different soup sorts, inter alia, did not try. Look at him. Just take a look at his head and give him a well-deserved name. Well, it is said that after a man has finished fighting, a woman takes over telling a story about the fight. To cap his folly that afternoon, the man targeted a full-to-the-brim cooler of fried meat provided for Ukoh's in-laws, hijacked it, and disappeared into the bush. The cooler was so full that its contents budged the cover and wouldn't let it close tightly. He was pursued by some young men, who recovered the meat from him, giving him a 'general beating' in the process. But before they delivered it, they settled themselves with enough meat in the bush. Yet the container looked intact. That was how excess its content was.

Now that his aunt had finally been buried, Ikenga left for Merogwu. And alone he went.

CHAPTER SEVEN
The Waylay

A responsible dog aspires to roar like a lion, not to mew like a cat. It desires to get bigger and better and braver by the day.

Nwabunna had just finished nursing his pain. His wound was gone. His toe was no longer hurting. His mind was aboil with questions. Too many things bothered him greatly. He knew he was not going to continue staying with an old woman, whose brothers-in-law were standing by, poised to take over whatever properties her late heirless intestate husband left behind. He was speedily growing into a mature man. Responsibilities, too, were hanging heavily on his shoulders. His body was long beginning to speak chemistry. So, he naturally understood his immediate biological need for a woman. However, Mama was more interested in his future than she was in his transient sensual desires. "It is too dangerous to dream of a woman when you can't buy yourself cream," she said to him. "And it's too pitiable, too."

She wanted him to learn a craft. Meanwhile, Oforbuike had offered to give him to a friend of his who dealt on general merchandise. But he told them he wasn't going to suffer again in the hands of a master. He had his fill with Obiuwa already, and he gave his mind to sentiment and prejudice. He told them – Mama and Oforbuike – he wanted to go to college. As far as he was concerned, what gave Ikenga's younger brother an edge over him was the little basic education the man had, something they called "Infant Two."

He dreamed of going overseas. Above all, he dreamed of going back to his grandfather. But he knew he couldn't, at least not any time soon. Was he missing the old man? One hundred percent. And was the old man missing him as much? Absolutely. And he was coming for his grand-boy.

Mazi Ikenga had been a simple, gentle, and generous man all his life. In his simpleness, he approached life situations with understanding and aim. In his gentleness, he kept himself from living in a way that would make it difficult to be of service or of help to others. And, in his generosity, he ensured no one met him distressed, and left without encouragement, strength, and comfort. He didn't solve everybody's problems, but he motivated all to walk on hope's world.

Moreover, Ikenga was not a maudlin man, a man who held onto the past and punished himself for his mistakes. He let go of everything and forgave everyone and himself. But the one thing he would not let go was his son's son, Nwabunna, and now, he was on his way to Merogwu, a place he last visited when Super Gnishere nearly collapsed like a cromlech, about two decades ago. Although neighbors, mainland distance between Baruru and Merogwu was fifty-eight miles. One of the things that made Nwabunna believe that by making a ford in River Omimi, through which he had fled, the gods must have viewed the thing he did differently.

Hoodlums waylaid him upon entry to Merogwu. Everything he had on and with him was taken away. It was a painful experience – yes – but he chose to believe it was all worth it. Going back was necessary but defeating, he continued from that waypoint. At-gun-point robberies, kidnapping, and recidivism were on the increase. Most of those who indulged in them were young men who refused to go to school and those who refused to learn a trade or craft. They wanted a jerry-built success. Bandits so much terrorized road users and made that terrain impassable that stopping them looked like a grail until community policing began.

That experience dredged up all Ikenga had suffered in life. Memories that were unsuitable at a time he was going to see his long-lost grandson. Life and people had always taken from him: his family, his farmlands, and now his optimism. A man of Ikenga's generosity, goodwill, and gentleness should not have had to cop all of those unfortunate situations. Not that he ever expected life to be fair. Not that his generosity was a stake for returns. Kindness was his natural character flaw.

He, nonetheless, was grateful they spared his life. For life – he believed – is worth more than wealth. His saving grace was a compassionate passer-by who hitch-hiked him with his flivver to the heartland of Merogwu, from where he would easily help himself through. He was going to have some food and rest before continuing, and he found both at a roadside eatery, where some people were in stitches when he arrived.

As he rested on a stanchion, he observed that a griffin statue which depicted Merogwu's deity, housed in a tall tower, some distance away, just tilted on its own. Knowing it was strange and ominous, he asked a man, "Did you see that?" The man was disinterested, as though he was a non-indigene too. So Ikenga left that place immediately.

As he hightailed, he remembered that a certain Igwe of Merogwu once attributed the deity with grim reaper and didn't survive it. But whatever the statue adjusting its posture on its own meant, Ikenga chose to concern himself with seeing Nwabunna alive at the end.

The lion half of the griffin represented fearlessness, the eagle half peace. But their current *igwe*, Igwe Udorji, lacked those two qualities; he was a chicken-shit and brought his people all manner of chaos and trouble.

Ikenga was still to continue his journey when the young man he had asked whether he noticed the tilt of the statue – the man who had been disinterested – approached him and asked to know where he was going to. Taking him for a perfect pick-pocket, and having been robbed earlier, a smart Ikenga ignored him. It was his own time to be disinterested. Why not? The young man was called Ekeledo. A properly poor soul, he used his breath as collateral and his creditors took advantage of that lien and turned him to a community liability.

How could someone be popular and poor at the same time? Ekeledo had at his disposal all the resources to fend off poverty, but was tardy and work-shy. While his mates plugged away to survive, he frittered his life away with wayward girls and tarts, until all he inherited from his father was exhausted. Now, he had become a human macaque – all he cared about was to have food in his stomach. The nimby tearaway would always wish he had foreseen this; if he had, he wouldn't have become a dish washer at a local eatery where he squandered his money, where he used to tip people, his type of people, of course – nimby ne'er-do-wells – who preferred being bought food to working to earn a living. And they were not ashamed of living such a shameful life. Shame!

CHAPTER EIGHT
Nancy's Pregnancy

A dog trained by a woman will definitely eat the eggs of fowls. And irrespective of how much it is loved, the owner doesn't smile at it for eating the eggs.

Mama's knee problems persisted. So a woman started coming to the house to treat her. One evening, she couldn't come, but she sent her daughter Nancy to take *ori* to Mama. Nwabunna was coming out of the bathroom when the Nancy girl arrived. He felt the urge for a woman immediately, seeing the compulsive invitation of her body. When Nancy noticed that he was looking at her, she shimmied her waist area vigorously. This aroused the guerilla commander between his legs and it ordered for the target. At such times, even a plasma rope wouldn't be able to hold it back. Strongly excited, Nwabunna covered his commander with the bucket he had just bathed with. But nothing is a more misleading compass than the waist of a walking woman. It lands men who depend on it for direction to a place opposite of their destination. It, also, saps men of their might at night. A man needs some heroics to not go for it.

Nancy, daughter of Molokwu, a Merogwu publican, had come to deliver shea butter to Mama as well as massage her knees with it. But Mama was in a here-but-afar sleep land when she came. Nwabunna wanted to wake her up but Nancy declined, maintaining she wasn't in a hurry to leave, that she wouldn't mind waiting. "Allow her to have a rich rest, please," she had said. Nwabunna first met her at her father's farm, where he once made two hundred and seventy five heaps within four hours. She had been the one who brought him 'work food' that day.

While they were waiting for Mama to wake up, only Satan knew what they told each other with their eyes. And Nwabunna drew her into his commodious room, which was two rooms away from Mama's, and she yielded like quartz fiber. They had a very steamy bed business that day. For well over an hour, they continued knowing each other in the biblical sense and Mama obliged them inadvertently, by not waking up on time. When the two opportunistic lovers felt that they had read and known all the chapters of the sensual bible, the emergency bible study dismissed. Then, Nancy, who said she wasn't in haste to go, earlier on, hurried home, without waiting for Mama to wake up. She ran home like a robotic motor, without a stopover anywhere, even Chinenyedi's place. They usually say that when a child eats that for which he's awake, he will sleep off. So she sped off after eating that for which she waited on a sleeping old woman. And for Nwabunna, he just found what he was looking for in an upper cave in a lower one. As the sales-turned-sex girl was leaving, Nwabunna continued to stare at her. He wondered what on earth the Creator wanted to achieve when he packed and padded all those flabs of flesh to Nancy, which gave the small girl such a big gift of a kind.

When Mama woke up it was already dusk. Nwabunna went to pick his clothes from where he spread them. He didn't know he collected a lizard as well. It was the same color as his trouser. That was the commonest adaption of most reptiles there – mimicry –disguising themselves to look like things around them. There had been a day, before he came to live with her, that Mama was bitten by a snake which had perfectly stuck to her wrapper. But, in Merogwu, venom of any kind didn't kill anybody. That was where their name came from; Meruo ogwu, meaning neutralize poison or charms. So, poison and charms didn't kill people. What killed them was wickedness, injustice. The gods of the land were always ready to punish men of mired mind who partook in charms and evil. Justice and clean hands were an effective anti-poison.

Three days later, Mama remembered that it was about time Molokwu's wife came to massage her knees. So she sent Nwabunna who was just returning from the river to the woman's house. That was only when he told her that Nancy came the other day. Mama was displeasured. She wondered why he didn't wake her up, allowing her to continue her sleep of pain. To placate her, he left with speed. He rode upstanding till he was near enough. As he rode, he remembered that his bicycle's back tire might not be able to carry Nancy should her mother ask her to go with him. Her weight, seventy-five percent of which came from her waist, would certainly be some considerable impediment for the carrier. He stopped and inflated the two tyres, adding more air to the already strong front tyre so that should there be a weight transmission from the back one, the bicycle would still be able move.

Just in time, he arrived at Molokwu's house, stood the bicycle by an *ugiri* tree which was replete with unripe fruits. Then, as he wanted to walk towards the passageway, Molokwu who completed a hedge work right round his house only the previous day walked into the compound. The palm leaves were still very green and so gave the whole place some curb appeal. He had gathered the leaves from his brother's pruned palm trees in his oil palm plantation. The pruning was to enhance its chances at fruiting next season. As they greeted, they overheard Nancy's mother's faint voice. It was suggestive of query and repugnance. In Merogwu, when a boy threw up, he was suspected of being febrile. But when a girl vomited, she was suspected of being pregnant. "You vomited scantily yesterday, and here you are vomiting again this morning," she queried Nancy. "I need you to tell me the truth now. Who slept with you and where? Talk before I send you back to your creator," she threatened. As they eavesdropped, Nwabunna was gripped with fear and wanted to run away. Molokwu saw some tanka of unease all over him, and as the woman who sold *ogiri* knew a blind fly, he knew the young man had something to do with the situation. However, in his maturity, he chose to calm his nerve-racks. So he began to ask him after Mama. Nwabunna answered all his questions vimlessly. "Let's go in so you can have some kola. The farmland you tilled for me some months ago has grown abundant crops. I expect a very large harvest from it."

Each step they took towards the door brought his wife's vengeful voice clearer and louder. "You have brought shame to this family, Nancy...you still don't want to tell me who got you pregnant?"

"*Nna-anyi* Molokwu, I have to start going now," Nwabunna said without ambition. Suddenly, Nancy emerged from the backyard, with her mother pulling her arm and ranting, "You must show me who got you pregnant today and I will show him his handwork." They both were taken aback seeing Molokwu and Nwabunna. And without further ado, Nancy pointed at Nwabunna. "He's the one," she stuttered. And a noose just appeared before a cow. What a bombshell that was. "He drew me into his room, placed me on his bed, and…."

"And what, Nancy?" her mother barraged her with a query.

"Is it true, my friend?" Molokwu asked Nwabunna, turning to him with stern looks. In Orient Gnishere, when a man called another "my friend" that emphatically, he just became his enemy.

"I didn't place her by myself. She positioned herself for me," Nwabunna defended. That sounded like the Adam response. The woman took the blame in both cases, and she tried to present herself blameless in both cases, too. Molokwu tentatively gave Nwabunna a decisive apprehensive slap which clattering sound assured his wife that they would get dowry soon. He tried to tie Nwabunna to a pear tree which was host to some ants of painful bite, but the latter overpowered him. Thanks to goodness that Ogubunka walked into the scene. There would have been a dead man at the end, otherwise. "So after tilling my farm, you began tilling my daughter." was what he recited.

"Why are you fighting with a small boy of yesterday, Molokwu. You don't have shame in your life." That was Ogubunka talking.

"He impregnated my daughter. This vagabond … this good for nothing and bad for something human being looked for a family to disgrace and it was mine that he found."

"Wait. Is that all about his crime? You should be grateful. You think it's easy to impregnate a woman these days? He only slept with your daughter and you're fighting. What will you do the day he will sleep with your wife? Boys are busy sleeping with people's wives and they haven't done anything to them. You're here fighting a boy for sleeping with your wayward daughter. Who doesn't want to sleep with Nancy? Her name is supposed to be 'Ukwu-chi-nyerem,' not Nancy."

"Come, Ogubunka, turn and leave my house. I can see you're the one spoiling our boys?"

"Who is spoiling our boys? Our boys are born spoilt these days. Nobody is spoiling them."

"Leave my house now. You're that old man who sits at home and watches a nanny deliver in the tether."

"When did you become a woman, Molokwu? You just heard that someone impregnated your daughter, and you want to jungle-judge him. You, didn't you impregnate somebody's daughter? Allow the young man to go, because impregnating someone's daughter is no more a new thing." Molokwu hurried and covered Ogubunka's mouth with his hand. He just scattered a bee comb. Turning to Nwabunna, Ogubunka said, "Well done young man. Your god doesn't sleep at night. In fact, he doesn't sleep at all."

"Who did you impregnate, Molokwu?" his wife accosted him.

"It doesn't matter, woman. What matters now is who is presently pregnant, not who was pregnant. He nabbed Nwabunna's bicycle and told him to go prepare for Nancy's dowry.

It was noon already yet Nwabunna hadn't returned. Mama was worried. The eyes of one who sent somebody on an errand should always be in the street. He was troubled in his heart as he traipsed home. What was he going to tell Mama about the bicycle, about the shea butter, and about Nancy? As he walked aimlessly, he saw Urudinanwanyi with her mother. They were obviously going to the market. He had laughed at her for not having enough *uru*, or flesh, on her waist area. Now that he saw and slept with a girl who had tumescent buttocks, he started mourning. Irony of life!

Whenever you see drunks respect them enough. They can transmit news, a rumor or fact, faster than the media. Trees, birds, and winds all carried the news: "Nancy is pregnant. Nwabunna, the Baruru taboo boy, is responsible." So, before he could get home, Mama had already heard about it. But it didn't shock or surprise her. She was attuned with worse things for the news to tickle her fortified ears. She waited for the hero to return. Some women who had never come around since she started ailing visited her this time around. And they wanted to stay back till the hero whose single shot had killed an elephant was back.

As Nwabunna wandered home, he developed a tunnel vision, because he was always trying to visualize what happened the other day. He took a detour at a T-junction in search of cashew because he was hungry, having not eaten since morning. After having his fill of the fruits, he sat back there. Thoughts. Bother. Burden. With a threnody going on in his head, he wondered how one bed meal had filled a girl with pregnancy. He slept off on that thought line. When he woke up, he was downright tired. He was in delirium. But he knew that the water which collected on the ground awaited the puppy. It had got to drink it. He wished that Mama never developed osteoporosis, that Nancy never came around to treat nobody, and that Mama never had siesta that day. But he must go home. He must face his fate. He must become a self-made man. Nancy was already carrying his baby. Whatever Mama's reaction would be, there was going to be no death penalty. Nwabunna remained in the bush till evening, by which time most of the women who had collected at Mama's house had left. They were women who tore a mat with gossip. Woe betided girls who were raised by or in the presence of such women, for they grew up to be bad-natured gadabouts. The fact that a girl who went to treat a woman of her pain but ended up treating her extra-biological son to pleasure was the vanity of it all.

The heinousness of the matter was that a girl whose dowry was yet to be paid hadn't received approval from the gods to bring forth offspring. So, pre-marital pregnancy was seen as rebellion against authority of the goddess of fertility. The girl's family was looked at as one that lacked values. Nancy was nineteen then but nobody, not even her mother taught her anything about her body characteristics, or something about knowing a man. The only thing, and the only time her mother went closest was when she told her, "That thing on your chest is breast! Stay here and be eating my food. Don't go and find a husband for yourself. When I was much younger than your age, your father and other men were already on the queue to marry me." Those words were more-or-less expletive, not educative. So, one could say that it was her mother's virago that put the girl under pressure to marry, and she finally wormed her way into Nwabunna's life. That thing on her chest was breast and so what! Female animals had breasts too. What difference did Nancy's make or have? As for Nwabunna, he had eaten what his heart ever wanted. But instead of having rest, all he knew was anxiety. The first and only other time he touched a girl was four months before he fled Baruru. He had slapped one Nma's buttocks in front of elders, who asked him whether he was really sure he was carrying that behavior with a head pad. In his boyish exuberance, he replied in the affirmative.

It was when Nwabunna remembered that Oforbuike told him to run to him whenever he had any problem that he decided to go home. At least, he had seen one person who would stand with him in the case. Mama served her fugitive son a very delicious meal when he returned – smoked ripe plantain and bush meat. She didn't bother him with any questions. It was Nwabunna who simpered after eating, his sobriety gone. But then, he knew that Mama must have heard about it. Next morning, knowing that Molokwu and his wife were coming, Mama woke Nwabunna from his sleep. It was very wee still. "How was your journey yesterday?" she asked him calmly, seated on one side of the *agada*.

"Yesterday wasn't the journey. Five days ago was. I slept with Nancy the day she came to treat you. But it was just that once. So how could she be pregnant for me already? I suspect that she had been sleeping with other men or at least another man before me." Mama was not amazed when he mentioned he wasn't sure he was the actual impregnator.

"The two of you are adults, and she might have been around her period when you slept with her. As it stands now, and as it concerns everyone, especially her parents, you're the one."

"Whoever is the one, she has to do something about the baby."

"What exactly do you mean, my son?"

"She should kill the baby now; she should remove it. That's what I mean."

"May the gods of our land deal with you their own way! May the goddess of fertility visit you in her wrath!" Mama was disillusioned in him.

"Mama, that child is not mine. How can someone knock open a door seven times earlier and wider."

Over there in Molokwu's house, the brouhaha continued. His wife, in her virago, pestered him to tell her whom he had gotten pregnant, according to Ogubunka.

"Get lost before I host another crowd in this compound, this time for your burial," Molokwu thundered, fidgeting his legs in fret.

"You must tell me who she is," she insisted, adjusting her wrapper knot. "No wonder! You no longer take care of me like before. You now give me money for food with your left hand, because your right hand has been holding a woman out there. And when the food is cooked, you reject it without a reason." When Molokwu saw that his wife's madness was at a critical point, he stood up, and he left the house for her.

Later, she placed her nose close to the ground and found out that it was Nkasiobi, a deaf and without-children grass widow that had been engaging her cheating husband on a night split shift and not his supposed night watch job. Molokwu, about eight months earlier, had told his wife that he would be taking up a security job in order to supplement the money he made from rents and taxes. Little did she or anyone else, except Ogubunka, know that he was actually visiting and sleeping with Nkasiobi over the nights. "What a nice night job you're doing," said Ogubunka to Molokwu the day he found out. He was a drunk, so he was given four bottles of Schnapp to seal up his lips.

Nkasiobi had stepped upon a serpent and was going to be bitten by it. Ola was out to reclaim her husband. Nobody was going to snatch him from her. Certainly not when her virago was more bitter than venom. "Nkasi is deaf but she is going to hear the one that is older than 'Beaty' today," she swore. She confronted the widow who told her that she was already done with her husband, having since gotten what she wanted. She simply wanted to have a child, and so having been impregnated, Molokwu's services were no longer needed. "Imagine?" asked the drunk. "Women are consummate baby-making strategists. Respect them for that and for every other exceptional thing they are perfect at."

Nwabunna accepted the pregnancy finally, after Mama had spoken to him. That evening, he was yet to drop his hoe when Molokwu, his wife, and Nancy came around. Seeing them, his heart dropped into his abdomen. One thing that got him most concerned was the fact that he was going to have to feed Nancy till, at least, she put to bed. Mama was the first to greet and welcome the visitors. The grace in her voice was suggestive that she was either pretending to be ignorant of what had happened or downplaying its enormity. And it was not going to be a friendly evening for both parties.

"I'm not welcome here," Molokwu replied. "How can I be welcome when the bad meat you brought from Baruru has brought disgrace to me. I mean, how can I be welcome when that seed from Satan, that bad meat that punches bad blows has shamed my name throughout the kingdom…."

"So what brings you to my house this evening?"

"Don't ask me that empty question. Does it mean that you haven't heard that Nwa, *em*

"Stop talking nonsense here, this man," Nwabunna interrupted him from his room, and he came out immediately. "Who has been sleeping with your daughter in the farm? It was just once that I slept with her, just once, and that was five days ago. In fact, she was the one who slept with me."

"Shut you up there," Nancy blurted. "You're the one who slept with me."

"You said you're preparing her for a rich man. Look at you. When I look at her all I see is a Warsaw waist and NATO breasts. You obviously don't know what is good for rich men."

"Well, I don't have time for you. Why won't you insult me having taken advantage of my nicety towards you. I have officially brought her for you. Make sure she is fine and well taken care of."

As Molokwu and his wife turned to leave, Nwabunna told them to go and bring the food Nancy would be eating. "From what I can see, she's the kind of girl that eats six tubers of yam at a time…." Nancy was disappointed in him for saying that. They say that the mouth with which people borrow money is not the one they pay the debt with. People coat their mouth with sugar while seeking favor. When it's payback time, they coat it with denatonium. They wear a sweet savor when seeking approval. Thereafter, they put on bad breath.

"Molokwu, come and take your daughter to Los Angeles for next year's Olympics. With this waist of hers she will win gold, if not diamond. A girl that got pregnant just at one bed game will be good at badminton." Turning to Nancy, he said, "just one slot-in and you took in, are you an automated pregnancy machine?" He said all these in insistence that he suspected some other man of being the actual impregnator of Nancy's.

"You," Nancy retorted, "the first time a girl entered your room you slept with her. Are you a poorly moderated machine? You should be ashamed of yourself." At this point, Mama left for her room. Her bed would do her more good than their 'bad mouths. "Begin to save for her dowry. Once she puts to bed, you go and pay it," she told Nwabunna off-handedly.

"I can't try that Mama. I can't marry this touch-and-take-in girl. She will return to her parents after giving birth." In Merogwu, a woman's dowry wasn't to be paid when she was pregnant. They believed that if the baby in the womb was a girl when born, the dowry payer had married her alongside the mother. They equally believed, like other kingdoms in Orient Gnishere, that until the parents of a girl received and accepted dowry for her, she hadn't been married. And even if she bore him a hundred children, they weren't a couple. They were mere cohabitors or housemates. And even when she died, her corpse was to be taken back to her father's house, save the man paid it posthumous. They were still waging the word war when Ndudim came to inform Nwabunna that his grandmother whose bush he was to clear the day that followed, said his 'work food' would be ready as early as 5 am, and that he would have to come pick it before going to the farm, because nobody would be at home to do that. Nwabunna was a farmhand people loved because of his strength and neatness of his work. As a result, he didn't look for jobs. Jobs looked for him, and most times they didn't find him. There were days he worked on three different farmlands a day. It was Ndudim's presence and message that ended their diatribe that evening.

The following day, Nwabunna went to pick the food. He got there and saw the old woman stirring the soup with a bunch of broom – a dirty short broom. The essence was to gather all the particles around the pot back into the soup so that it would last longer. Nwabunna rejected the soup. "There's nothing I've not seen and there's nothing I'll not see in this community," he thundered. The old woman gave him some money in place of food. Later that day, Mama sat Nancy down and began to counsel with her.

"Nwabunna is now your husband, or at least the alleged father of your baby."

"Mama, he's the one…I've never slept with any other man all my life." And she started crying.

"Tears can't reverse the situation, my daughter. In fact, tears are joyful about what has happened. All you've got to do now is to be kind to yourself and respectful of him. Nwabunna is a very hardworking man. He will take good care of you. I know it. He's been saving for some time now. Love and respect him. That way, you will win him over. Men are subtle and they are soft as well. People, especially your peers, are going to say certain things. That shouldn't reach your heart."

When people heard that Nwabunna had taken in Nancy, it became a talk of the town. Different folkloric narratives and jokes were made out of it. One young man went to a lady and said to her, "Let's take our love to Nancy-Nwabunna levels now." Some women began to call Mama a mother-in-law. And she was one in some right. A woman that took the risk of keeping a convicted fugitive and had continued to guide him could be said to have given birth to him. Nwabunna returned in the evening. He was listless, because he didn't really eat at work. He only bought groundnut and later ate some wild mangoes. He was given nineteen pounds by his hirer, but he kept the money. He suddenly became thrifty. With the arrival of Nancy, he knew that his responsibility had doubled. And whether he liked it or not, he had to take care of her. Nancy noticed that hunger was in his body; such a hunger that could make a man to finish a plate of white rice before arrival of stew. She served him 'swallow' with *egusi* soup. He liked and enjoyed her food, but he was yet to get over the reality of his imminent and unplanned fatherhood. Later in the night, he made love to her, taking a full and firm grip of the same waist he called worthless in the morning. Men and conjugal hypocrisy; they call the doohickey nonsense in the morning, but when they get to the climax of it at night, they make a joyful noise unto the Creator.

CHAPTER NINE

A Triplet

T he confidence of a dog is in the strength of its teeth, not in the hardness of the bone before it.

Nwabunna went nowhere the next day. The job he was supposed to do was cancelled. The owner of the farm was disappointed in a woman who was supposed to have properly prepared it for tilling. Nwabunna had no problems with the development. He hated to till soils that had debris or refuse on them as well as those which had grown grasses on them. There was a day he had gone to till such a soil in the past. It was full of stumps. He knew he would be doing a bad job should he make heaps on the soil in that condition. That would destroy his reputation – one he had built over the years. So, he took his time and prepared the soil well, removing all the stumps and other 'removables' before tilling it. Whoever cleared the farm initially did a bad job. Grasses left uncut were greater than the ones they cut, and after burning, they constituted sharp masses – thorns. The person must have lopped off branches of trees before cutting the grasses underneath. They fell on the latter, making it difficult for his cutlass to access them fully. What a poor job he did. After doing the two-in-one job, Nwabunna went to the owner to explain everything to him, hopeful the man would show some understanding; he thought he would double his pay. The man didn't consider him. He told Nwabunna that he only asked him to till, not uproot stumps from his farm. Cantankerous, Nwabunna smashed the earthenware with which he had brought him 'work food.'

The heat-resistant enamel was commonest cutlery in those days. Despite seeing his plate in pieces, the man chose peace and paid him a day's work wage. When the for-wage worker insisted his pay be doubled, the man told him that the damaged plate was worth a day's wage.... "Let that which will happen tomorrow happen today;

let it happen now." Still angry, Nwabunna threatened the man in firm anger: "Don't sow anything on the heaps I made unless you pay me in full. I'll destroy your crops if you do."

"Same way you destroyed the crops in your own land and sold your people to famine. Lost cause of a fugitive! What a shameless soul you are." These wordy grenades got to Nwabunna's yellow marrow and nearly caused him a brain stem stroke and paraparesis. He was curled up. He went home disarmed and undone, daunted and haunted. With his mouth Obierika just told him his world and his god. The Baruru pestilence was known everywhere. Most people fled because of hunger. Salvation from their starvation only came when neighboring kingdoms, including Merogwu, sent them relief provisions in exchange for their palm oil. It was later learned that Umuakaekpe, seeing the severity of their plight and knowing that they were desperate for help, made them to agree to a pact that saw them handle their oil mills for six months, and keeping the revenue to themselves, in return for bags of garri, grains, and tubers. When Borealers heard this, they laughed at Orient Gnishere, calling them leeches of their own people. "A brother that doesn't help his needy brother, is that one a brother or a spoiler?" This was their gloating of Orient Gnishereans. Height of the famine was that it happened in the year of *aju*. As a result, people had no food reserve at all. *Aju* was a cultural festival which was observed in April and October, once in four years. Throughout those periods, families cooked choicest meals for their ancestors. It was also a period within which people were not allowed to die or bury their 'dead ones.' If someone died before the festival commenced, they must be buried before March 31 and September 30. Those who did die within that time – and they rarely did – were buried after the events. People rarely died in April and October because their ancestors wouldn't welcome or receive them to the other realm of existence, being too busy feasting and celebrating and being celebrated. And such people were seen as killjoys, and therefore were given 'wretched,' or unceremonious funerals.

Nwabunna was really debilitated because of those words from Obierika throughout that day. It was in order to avoid such words that he chose to stay home this time. In fact, each time he remembered those words, he forgot his world and his god. Could it be that he was an Icarus in Merogwu after all? Of all blue-collar jobs, it was tilling people's farmlands, a thankless and sinews-wasting endeavor, that worked for his hands, after what he did had destroyed crops in Baruru.

Moreover, vagary things had been happening to him ever since he arrived in Merogwu. He was working hard and was earning fairly great wages but he couldn't account for the money. He seemed to be seriously suffering from what they called *akpatetufuo* syndrome; he earned money and "threw" it all away. Other young men who did same and similar menial jobs fared far better than he did. They all had assets and investments. Some tilled soils for a year or two and established enterprises with their wages, and then quit. Certainly, Nwabunna knew that an enigma was following him. He even began to suspect his soul of being the enigma, and that although he had managed to escape the mortal penance for his cardinal sin, the gods weren't appeased yet. He had the guts to offend the gods, but lacked the grace to appease them. One bone this dog didn't bargain for was the native hate and rejection by his people back home. But he trusted the enamel of his teeth to crush it at the end.

Nancy didn't actually know how to address Nwabunna, initially. And although they made love the previous night, she knew he was still uncomfortable with the reality on ground. By-the- way, sleeping with her didn't really set a man's heart to love a girl. It only shed some emotional weight off his body. That was the reason men who took decisions while atop a woman were more unstable than drunks. Their minds were cobwebbed in indiscretion. Drunks sold their thoughts for a bottle of liquor. Voluptuaries exchanged judgment with erratic.

Nancy was sweeping the surroundings that morning. Nwabunna stood by a guava tree, a branch of which he made a chewing stick from. The stick was as long as his humerus. She didn't know whether she should call him 'Sir' or Nna-anyi, or just his name − Nwabunna. So she just greeted him: "Good morning." A man came from somewhere that someone didn't know about. He met Nwabunna at the entrance of Mama's house and told him he was looking for Nancy, his wife. He took a long, protracted look at the man and replied: "You're looking for

Nancy, your wife, right? Her father sent you to come and look for what you will hear from my mouth, right? The one I told him yesterday was not enough for him, I can see." When the man told him that he came to pay Nancy for the ori he had bought from her for a very long time, Nwabunna told him to go and give her mother the money.

Nancy didn't come with trousseau, but that didn't matter because her lobola hadn't been paid. Mama had given her some clothes, including four sets of wrapper, gowns, and skirts, one of which she wore as she swept the surroundings that morning. They were clothes which vicissitudes of life did not permit her to wear. Married in 1959 to Nnochiri, a minstrel at a magistrate court, she knew the sweet side of life. The respect given her husband reached her also. They enjoyed a pretty happy domesticity until when the Inter-kingdom War broke out. A beau himself, Nnochiri was fond of buying his beautiful and beloved wife various kinds of garb. He loved her so much that he did everything he could to keep her happy. She was a responsible possible adorable wife and duly requited the love. And that attitude of love enabled the couple to achieve impossible feats together. They were a colorful couple, who enjoyed some custard of intimacy and a culture of understanding. Their bond was so strong that death needed life and its strength to break it, but it couldn't.

The skirt was very good on Nancy, unlike the one she wore on the day of their mutual temptation, which resulted in their marriage of chance. The skirt did not only show Nwabunna anatomy of her nether regions, it also showed him their accessory routes. Don't blame the young man too much for being unable to resist her infatuation. Only a few men could have, because Nancy came looking very 'nwunye-Potipharous,' and Nwabunna was no Joseph to say no when nudged. And while the Bible Joseph had a clothe on him on the day of his own test, Nwabunna had none. He just came out of the bathroom with a mere underwear.

Their relationship grew with time and Nancy began to call him "My good husband". But the very first time she did, he didn't behave like a good husband of hers. He snubbed her, and later, he said: "For now. 'I'm your good husband' just for now. Once you put to bed, you go back to your good parents." But she got a masterstroke of a reply for him. She said, "There's no problem, *Ezigbo Dim*. Let me be your wife for just two years. And if you're not happy with me after that, I'll gladly go." He soon embraced his reality. His hope of ever going to school ultimately gone, he concentrated on the tilling work. He began to secure bigger and better jobs, and so had to regularly engage in three different jobs daily. His savings were growing. By Nancy's second trimester, he stopped her from selling *ori*. He took care of her some more. Her abdomen burged forwards and her buttocks backwards, giving her the irregular shape of cocoyam. It kept getting bigger and firmer by the weeks.

Mama was happy about their improved relationship. She was pleased to run errands for Nancy. The joy she derived from the development soothed her aching joints. And more than ever before, her body regained its muscular and skeletal functions. Somehow she was going to be called a granny. She had always received Nancy since her parents brought her around and her love for the girl got larger with every beat of her heart.

Later, in the seventh month of the pregnancy, she had pain episodes around her womb and waist areas, so she thought she had miscarried her baby. It recurred after two weeks and was followed by some lightening. Everybody thought she was going to put to bed prematurely, best off. So Mama massaged her gently with the anodyne balm she used to sell. Nwabunna was greatly petrified. He was afraid of pre-birth complications. "Don't bring me trouble in this land, Nancy," he warned her. "Just mind yourself. Deliver in peace and go back to your father's house…." That was his visceral irrational response.

"Shut up, you silly boy," Mama scolded him, "that's unkind of you to say." None of them, not even Nancy, knew she was pregnant with multiple babies. And after she survived the near miss, she bounced back to full health and energy.

And when the day came for the snake to vomit all it had swallowed, Nancy got a surprise for everybody. Like taking candy from a baby, she brought forth three babies – boys − sons. The news broke and burgeoned across Merogwu. Nwabunna was somewhere working. He felt it before he heard it, and when he confirmed it, he broke out in joy, like a puppy which was just released from its chain. He left his implements in the farm and ran to the local maternity, wondering how only Mama and Nancy's sister were able to take Nancy to the birth room. It was still early in the morning, so owners of the farm he was tilling hadn't brought him 'work food' yet. When people saw him beside himself with joy, they were surprised and impressed that there was one thing in life which could ever make him happy. He had been bolshie and indifferent since arriving in Merogwu. Two facts were testament to that. One, he mostly worked alone, no matter the size of the farmland, almost always. Two, he always walked away when farm owners didn't buy into his suggestions. These made the people of Merogwu to wonder what gave a fugitive, a young man who was on the run from his native land, a sheer gut which saw him dictating things in their affairs. But while cats and rats use their vibrissae to detect the presence of an enemy, a dog uses its own whiskers to build a daring boldness against daunting bones. When he got to the maternity, he saw an overjoyed Mama jumping and leaping like a marsupial, forgetful and unconscious of her 'porous' bones. He went straight to the delivery room, and before the midwives could know what he was doing, he had already reached for his just-born boys with his dirty body. "You're welcome, my boys!" he greeted the neonates who inadvertently replied with giggles. And he was grateful.

"They're now yours?" Mama countered him. "Not when their mother is not your wife. Not when she is to return to her parents."

"She's my wife," he said, adjusting his breeches, which had always been his work clothes. "She's my wife, please. My Nancy, my fancy!" He went over to her and cuddled her so dearly, still with his dirty body and clothes.

"Can you leave a woman that just returned from the spirit land to regain herself?" That was an order from the chief midwife. "In fact, get out, *oga*. Go to the reception and wait. There at the reception, he continued to go crazy, singing all manner of praises he knew. He so much entertained those around that they dispelled whatever not-too-good an impression of him that had formed in their hearts. Meanwhile, Nancy's sister had left to buy additional layettes to add to the ones they provided for a single baby.

CHAPTER NINE

When Oriuwa's wife, whose farm Nwabunna was tilling, heard the latest, cheery news, she went headlong to see them. She had brought Nwabunna his 'work food,' which he received from her at the maternity and guzzled down his gullet immediately. He believed that a worker was deserving of both his food and wage. And he was an efficient eater of foods. Families who had his kind of consumer in two people would rarely have leftover for the dustbin.

Theretofore, Nwabunna had been planning to estrange Nancy once she put to bed, but the arrival of the triplet poppets changed everything entirely. It changed his interests as well as his fears. His love for Nancy became real, essential, and substantial. It evolved into an organ and formed an extra pair of chambers in his heart. Now, he had come to like not only Nancy's waist but her ways, too. You needed to see the nerve, the verve, the joy, and the domesticity. He turned into a Baroque composer that night, singing a serenade of her name. He continued it the days that followed.

When Nancy saw the change in her husband, it entered her head, which swelled and became bigger than her waist. She began to behave like a harridan, exhibiting her mother's virago. But she was vindicated. She had the exoneration. Her god just placed a seal of honor and one of worth on her head, and a royal diadem on her neck, too. What more could a woman have wanted after going into the birth room and coming out with three bonny boys? Nancy brought forth her boys without assistance from any doula. She did it so 'stresslessly' that Mama had to say she peed out her babies. And the children were grateful somehow that they were born safely. Nancy created three records with that delivery, viz: One, no one had ever had a multiple birth in Merogwu before then. Two, Merogwu firstborns were usually females but she got boys in her first pregnancy. Three, she was the first girl in Merogwu to give birth from a pre-marriage pregnancy, something that people called "guinea fowl pregnancy." And while her pregnancy was not applauded, its outcome was celebrated, because its glory outshone its initial shame.

CHAPTER TEN
Igwe Dimanochie Is Dead

S ame curiosity which killed a cat kept a dog alive. That was because while the cat ate fish because of hunger, the dog took up bone for courage. And to be alive a man needs strength for every struggle. He needs adequate inner strength through good and bad times.

Nine years after the famine, the people of Nsogbubaruru still hadn't recovered from it. It wasn't really because it was too severe. It was just because they were so bent on revenge. They were so obsessed with and carried away by such thoughts that their minds had no space to brood enterprise and ingenuity. As a people, they didn't come together to strategize towards the advancement of their kingdom, and as individuals, they didn't plan towards self-development. They were waiting for the day Nwabunna would return for them to stone him to death. There was a day a woman mentioned his name in a small talk while passing. A man lifted a stone in agility, looking about the whole place for him. When he learnt she was only kidding, he was disappointed. "Let me still preserve this stone," he said. "I owe him a cast of it whenever he is back." Instead of building houses with stones so as to have shelters over their heads, they piled stones up for Nwabunna's head.

Despite aids and reliefs from humanitarian bodies, they couldn't move forward like other kingdoms. They were held back by mental inadequacies which manifested in the form of bitterness and malice. Poor philosophy was their problem. When Ikenga saw that their hearts were covered with shade of darkness, he knew that Nwabunna needed to be more careful wherever he was.

"If we wait for him a little more and he doesn't come back, we will trace him, bring him back by ourselves, and kill him accordingly." That was a suggestion from one of them. Another said: "Better still, we'll make his grandfather pay for it. He must have been the one who told him to crack kernel by that time." That was their resolve for revenge. They were so carried away by vengeance that they couldn't see many carts of opportunities being carried by other kingdoms.

Nwabunna was long beginning to find his footing in destiny in exile, but his mates were going extinct destiny-wise, back home, because of malicious tendencies. When they heard that his wife gave birth to three sons, they were embittered the more. They said, "May hunger kill all of them same way it killed our children. *Iseee!*" Later, a mob of youths led by Baruru red cap men invaded the palace one early morning, protesting that Igwe Dimanochie should go liase with his Merogwu counterpart in order to repatriate Nwabunna. "The gods have refused to bless us with rains and grains because we are yet to bring that boy to book," they pursued. "Go and get him. That's what makes you our igwe — to protect our interests and defend our cause."

"My children," Igwe addressed them, "none of you are more interested in the Nwabunna case than I am. However, mortals don't have to meddle in the jurisdiction of the gods." He told them that the gods would someday punish Nwabunna their own way, same way they dealt with white men who desecrated their land. "The gods unleashed mosquitoes on them and the resultant malaria epidemic sent them home." But the protestors weren't going to be talked out of it. They insisted on going to get Nwabunna back. "He has to stop breathing for our soil to start yielding again. Stop talking like an accomplice and like a stranger. You should be sensitive enough to know that the gods are raging against us."

Some days later, a presidium led by Nze Afuonu went to negotiate with *Igwe* of Merogwu to turn Nwabunna in. But he declined. He told them that he wouldn't grant such a sensitive request without the imprimatur of their own igwe. "I respect his throne as much as I have awe for the gods of your kingdom," he told them.

"He has no throne of his own. All he has got to do is listen to us …."

That was the second scandal Igwe Dimanochie was having to deal with. The first was allotting huge hectares of land to a troupe of Borealers for permanent settlement, three years after Uba and his brothers had left, saying that "We all belong to one Super Kingdom Gnishere. The Borealers are our brothers, therefore. We need not have a tribal reservation against them. So, let's live and let them live." His people were disillusioned in him. They were ashamed he said those words. They said, "Are you sure this man ever tasted breast milk? How could our leader, the mouthpiece of our kingdom, not defend and fight for our common cause with the last drop of his blood. What a cheaper-than-cowry coward he is." One of them went further to say that it was possible that Dimanochie wasn't a true seed of their earth. "...Where did they bury his belly button? And to whom did his father ever give a yam seedling to cultivate?" Their cage was rattled. Dimanochie was unmoved howbeit. He said to them: "Go home and think, men of Nsogbubaruru. A man who doesn't think before he sets sail sinks in the sea of uncertainty. If you continue to pursue this case, the entire Orient Gnishere will lose whatever favors we enjoy in the hands of the central government...."

When they investigated into his provenance, they discovered that Dimanochie's grandfather was actually a Borealer who impregnated a true Baruru daughter that resided in his province, where she sold firewood and coal. When the circumstance would not result in marriage, she brought her pregnant self home, before giving birth to a son who lived all his mortal life in Baruru. When the boy grew up, he had Dimanochie with one of the maidens of mercy. So, by implication, he wasn't supposed to have become a royalty, because he didn't spring up from the real lineage of their fore-fathers.

Maidens of mercy, in Baruru land, were young girls who had one or more conditions that made them believe no responsible man would desire them for a wife, ordinarily. Some of them had deformities. Others were family rejects. They were usually married by the hoi polloi, who couldn't afford a woman's bride price, men whose own brothers called *efulefus*. Maidens of mercy were women of no self-worth – women with a wrong self-definition. But they actually were maidens of pity – self-pity and low self esteem – not mercy.

One of them, Nnenne, however, rejected that tag and fate and took her destiny in her own hands. She put her brain to use and got a rare selling skill, in spite of her disability – lameness – and by the time she had established herself, men of resourcefulness fought for her hands in marriage. And you know what? She chose not the richest amongst them, but the kindest. That was when others began to wake up. That was when they began to believe in themselves; when they began to embrace the real desirability of a woman – the power to create taste out of fustiness and love out of hatred. That her being beautiful: appreciating herself for being too inestimable is to be despised. By the next rite of passage, there was no lady to be called a "maiden of mercy" in Baruru. All thanks to Nnenne, who challenged destiny and taught others self-belief and armor proper.

The subjects wanted to depose and banish Igwe Dimanochie, in a raucous protest, but the gods said no. The people accused Ezemmuo of perfidy and the gods of bias. As far as they knew, there was nothing they were enjoying from the central government, which simply saw Orient Gnishere as its lapdog and scapegoat. Consequent upon that, the presidium began to sabotage Dimanochie's economic efforts, by diverting revenues from palm oil sales. That way, they succeeded in turning the burghers of the kingdom against the Igwe. This latter revolt pressured him beyond his bearing point.

Distraught in the gods of the land for literally siding with the Igwe, the red cap men went and took foreign gods from other places. "The gods of our land have become selfish and corrupted and influenced by mortals," they alleged. "They now protect what favors them and no longer the interest of the land."

"Clowns drown in the cauldron of their stupidity and don't notice it," Igwe rebuked them. "How could you people have done that?

"Do you want the gods of our land, the gods of our ancestors, the very heritage of our souls, to turn their backs on us? Would you rather prefer calamity to befall us all?"

"I give you all until the next Eke market day to rid yourselves of all the useless gods you have introduced to our land."

"Do not listen to that damned man," Chief Afuono told others.

"He must have sold his mind to the wind. Adultery and alcohol seem to have spoilt his head. You tell these *igwes* to take it easy with women and wine they refuse. I'm keeping my own god. It's time to protect myself and my family with juju." Nothing caused Dimanochie a more penetrating sadness and depression than the fact that he lost the loyalty of his cabinet and goodwill of his other subjects. Alas, his throne became like a tomb in his eyes! Sitting on it felt like sitting in a cold room.

Things continued to get funnier, sadly funnier, for Igwe Dimanochie by every second, simply because he prevented them from meting out subjudice on Mazi Ikenga, and because he refused to request for the repatriation of Nwabunna from Merogwu. He continued to maintain his stand that the gods had got to fight for themselves and that if Ikenga did mastermind the kernel crack incident, the gods would feed him for his pains. They kept and worshipped their foreign gods. Of all people in Orient-Gnishere, the men of Baruru were most anthropomorphic; they believed that the gods should feel their plight at all times and therefore give them sympathy and justice.

"Men are the mouth and hands of the gods. The gods should be the minds of men. Allow us to handle Nwabunna by ourselves. Allow us to fight this one battle for the gods."

The resultant disunity in Nsogbubaruru made the central government to suspend their monthly allocation. This terrible development disturbed Dimanochie greatly. He told them to drop the protests but they wouldn't hear. So, the conniption continued. The continued agitation put Igwe Dimanochie on the canvas already.

When the Central Governor learnt about it, he interfaced. Dimanochie knew he had a personal interest in Baruru's oil palm and that the agitation was favor of a kind to him. He asked the Central Governor to go away, alleging that he had come to destroy their tradition with politics. Dimanochie and the dissent group reached a compromise when the central government gave them a ten-day ultimatum to resolve the argybargy. They agreed that he would officially request of Igwe Merogwu to turn Nwabunna over while they drop the conniption. But Afuonu had another plan. He knew Dimanochie was never going to do that. So, he connived with his second son who was Dimanochie's butler to poison his drink. A death that has come to kill a puppy, they say, doesn't let it perceive feces. It makes it to stop at nothing until it has tasted it, even when it knows something harmful might happen to it. They schemed it carefully, and on the D-Night, the most unusual thing happened in the palace. Guess what? Igwe invited all palace attendants and equerries to the dining table. Before then, Afuonu's son had already dropped some lethal crystalline substances into Igwe's wine. As they dined, Dimanochie said he had chosen to use that opportunity to thank them for their services to his household so far. "I have the pleasure to share my choicest meal with you just to thank you all for your unreserved services in this palace these whole years." He signaled his butler, Afuonu's son, to stand up. And when the young man did, Dimanoshie said, "I am not trying to stir up jealousy amongst you, but I am going to say that this young man standing up has been more exceptional than anyone else. He not only makes sure that my drinks are fresh, he also ensures that my thoughts are always clear. He doesn't drug me, and he doesn't get tired serving me.

"So today, I'm going to let him have a sip of my drink." He handed his wooden horn-like cup to the young man who was stunned at the offer. He never assumed that Igwe would on any occasion, or for any reason, ask him, or any other servant, to have a sip of his royal wine. The very last thing he was ever going to think about was that. And Igwe wasn't suspecting him of poisoning his drink either. If he was, he wouldn't have tasted the drink first. So while everyone looked on with admiration, the butler placed the cup on his lips carefully and pretended as though he took a sip of the liquid. He licked his lips and smiled, saying, "Thank you, your Highness. It's a rare blessing to have a taste of your choicest drink."

By the witching hour, Igwe began to have a disturbance in his stomach area, like that from a neried worm. Before no time he was really in a catatonic state. By sunrise he was dead already. When it was recounted that he gave his staff an unusual feast, where he thanked and blessed them for their services the previous day, the people believed his death was natural – that his god had called him home. Nobody, therefore, thought along the line of making an investigation into the cause. But somehow, a suspicion was going on in the heart of his valet. He tried to figure out what must have actually made the Igwe to ask his colleague to have a sip of his drink. And he knew the butler didn't actually taste the drink. At least he didn't swallow it. But he had no evidence. So, he chose not to sail close to the wind.

Igwe was given a befitting funeral, despite the fact that most of his people got displeasured in him during the last years of his reign. At least, they knew he was a good man. His burial happened in eight market days' time, and it was a three-day event.

Meanwhile, Mazi Ikenga was joyed and buoyed by the news about his next generation over there in Merogwu. It gave him a nirvana, an eternal bliss on earth. It was a consolation for him in the midst of his many mists, which tried to stop him from seeing something good about the future. The red cap men had done everything they could to kill him. But nobody was going to kill a man whose god had kept alive. They laid traps here and there for him, but his destiny said no. However, he knew that someone surrounded by enemies should always sleep with an eye of his open. So, he was very careful. He calculated his every action and restricted his certain movements. As for him, "Wisdom is the first pass to live on earth." That, too, was a lesson his father taught him.

CHAPTER ELEVEN
Nancy's Dowry Paid

A dog once said that the real reason it followed a pregnant woman head-on-tail was because if she didn't poop, she would vomit, and definitely something must come out of her. And this dog hoped that the woman was actually heavy with a child and not just big with something to chide her for.

Nancy developed a post-birth ailment, which was characterized by fever and lumbago of slow pain. It started after a second 'word war' with her husband. What happened was that Nwabunna returned from work a certain evening and saw Nancy splitting firewood with an axe. It was only four days after her delivery. Seeing her doing that, Nwabunna was heart-rent. He thought it wasn't safe for her health, especially because she was nursing three babies at once. Since the third trimester of the pregnancy, he had been making sure every thing she needed was provided. He fetched enough water every evening, after work. There were even days he went to the stream when it was stark dark in the night. He was a brave man. Nothing was ever going to petrify him. There was a day he got to the river by past 8 pm and he ordered "Mummy Water" to come out if she really thought she was powerful. He threatened to kill the water woman if she emerged. But she didn't. That was when rumors were rife around town that a creature — half a woman, half a fish — was spotted in the middle of the river.

So he wasn't happy that Nancy chose to split logs by herself instead of waiting for him to come back. "You're so determined to bring my feet out to the city gate, this girl," he blasted Nancy. "When you get hurt now, your bad-mouthed mother will start insulting herself and not me."

"You dare not call my mother names," Nancy returned the insult. "You're insulting a woman you've not bought a wrapper since you started living with her daughter. You've not even bought her ordinary waterproof before."

"How can I have bought her waterproof? Is she ice fish?"

"E-eeh! You called my mother ice fish!" A word war rallied.

When Mama heard those words from their mouths, she was ashamed of their immaturity. She came out of her room and saw the two guests of gory circumstances bandying words, as Nancy held Nwabunna by his mangy breeches, daring him to beat her up. The murder of a man, they say, is better than the insult given him. So, Nwabunna lifted a log for Nancy's head, but Mama intercepted it with her hand, and she removed Nancy's hand from his codpiece. Little did Nwabunna know that it was Nancy's antics at getting him to go pay her bride price. And she got it.

By mid-morning she woke Nwabunna up with groaning, like that of a colic. He initially ignored her, telling her to go and insult her father and that she should call her father for help. Mama heard her cry from her own room, and she knew it was no false alarm. So, she hurried her to the cottage clinic, where she delivered her babies five days earlier. It doubled as a surgery room, too. None of them knew that Nancy still had a baby in her, which was due for birth. She had superfetated and knew it not. Her womb hadn't collapsed yet. And while midwives were still trying to figure out what was troubling her, she brought forth a baby with her usual aplomb. Everyone, including fearless Nwabunna, was shocked. "This must be a dream!" they sotto voced.

"What kind of woman is this?" Nwabunna wondered in his displaced heart.

"...but she just gave birth the other day," the midwives enquired from no particular one, confused. Even Nancy was gob smacked.

When Nwabunna saw that it was a girl, he said within him, "Birthmother, the queen- goddess of my ancestors must be asking me to return home. I must have been forgiven. She's most probably asking me to come back to Baruru.

"If true, Birthmother, give me another sign. Prosper my lot. Give me wealth in this land, the type of wealth that will make my people desire me and ask me to return." Nobody heard it but it was going to be answered. Humbled by what just happened, he went to Nancy, bent unto her, and said, "I may not have been wonderful to you all this while, but I have come to really love you. Please, become the love of my life." Tearful, Nancy held his hand firmly, but couldn't utter a word, still lying on the birth bed.

Nwabunna rushed back home to see his sons, who were watched over by Nancy's sister. Her mother hadn't come for omugwo yet. Maybe, she was still busy fighting off those women who were out to snatch her husband from her. The boys were sleeping beautifully when he arrived. He thanked his god that he returned at that moment. Something tragic would have happened, most probably. His sister-in-law had stood a kerosene lantern close to a cloth stand from which a head- tie fell unto it, and it was getting heated up already. He removed it immediately.

A day later, Nancy returned with her baby girl. She felt for her boys, who had to spend a day without her. She had to lay down her milk into a feeding bottle which her sister fed them with.

Nwabunna could not afford not to go to work the next day. As he tilled, a thought evoked his mind that a man who hadn't settled with a woman's people wouldn't be recognized as a married man in the company of his kinsmen, even if he had received the highest title in the land. He knew that, according to their tradition, Nancy's children belonged to her father, Molokwu, until he had paid her dowry. So, he began to plan towards doing that.

Coincidently, as he was going home in the evening, he overheard a Merogwu woman telling another that she was returning from Mama's house. And when she was asked what she had gone there to do, she replied that she went to greet Nancy's "love children". This impression angered Nwabunna, who was not seen by the two women. It pushed the obligation up his heart's preference scale.

Immediately, he diverted to Oforbuike's house to tell him of his intentions. The man was pleased to hear that. He felt honored he was going to be Nwabunna's stand-in father. A few days later, Oforbuike took Nwabunna to Molokwu, with two kegs of palm wine, a bottle of hot drink and some kola nuts, as custom demanded. Molokwu's kinsmen told him that since he had decided to properly marry their daughter, there was no need for iju ase. Nwabunna told them that he wanted a full traditional marriage, not just dowry payment, saying, "Nancy has made me proud, I have to make her prouder." Oforbuike was very happy because Nwabunna was becoming perky by the day. He was becoming a changed man; his hauteur and hang-dog expressions were going away.

However, he was concerned about the young man's finances. "That's pretty good. But how do you plan to fund a full traditional marriage, my son?"

"Don't worry about that. I have already saved enough."

"That's right. But you have four children already, and then your wife. How are you going to take proper care of them? Savings are for investments, not merriment. You don't save to later spend it. You save to invest it in something that will yield you fortune. That's how wealthy men do it.

"You see, the undoing of any man is to overspend his pause weight. After paying Nancy's bride price, you have incurred her parents' asking price. Or do you intend to sell your children one after one?" They were still chatting when his son came in from the outhouse, holding his head as though calamity just befell him. Three days to the marriage, Nancy moved down to her father's house with her children and sister. Her family was proud of her, as was everyone else, save a few women who were disappointed with the fact that she was getting married. They were bitter that their own daughters who had kept themselves from men to show they had a good home training hadn't gotten married, yet the one who did otherwise was being celebrated. They had expected Nwabunna to send Nancy away after her putting to bed. They never understood that destiny is both discrete and determined. Another thing they didn't grab was the fact that "the ultimate virtue of a woman is to help build a man and not just to keep herself from men." That was what Mama learnt from her mother. So, when she saw that Nancy was building Nwabunna into a man of thoughts and results, she supported their getting married.

Nancy's mother, who had apparently recovered her cheating husband from the coop of his kept women, celebrated her grandchildren greatly. "My beautiful children, you're welcome. I'll kill four fowls for you, one for each of you." On his part, Molokwu, who had regained his senses from the sex box of strumpets, vowed to make his daughter's marriage the most outstanding outing in the history of Merogwu. He provided everything that was cooked. Ever since he stopped seeing his 'outside' wives, and ever since he started eating in his house, his finances started growing. One of those women threatened to kill his wife for asking her to steer clear of him. When Nwabunna heard that his father-in-law had catered for everything that needed to be cooked, he was grateful.

On the eve of the marriage there was food everywhere. Molokwu was keeping to his words. Seeing the lashings, one middle-aged man kept a jar of palm wine for himself as well as three plates of yam porridge. Another asked him: "Are you sure you will be able to finish all you've taken?" He replied, "With God all things are possible."

"When did you become a believer? I thought you're the first son of your family and as a result are supposed to serve the idol your father left behind."

"Leave me alone, let me enjoy myself. It's not easy to have an in-law to whom our daughter has given four children in one pregnancy. Chai! That young man is powerful and our daughter wonderful to have converted one shot to three sons."

"It's just their luck. The Creator of the universe chose to favor them."

"Our in-law is an in-form shooter of shots. That's what I know. That boy can overshoot world population by thirty percent in six months. Just give him fertile girls." That was Adindu, a new church goer in an orthodox church, who, howbeit, refused to do away with his father's idol. He was simply going to church to observe Christians, not to become one. First day he went to church the priest preached on the topic: "With God all things are possible." And one of the things he believed was possible, was being able to exhaust everything Molokwu was going to bring out that day. "After all, he promised that we will eat shasha," he further alluded.

"Don't kill yourself with food. That's my concern. Don't bring bad luck to tomorrow's event. You can go to your house and die if you like."

"Don't worry. My stomach is elastic." Adindu was the father of Obilor who was born the same day as Nancy. He was the one who plucked all uha leaves that were used to make soup for the marriage. In their subculture, uha leaves must touch the soil when plucked. Otherwise, they tasted bitter and ruined any soup made with them. So, nobody plucked them high up and carried them down in their hands. Nor were they caught in the air. It just had to drop on the soil before being picked. Also, Obilor was the one who ground all the egusi and pepper that were used in making the soup. He did all of that to show his birth mate, his only village coeval, goodwill as she moved to her husband's place. He had been close friends with Nancy since their pre-teens. They were from the same hamlet, so were marriage-tied. "A man doesn't marry his own sister irrespective of how much they love each other," he had told one of the women pounding fufu. "Save that, I would have married Nancy a long time ago. We just have to respect our culture." Those words were still in his mouth when he felt a peppery sensation. So he cried out loud: "Pepper o! Pepper!"

"What happened to pepper, Obilor?" one of the fufu pounders asked him. "My eyes! My eyes!" the girlish boy cried on.

"Ewo! Sorry, you hear?"

"Bring some salt quickly. I'm about to run mad!" They dropped a pinch of salt into his mouth to neutralize the peppery effect.

"Don't run mad, please," one of the women said. "My daughter's hands are waiting for you in marriage. After marrying my daughter you can then run mad in peace."

"I don't understand what you're wishing me, Mama Adaobi."

"I mean that you will make a good husband for my daughter. You will be madly in love with her." Looking at Obilor's physique, one would think he needed a husband himself. He was too effeminate for manhood. When his eyes, which he had rubbed red and hard with his hands, cleared of pepper, he continued his voluntary job.

Ikenga had arrived in Merogwu earlier that day, alone, and robbed. He saw a boy named Eme and asked him about how he could find his way to "the man whose wife gave birth to three boys at once." The lad led him to a crossroad and that was the farthest he could go. He was on an errand. "My mother will flog me if I don't return home on time." He tipped the boy some coins which he rejected, to his surprise. "My father told me not to accept strangers' gifts, especially food and money."

Ikenga was still trying to reconcile with the boy's conviction when he saw a girl sauntering down the road. He asked her whether she could take him to "the man whose wife gave birth to three boys at once". She agreed and did. They reached Mama's house and Nwabunna's tent of sojourn in twenty minutes. Ikenga's grandson was sprawling on a bamboo back chair when they arrived. He jerked up from the chair seeing his grandfather for the first time in over a decade. He ran to him and they locked up each other in a firm hug. It was a reunion of blood, a reunion of friends, and one of hopes. Ikenga kissed him on his forehead and they hugged again. Their contact got Mama out of her room. The last time she heard such a clinking sound was when her conscripted husband kissed her, before leaving for the Inter-kingdom War, which 'ate' his head and those of his children, eventually. She saw the two men locked in a bear hug and she smiled. "Mama, this is my grandfather," Nwabunna announced.

"I know him," she replied. "Who doesn't know Mazi Uche Ikenga across Super Gnishere. He's an unsung hero. Welcome Nwoke Bu Dike." Despite his age, Ikenga was looking sprightly, bubbly, and assured. His frog money was showing on him. He chose not to come with his car. And he chose not to take his wealth to Merogwu. As far as he believed, "A man doesn't put his life into a vase stuck in another man's house. If he does, he will have to become his slave for life. Also, a man doesn't fetch water with his enemy's container. He either spills it or denies him a drink of it." These were the words of the elderly during his youth.

It was when Mama and Ikenga began to talk that Nwabunna turned to thank the girl who brought his grandfather. He recognized her quickly. It was Urudinanwanyi. He was grateful to her and invited her to his occasion. As she turned to leave, he noticed some transformation that had occurred in her. The joy of seeing his grandfather overwhelmed him. Mama, who since the birth of the babies had become more energetic than ever, served them some food. When Nwabunna, who was yet to learn about his frog business and resultant fortune, asked Ikenga how he subsisted, he replied that the gods spared him. "The word is spared. I owe late Igwe Dimanochie a lot. He stood by me when it mattered most. In the face of insurrection, he refused to turn me in nor did he come for you."

After the meal, Nwabunna took Ikenga, who had wanted to return to Baruru same day but for the marriage ceremony, which he didn't know of theretofore, to Oforbuike who was due to leave for the house of one of his clients. He postponed it seeing Ikenga.

"The great Ikenga himself!" he hailed him. "The man who defied fire and rain and wind and saboteurs in the struggle to free Gnishere from colonial constraints. I'm honored to have you under my roof. The eyes with which I've seen you will never go blind... If only my daughter had seen your heroism, she would have been cool-headed...."

"Thank you so much," Ikenga replied.

"He has been my father since I arrived here," Nwabunna said of Oforbuike. Ikenga thanked him for that. "No one raises their child alone. You have done for him what none of his parents was allowed by fate to do for him."

Oforbuike told Ikenga that it'd be good for Nwabunna to stop tilling and start a known business. "He can't continue to till people's farms. He's now a man, a family man with children and a wife. He's got daily bounden responsibilities to shoulder." Nwabunna looked at his grandfather and then nodded.

"Again," Oforbuike continued, "He can't continue to stay with an old woman in her house, too. What if she dies today? Where will he stay? Or don't you know that her husband's people don't want to see her with their eyes?"

"You're right, my friend," Ikenga concurred. "But his neck must not break because he's getting married, or because he's had four children. It is one load at a time, for his neck's sake."

When they returned home, it was dark already. Mama provided a mattress for Mazi Ikenga. And with Nancy, her children, and sister absent, there was enough space for him. And he eventually slept in a kennel because of the dog he truly loved.

In the morning, Molokwu's house buzzed with excitement. Wontedly, Merogwu women were bringing food materials with their basins and baskets to support the host family, as they prepared to give out their daughter in marriage. Nancy's mother provided a big sisal bag into which the women poured garri. And this caused the community's fiercest quarrel ever between Olamma and Olaedo. The latter stood by, waiting for the former to empty her basin of garri and give her space to do so herself. Olaedo then said to Olamma "Your garri looks as though it is burnt."

"What are you talking about this woman?" Olamma rebutted, already angry. "Garri that I fried by myself burnt? Garri that I fried the day my good husband made me happy for the first time in five years? You think that I'm your shameless self that doesn't know how to fry garri?"

When the quarrel was quelled, excitement returned to the surroundings. It returned with Ogubunka's arrival. He saw many young men around and knew they were sharing some money which was their right as youths of the town. As custom demanded, youths were given twenty- seven naira and some drinks before dowry payment proper. "We're the ones who protect our girls until a suitor comes around," they bragged. As he entered, Ogubunka began to sing one of his self-composed poems:

I'm looking for a fifteen year old girl to marry

To marry — yes to marry her

The ones I see look old even at their young age

They don't greet elders again

Always looking at their 'backface' as they walk
Forgetting that their waist isn't theirs after-all
My father begot me late enough
Didn't marry as early ...
I'm already old in my youth
But I'm looking for a fifteen year old to marry

The women began to laugh hard. Before he came, the garri quarrel had threatened their joy. But here they were, excited again.

"You see those girls over there?" Ogubunka continued, pointing at some maidens who were waiting on Nancy. "They belong to strangers. The strangers then become our in-laws, friends and brothers. Is marriage not a wonderful something?"

"It is a wonderful something indeed!" they chorused. Although habitually drunk, people loved Ogubunka for his 'hillarics' and fun tricks. Anyone who met him and didn't laugh was believed to be receiving a reward from hell already. He called out one of the fufu pounders and said, "That's a typical job for men you're doing. Why not ask some of those hungry money sharers to do it. It's not only pami and ego obi nwanyi that they should partake in. Give them jobs too."

The woman she was talking to was Julius' wife. Called Julius of Nazareth, he was known for eating any kind of animal whatsoever: snakes, cats, dogs, frogs, rodents, name them. He ate his thing and didn't mind which was which. When one of the believers saw it, he remembered where it was written, "Can anything good come of Nazareth?" So he began to call him Julius of Nazareth, because he didn't see anything good going into the mouth of such a man. Others followed suit. "Your husband will eat human meat someday," Ogubunka said to Julius's wife. "I love cannibals anyway, and it'll be interesting for Merogwu to have one or two or even three cannibals. Why not?"

"If you don't move your drunk self out of this place, I'll pound you like yam now."

"Are you serious? I've been looking for a woman to pound me. So, see me here, Madam Pounder. Pound me. Come on, pound me like yam. I love being pounded, and it's been so long since I was last pounded. Madam man pounder like you. Can't you see you've pounded sanity out of your husband and now he eats anything that comes his mouth's way." Ogubunka held onto her pestle as she, as well as other women, was dying in laughter.

"You're both a simpleton and a singleton at your age. Shame on you."

"To marry is not an end. Money is not even the problem."

"Then what is?"

"I want to first find a girl that my destiny accepts."

"Please, carry your world and your god and go away. You men think that a woman is something you just can go somewhere and pick on your way home. You people are cold wrong. Women are the beauty of creation, the beauty of life, and the wonder of the world. That's why we are rare."

"You rare? You in particular rare? You're not serious. You that Julius just picked at a… in fact, let me close my mouth. Your husband will find my meat tasty if I expose both of you. I will still do that though.

"Allow me to take my time and find a fifteen year old girl. I don't want to suffer same fate as my father. He married in a hurry and died early. If he hadn't married at all, he would have been here with me today." What a crapulous fable that was.

"Go and face your own fate and stop deceiving your heart. Old young man like you. There are too many fifteen year old's out there. You are the one who knows what your heart is looking for exactly."

"I can't find them o. I see fourteen and sixteen year old's. But those little children know what their mothers don't know. I give up on them. I give up on marriage in fact.

At the other end of the compound the umuada, some of whom were going to be Nancy's ashebi, were busy preparing their make-up kits of uri, nzu, and tiro. Gossip was their companion during the preparation. "Imagine Nancy of all Merogwu maidens; she's getting married ahead of us all. And she has four kids already," one of them had begun.

"I see luck's hand in all of it," Chinenyedi submitted.

"Remove luck from it, my sister. Nancy is smart and I like her theatricals. When a woman knows where what she wants is, and goes for it, she gets it. That's exactly what she's done," Nkiruka lent her thought and continued. "Her mother taught her well. She's always telling her that the thing on her chest is called breast but my own mother, all she keeps telling me is that when a girl keeps herself and behaves aright, men will queue up for her. I've been keeping myself and behaving yet men are not queuing up."

"Imagine my own mother always asking me to carry water on my head; an entire me carrying water on my head. I have suffered. I have eaten sewage," Chioma, who just came out from Nancy's boudoir joined in.

"That's because you're still in your father's house, still eating from your mother's kitchen," Mgbenkwo submitted.

"If that's the case then, I won't stay in my father's house beyond next year."

"Where will you be going to then?"

"I don't know yet. If he doesn't come for me, I'll go for him. I'll do my thing the Nancy way."

By noon Molokwu's compound was already chock-a-block. Although Nwabunna wasn't an indigene there, the natives turned up greatly. They were mostly people whose soils he had tilled, and those whose sons he had turned to rocks — boys he taught hard work and they became men consequently. They were impressed by his recent thaw which made them begin to talk about him positively. They came out in their numbers and were now waiting for their in-law and his company. They arrived later and were warmly welcomed. The royal presence of Igwe of Merogwu humbled Nwabunna. He came uninvited. Everybody marveled.

The marriage started with a monkey's wedding, which stopped after a while. Then, the occasion went on. When Igwe was given time to say something, he made a statement that ended up becoming the

COMMENT OF THE MOMENT. He said that it was Nwabunna's sons who invited him and that he was impressed with his work culture of honesty and diligence. "… And again, you have never broken our laws or stolen from any of us since you arrived here. That's why I have protected you from your people… You can see how hugely the gods of our land have blessed you. It's because you chose to be law-abiding here."

"It's because he's been drinking the waters of our girls and nobody knows," Ogubunka interrupted Igwe. "The waters of a woman cool down the heat in a man. And in Nwabunna's case, his heat was beyond limits but our daughters' waters have cooled his head." And everybody laughed out loud. "He tills our soils and tills our girls too," he continued, seeing that his vain talk enthused the people. And everybody was exhilarated, except Kalunta who wasted no more time in rebuking him. "Will you shut up your smelly mouth, you drunken thing. When did children start talking in a gathering of the elderly?"

"I'm not the one who said it. I heard it from Molokwu's mouth. He said that Nwabunna tilled his daughter after tilling his farm. In fact, it is the result of that tilling that has gathered us here today."

"If you don't stop talking now, I'll make sure you don't taste any food here today."

"Allow your brother to express himself, my friend," Igwe said to Kalunta, trying to restore calm. "You see, although alcohol has spoilt his head, he's still our son. A man doesn't deny his son a portion of his soil because of the boy's stupidity. Our people, is it not so?"

"That's how it is, Igwe. May you live long," the people replied. And Igwe continued. "Report to my palace tomorrow evening, Nwabunna. I'll have a gift for your sons."

Nancy came out to greet the people, led by her ashebi. Adorned with beads on their waists, ankles, and wrists, and with nzu and uri, local rouge, they danced vigorously to some melodious cultural music. As she danced, she swayed her waist of contentment so contentiously that most of the young men around shouted, "Is this what our stranger-brother enjoys all alone? The bride price must be doubled." But it was all in admiration.

When the two parties had settled on the dowry, her mother came out to greet the people too, like her daughter just did. She appeared from a passage, looking elated and elegant. She had to be happy. It was her first daughter's day. And although she got pregnant before her dowry rites, the incident led to the exposure of her father's adultery and his subsequent apparent eschewal of it. She danced and danced as though she was more sloshed than Ogubunka. Her well-wishers hailed her on and told her to get her waist lower. On the other hand, her perceived enemies, one of whom was Ngadimma, the woman who had threatened to kill her for warning her off her husband, sighed in contempt and smirked in envy. But she didn't even notice them, and all those nuances didn't get to her. She was so lost in joy that even a jab from them wouldn't have been felt by her skin. And, besides, the cheers of 'good wishers' swallowed up the jeers of 'bad belly' people.

Nancy came out again with a drink, this time to 'find' her husband and to officially declare her acceptance of his proposal. She wore an azure dress which was hewn with celadon. Her hair was filleted with tiara and her face shone with rouge. This time, her pace was even and majestic, in congruence with an adagio. Men beckoned her to give them the drink, saying, "I'm the one you're looking for. I'm your husband. I'm Nwabunna." One of them even told her he was the real father of her four children. When she finally 'found' the 'missing' man, she gave him the cup which he drank dry and refilled with money, to the applause of the people. Then she led him to her father, who blessed them. It was when they stood up after the prayer that Nancy noticed that Nwabunna was badly dressed. He was just looking like a beginner tapper of wine. She was disappointed. The young man had wanted to make a new clothe for the occasion, but what Oforbuike told him about life after marriage seemed to have found meaning in his head. So, he chose to save up the money and repeat one of his wears. Nancy had expected him to be in a native wear. She showed composure and decorum nonetheless.

After the marriage, the couple seized the occasion for the naming ceremony of their children. Nwabunna gave his sons the following names: Agurubuike, Onwubundu, and Nsogbubaruru, and he called his daughter Adabuasa. People's reactions were mixed. What on earth informed his initiative to give them those names? Was he under the influence of narcotics? Then, he began to explain, "Agurubuike means hunger is strength. It was hunger that tempted me to break the kernel crack law and consequently flee Baruru. And I came over here and the gods have blessed me. I wouldn't have probably met a woman who could've given me four children in four days if I hadn't come to Merogwu. So hunger gave me the energy to move on and locate my destiny." The people applauded. He continued. "I have chosen to call my second son Onwubundu, which means death is life, in order to honor the memory of my parents. They're gone, but they live in me. That's why I'm brave and brilliant." He turned to Ikenga who looked troubled by those words. He was a man who had taken both smooth and rough routes in his chequered life. He made a sign with his mouth as though he said to Nwabunna, "It is your father that begot you indeed." Going further, Nwabunna said, "And I've chosen to call my third son Nsogbubaruru in order to appreciate how I have come to marry Nancy. We put each other in trouble, and when I thought the worst was in sight, the best thing happened to us." He wanted to mention that he had intended to have the pregnancy aborted, but his sixth sense told him that a host of a party ought not to get drunk before his guests. "Also, I chose that name to always remind myself that under no circumstances should I do what I did in Baruru here in Merogwu. As long as you allow me to stay, I pledge to observe your laws and your subculture." This assertion appealed to Igwe Udorji so much.

"What about your daughter? Why have you called her Adabuasa?" someone asked him from amongst the guests.

"Oh, that's simple! She's just a beauty and she's my first daughter. She's as beautiful as my mother (God grant her soul a peaceful rest). She's also as beautiful as her own mother, the woman whose waist wasted my night and profited my morning. And these days, it profits both my mornings and my nights." And they all laughed with bug and energy. Igwe just saw a brain tank and he was grateful he came. He stood up and took his leave. He was led to his car by beaus and servants, as a group of hysteric people, who abandoned everything else they were doing, sang and danced his praise. Pomp and pageantry, they say, is the awe of a king really.

Food was served unsparingly and people began to get themselves on it. It wasn't long and the most disgusting thing happened. A breadfruit tree was so close to a soak away and two 'heads' of it fell and split open. It was in Molokwu's backyard. He was the first man to build a cistern but it was made with mud blocks. Before no time, a strong disturbing fetor from it saturated the whole place. Everybody took to their heels — rats in the bush, lizards in the paths. Ogubunka didn't know whether he should take some bottles of hot drink or pack as many wraps of akpu as he could carry. His unfastened trouser was busy wobbling on his hips.

"How could Molokwu have built soak away with mud? Is he mad?" one of the guests asked everyone who could hear his faint voice.

"Don't mind that yeye man," another replied. "My concern is that I couldn't take time to eat. I was still trying to loosen my belt when the odor hit my nose."

"That their rice is delicious, I swear."

"Take solace in the one you ate yesterday."

CHAPTER TWELVE
The Run Man Now a Yeoman

A man who swallows saliva when he sees a sweet-looking lady doesn't starve his dog when it craves for big bones. He is always generous to his dog, because he understands that his desire for a woman and the dog's need of a bone are both impulse-driven, and therefore deserve to be met equally.

Igwe Udorji Obike, *Aku-Uto* I of Merogwu, had been hearing things about Nwabunna — how he fled his town, how Mama took him in, how he had adapted ever since arriving; his hard work, finesse, and his determination at success. He had heard about how Nwabunna did three different tills a day, which made one of his hirers dub him 'Nwoke-ezuike.' And true to that alias, he was a man who rarely rested. And yesterday, he saw everything with his eyes. He marveled at Nwabunna's wisdom, vision, and courage.

Igwe Udorji had a far-from-fine childhood himself and struggled through a larger part of his youth before he got out of the ruck. So, he decided to help struggling Nwabunna big time. A man who has defied oddities to live should be helped to have a comfortable living. Udorji was going to do that. A factor that particularly endeared Nwabunna to him was the fact that he had never violated any Merogwu laws. He wondered what on earth had pushed him into breaking one in Baruru. Whatever enigma it was, Udorji believed that the young man was only a victim of an unfortunate tradition. That was why he resisted every pull to repatriate him.

Nwabunna arrived at the palace on time. He was happy and assured. Nobody meets a king and remains in his current status. His worth either increases or decreases afterwards.

He hadn't offended the ruler. He wasn't in his bad books. So, he knew he was going to increase in worth. His name had automatically changed to *Papa Ejima*. And, according to Oforbuike, "that's not a name one can bear with an empty mouth. A father of multiple births has got to fasten his belt tightly round his waist. His trousers have got to be firm on him – yes." The palace was a large building with five to six outhouses.

"Our people usually say that a sand-laced hand brings about an oil-dripping mouth," Igwe began. "You have kept your hands clean since coming here and you've used the same hands to work your way to survival. I'm impressed."

"Thank you, a lot, Igwe," Nwabunna responded, throwing himself on the ground. "You will live long, Igwe."

"I actually called you to tell you that the land which overlooks the village square is now yours. All of it. Here are the papers. It's the token I have for your sons. They are unique and adorable."

"What! Igwe, did you really say what I just heard? I mean did you…oh, I'm grateful, Igwe. You must live long on the surface of the earth."

"You will live long too. You will live and raise your boys and you will live to reap the rewards there are in children."

"When you give a child something that is bigger than his eyes, he will ask who you want it given to." That was what the people of Orient Gnishere said, and that was what Nwabunna did.

Nwabunna left the palace with a specific-yet-terrific joy and made a beeline for home, almost taking ollies. Ikenga and Mama were seated on a stoep having a discussion when they saw Nwabunna approaching. His stomping feet made them leap off the platform. They wondered what a thing it was that put him on that celerity.

"Papa! Mama! Good news. In fact, best news – best news ever."

"What is it? Tell us please."

"Igwe has given me the tract of land opposite the village playground. He said I should build on it and live comfortably."

"The gods are gracious," Mama said, dancing. "You see it? When a man is in good terms with his god, he makes men to favor him."

"Was that the reason the statue adjusted its position when I was coming?" Ikenga thought to himself. The news blessed their souls and they joined in his joy.

They were still celebrating when Nancy and her children returned. She had wanted to spend more days with her mother but the pong outbreak wasn't too good for her tots.

Nwabunna took the news to Oforbuike. As he went, he relieved Igwe's words. He realized that Igwe was always mentioning his sons only. Was his daughter not one of his children? Was she not a part of the spectacular birth, if not the utmost amazement therein? He wondered widely. He liked his *ofor*, however. He had always prayed to live long in order to love and train his children. He wouldn't want them to grow without parental presence and cover like he did. As he approached a flea market which landmarked Oforbuike's house, he saw the wonder of his émigré life, which was also the drama of Merogwu's history. Guess what a thing it was? Lady Unshakable was finally shaken and shattered. He saw how a young man dealt with her until she surrendered, amid tears she couldn't stifle. Every strong man has got a day of humiliation and every oppressor a day of self-sorrow. And that day, her waterloo had to live with her.

What happened was that the lady of undaunted gut and numb sense of respect for others had repeatedly displaced one petty trader after another from their rightfully allotted shops. And that day she carried her 'bad world' to one random woman, not knowing her cup would get chock-full with that single fill. All polite pleas by co-traders and intervention from market regulators for the chit to allow the woman to sample her goods on her rightful stand were not considered. When the woman saw that Lady Unshakable had already sampled her own wares on her stand, she improvised a makeshift stand near a dustbin.

When the victim's first son heard it, he was infuriated. He asked what was to happen the next day to happen at that moment. "A shot of archery hits the pit toilet. Another shot is released and it also hits the pit toilet. Is latrine the target of the arrow?" the young man fumed on. When people heard he was going after Lady Unshakable, they tried to hold him back. "That girl is a bony soul, remember. She will kill you with her bare hands. *Heeeee*! Come back, Obinwanne." But he wouldn't hear. He knew that his own arrow was not carved for the pit toilet. He felt that it was time for Lady Unshakable to give back the surfeit she had taken. His father had told him when he lived that, "a man doesn't steer clear of a battle because of shooting and that what a man does resides in his heart."

When he got to the marketplace and saw his mother relegated to the dustbin part of it while Lady Unshakable sat in her rightful place, his anger exploded immediately. So, Obinwanne lifted all that Oforbuike's daughter had to sell, dropped them on sand, and stamped on them. She smiled contemptuously, thinking it was going to be her as-usual business of beating her victims, not knowing that fire would always have a thing or two to do with a rat's ears. As she jerked up like someone stung by a scorpion, Obinwanne unleashed seven successive karate strokes on her. While she tried to figure out what was happening to her strength, the young man was already smacking and whacking and jabbing her. Then, he went for her stranglehold and held on to it till she surrendered. The thrill was a trail. The market people were so much entertained, and it made up for the 'bad market' or low sales of that day.

Before he left, Obi reinstated his mother, who was pretty proud of him, on her stead. As he took a walk, he was hailed: "it is your father that gave birth to you!"

In no time, the news spread everywhere, through different furrows, channels and networks. "The disagreeing one has finally agreed on the mat of agreement," they gloated at her. Others said that "the cow has finally been brought down by a noose. Obi has just shown us how to do it." Shaken Lady Unshakable shed the tears of a wild pig that day. She wept until her eyes turned cerise.

Nwabunna overlooked her and continued his ride to her father's house. The bicycle seemed to be functioning better since Molokwu released it to him. That was a day after he agreed to pay Nancy's dowry. He reasoned that since Nwabunna had agreed to pay for what he ate, he didn't have to continue keeping it.

He arrived as Oforbuike was boiling some decoction in a cauldron. "You're welcome, my son. How are Mama and Mazi Ikenga, your children and wife, and everyone else?"

"We are all fine. The Creator continues to be kind to us." He deliberately forgot to tell Oforbuike about the market melodrama involving his well worked over daughter, who was yet to return. He knew it would take him away, or at least kill his affect. He needed to have him in the heart he was in when he arrived. Besides, he felt that the information he brought him was more news-worthy than the humiliation of his daughter. Although Oforbuike wasn't proud of her daughter's misbehavior, he was attached to her. He wouldn't forsake his farm because of weeds. Only oafs would do that. Oforbuike was happy about the news. He congratulated Nwabunna and prayed the gods to bless the Igwe with the strength of a donkey, the health of a baby, and the wealth of the aged – wisdom. He was proud of himself because his fatherly efforts towards Nwabunna were yielding great fruits. Igwe had praised his protégé but didn't know the hand that was tugging the drum. The credits should go to him. Nwabunna knew that. He had back-talked to him when they first met, but Oforbuike treated him with a fatherly understanding and grace, instead of with barb and snarl. He had wanted to treat one of his clients but postponed it until the overmorrow, so that he would go see the land with Nwabunna.

The bosky land was located in Agbani, a pediplain with rich, lush and verdant vegetation. It was seventeen miles from Ugwuewu, a community of 'idiotics' and lunatics, who were characterized by a blue skin and yellow hairs and green eyeballs. They were originally normal people until they betrayed their father's confidence, conniving with his enemy to kill him, in return for fry-ups. That was when the discoloration and other anomalies started. Those 'idiotics' and lunatics appeared gentle and oleaginous, but were actually violent and contentious. They used to dispatch their radical and lunatic natives across Gnishere to raise hell. But a time was to come and they were resistant to stop. They ate grasses and drank exudates of trees and shrubs. Until the nineteenth century, they were sub-humans – half human and half orangutan. Narcotic addicts, they used to torment and sack their neighbors until 1919, when they suffered an intra-ethnic war, a self- harm that reduced their preponderant population drastically. That was when their neighbors, all of whom were of minority strength, heaved a relieved sigh. The awe of the war instilled humanity in the remnants a bit. Their blood thirst ceased, but their irrational tendencies remained. So, they continued to do things that only befitted animals. They needed light, the light of knowledge, to come out of the darkness of ignorance. But instead of education, their leaders taught them abomination. They taught them hate for others. Sad.

Oforbuike and Nwabunna surveyed the land manually and marked out its boundaries with stones. A man came by and greeted them and they greeted him too. He was returning from a woodland where intensive lumbering was taking place. That was what Merogwu got – timber. Trees were felled and sawed into logs of different shapes and sizes, which were then sold under strict regulations. Also, the likes of castor, eucalyptus, and patchouli oils were produced by Merogwu factories, and exported. Although they made huge revenue from timber and its by- products, they ever envied Baruru's coal, soda, and palm oil.

"This one you people are pointing here and there. Who is buying and who is selling a portion of land?" the man from the woodland enquired.

"Nobody is buying and nobody is selling any land. But somebody just became a land owner."

"What exactly do you mean, Mazi Oforbuike?"

"Nwabunna found favor with Igwe, and he graciously gave this land to him."

"O my son! Congratulations. May the Igwe live long!" The man was reserved though. He was half-hearted and disappointed in Igwe Udorji, deep down. He couldn't quite understand how he should give three plots of land to a fugitive ex gratia. His name was Ikele, a mat maker and supplier. "This our *igwe* is mad...very soon, he will step down and give up his throne for another stranger. And this Nwabunna of a boy is rooting deeply into our soil. Three sons already from our daughter. He's more popular than our illustrious sons. If we allow the gods to continue to favor him, a time shall come when he will be the one marking out the boundaries of our own land."

That was the genesis of hate and envy against Nwabunna. In fact, his troubles just started. Ikele began to sell those thoughts to other people.

"It is the fault of that widow who took him in," one of Ikele's disciples of disparage said. "Her husband's brothers are keenly waiting to take over his properties and put them to good use, but she has refused to die."

"Well," another said, "while I want us to stop Nwabunna's prosperity in this land, I have nothing against Mama. She has done no wrong in this matter. If it's a small holding that Igwe has given him, it would have been bearable. This one is three plots of our land."

Fair enough, a man's deeds, good and evil alike, live down his lineage. Ikenga, Nwabunna's grandfather, lent a stranger his land just to help him settle and survive. Here was his only survivor enjoying even fatter favors in a strange land.

After surveying the land, the two began to go home, discussing interestingly. At a point, Oforbuike resumed his insistence on Nwabunna quitting tilling. "It is time to get your hands on something novel and noble. I said it the other day but neither you nor your grandfather said anything significant."

"Something like what exactly, *Nna-anyi?*"

"Something like anything-else, something that will reflect your status as a married man. Do you think you'll continue to have the strength to attend to two, three different jobs daily? Look for a business like palm oil business. You can start with two or three drums. Or you can partner with someone. And, whether you take it up north, or sell it in the bush markets around, you will definitely fare better than you do now. Stop enjoying your suffering under the guise that things will get well soon. They don't until a man turns the neck of his ways around. Hope is not stupid. And faith is not lazy. Do a business. Save from its profits. Before you know it, you will have built a house."

"I have heard all you've said and I will do something about it."

Nwabunna began to turn down jobs from that day onward. Decidedly, he was going to hang up his hoe after completing the many jobs he had already agreed to do. If it were possible, he would have withdrawn from them. But he didn't want to hurt feelings. He applied for that year's palm fruit lease, later, which allowed people to own a specific number of palm trees on communal lands. Also, he applied for more lots through other people with whom he found favor in Merogwu. When people heard he was going to quit tilling they were disappointed. However, other young men who ate with tilling were happy. Nwabunna represented a constraint that denied them of jobs, because people preferred him to anyone else. And it wasn't sentimental. Nwabunna did his jobs neatly and never cheated anybody with time or money. Weeds didn't attack crops grown on the soils he tilled the way they attacked those growing on soils done by others. He did his jobs with all his sinews and with all his heart, enough as though it was something his ancestors adjured him to do. As a result, his hirers didn't see any bummer in their farms. Instead, they had bumper harvests. Only those who felt that the time he gave them was too far hired those other till-men.

All persuasions to make Ikenga to spend more time in Merogwu failed. Not even threats from Afuonu and his men deterred him from returning to Baruru. He was yet to see anything or anyone who could scare him in Gnishere. "They have not born anyone who can do that," he said defiantly. He told Nwabunna that he would send him enough money with which he would start the red oil business through Nwani. Why wouldn't he do that? He had no other immediate kin to will his wealth. It's either Nwabunna got the money he made from frog business or enemies would. His goodbye words caused some misunderstanding between Mama and himself. He had said of Nancy's children, "my children would love to visit their homeland someday."

"You just lied, Ikenga," Mama disagreed. "Is that the gratitude you have for me?" she heckled. "Is that your way of thanking me for picking up and taking in your mooching grandson, a boy you couldn't train in trade or craft?

"Is that what I get in return for giving him a life; for my shelter and food and some other things until he started earning? I love it that you have chosen to call me a fool instead of appreciating me. It's not your fault, Uche. Since the Creator humbled me this low and decided not to be merciful at all, why won't you and my husband's people treat me disdainfully? Now, for your information, those children are mine and they belong to Merogwu. Neither you nor Baruru has any right over them."

"I never came to Merogwu to negotiate ownership of children," Mazi Ikenga entered. "I'd be both stupid and ungrateful to do that. However, whenever the time comes, the children will find their way back where they truly belong. Even if they don't want to, circumstances will make them do it."

Nancy was pleased with Mama's position. As for Nwabunna, nativity of his children wasn't a problem yet. He was just interested in seizing all the opportunities he was seeing. So, he sat on the fence while the fulmination lasted. What if he took sides with his grandfather and Merogwu asked him to vacate their land? Baruru didn't want to see him. And, conversely, what if he took sides with Mama and his grandfather changed his mind about the money he just promised him? For him, wisdom was way better than butter.

As Ikenga left, he tried to fathom between him and Mama whom the gods had humbled more. In the days that followed, Nwabunna began to expect Nwani to bring him the money promised him. When he met Oforbuike much later, he raised the issue about Mama's position on his children's real nativity. "Your children don't belong here," the father-figure answered. "Never in the entire history of Merogwu has a woman given birth to a son in her first pregnancy. Never. Our first borns are usually females. But your wife, our own daughter, got not just a son but three of them in her first pregnancy. Nsogbubaruru is the third kingdom in Orient Gnishere. Doesn't that tell you something? Besides, all of them came with six fingers and six toes on each hand and toe. Merogwu babies have never had that.

That alone tells everyone the answer. However, they are Merogwu aborigines, but not natives. When they grow up tomorrow and decide to relocate to Baruru, nobody will stop them. If they choose to die here, nobody will stop them, too."

"Igwe Udorji has always left my daughter out each time he is talking about my children. Why does he do that?"

"I see nothing in there. Like her brothers, she's your child and she belongs to Baruru."

"Mama said she had expected me to name my daughter after her. And I think she's asking for a lot. I'm not happy that she feels under-appreciated."

"She is not asking for a lot, and she deserves to feel anything, my son. She is somewhat right. I see reasons with her, but I still love the name you gave your girl. Mama has helped you as much as you have helped her in turn. Justice tilts to her side. My only problem with her is timing and size of her dissatisfaction."

"I never knew she was interested in that. If I have another daughter, I'll allow her to give the girl any name she may desire."

"You owe her that. She lost her family too soon. Then she picked you up. She has provided you with goodwill and guidance. What more do you need? My son, things happen to drive home the message of the gods to us. Although Udorji has asked you to settle here permanently, still see yourself a stranger, a sojourner in a tent waiting for dawn to continue his journey home. The gods of your land want you home. Besides, a new Igwe may come on tomorrow and revoke what Udorji has done. So think it out, my son. A man's spirit sinks when he doesn't think. You must have heard that before."

"I have. But, if the gods of my land want me back, let them clearly order my people to drop the charges against me. Or, do they want me home to have me face the penalty?" There was a scorcher, and so the house heated up. So, a drink from the earthen pot was desirable, and Nwabunna served himself good. Why not? Oforbuike's house had long become his as much. Drawing up the lace of his full-frontal breeches, which made him look like a wide boy, Nwabunna told himself that his children would definitely return to Baruru. "Although we believe that the soil is one, each man has a particular spot of it to call his own." That was his thought as Oforbuike talked on.

Oforbuike was an honest man. He's an objective progressive with constructive perspectives. He was saddened by the fact that although Merogwu people were smart enough, they had less working-class people, vis-a-vis other kingdoms in Orient Gnishere. Despite being grateful to Udorji for his benevolence towards Nwabunna, he was disappointed in him for channeling Merogwu's resources to Umuakaekpe, his maternal home. This made their sons follow their sisters elsewhere, in order to find jobs. A drama happened at the palace a certain time in the past. Igwe Udorji had received a letter from the Central Government one day and needed to know what message there was therein. But when they couldn't find a reader, their literate children having all left the kingdom, one of the red cap men decided to attempt it. The meeting had to dismiss when the man pronounced "allocation" as "arrow-*nkechi-onu*," which translated as "an arrow that tied up the mouth." And because the correspondence had read: "We shall continue to send you allocation always," Udorji and his people became afraid, thinking it was an arrow as during the inter-kingdom conflict, which was laden with offensives and reprisals. That was what Oforbuike heard and decided against attending a garden-eggless gathering in his life again.

CHAPTER THIRTEEN
Fun Turns Folly

H ow sad it is that after a dog has barked a suspected danger away it eventually does greater harm to its owner than the stranger could ever have done. Terribly sad!

Nancy's affair with and eventual marriage to Nwabunna changed the course of chastity in Merogwu. The very way in which they married introduced unhealthy and undefined boy-girl relationships in the land. Whatever restraint which formerly prevented that was removed completely. As a result, pre-marital sex, in-my-father's-house pregnancies, abortion, and of course, single parenthood became commonplace. The Nancy-Nwabunna thing became a template for young persons. "Why not be my Nancy and I your Nwabunna!" became a wooing cliché with which boys brainwashed girls, who encouraged one another with sentimental statements like, "After all, Nancy did it and nothing happened to her. Instead, the gods blessed her with four children."

It is said that when evil lasts for a year, it becomes a tradition. And every nation is either famous or notorious for a tradition. And a tradition as repugnant as this is a nation's bane and destructive vane. Nothing could have been more unsightly than a picture of a boy and girl having a heavy-petting in bushes and river banks, something that made elders of Merogwu spit and flick their fingers in disgust and angst. But the young girls didn't care. They just discovered a new world they thought had to be explored. But then the schadenfreude they had on Nancy returned to them. While Nancy finally got married to her opportunistic lover, most of them didn't have such an end result. They were 'tilled' and spilled afterwards.

The first girl to get pregnant out of wedlock, after Nancy, was Chinelo, daughter of Merogwu's finest tanner. Her mother sold comestibles. Consequent upon that, her father was barred from talking in umunna gatherings, while her mother was made to sweep the village square with a bush broom for a month, at a time trees shed their leaves. So the job was an arduous, thankless one. Thereafter, she took a cylinder of powder and a basin of calabash chalk to the river in order to appease the goddess of fertility on her daughter's behalf for "taking a baby from her hands forcefully." That was the belief. A girl who got "pregnant in her father's house" was adjudged to have stolen or snatched a baby from the hands of the goddess of fertility. When a married woman took in, conversely, she was said to have been given a baby by the goddess willingly. The former was loot, the latter largesse. The first was an act of rebellion, the second cooperation.

In Merogwu, an untrained child was seen as society's greatest threat. So, although they gave birth to many children, men ensured all of them had something legitimate doing. As early as eight years of age, a child had already discovered which way his destiny should walk in. But nobody was interested in training a child his daughter bore out of wedlock. That was why they tried to use severe penalties to dissuade girls from it.

Two weeks into Chinelo's mother's penalty, Nneafor joined her, after her daughter was confirmed pregnant. Her daughter's pregnancy had long been forthcoming. Called "Jarcas the Gbaza Queen," she was always 'throwing' herself on boys. So it wasn't a surprise when she gave birth in her mother's kitchen unassisted — something the red-cap men called a woeful abomination, unbeknownst to them that it was coming to their houses one after one. When they saw they and their wives were simply taking turns in the consequent punishment for one's daughter getting enceinte at home, the penalty was overturned. They chose to allow everyone to go wherever they bathed to pick their wrapper by themselves. This happened when Igwe's daughter became pregnant for Mmeregini, a tapper of palm wine. Of all people, a palm wine tapper did that. Badness! The meaning of his name — what did I do? — made the whole thing dramatic and funny. After what he did was resolved, it became a subject of joke. People would ask him, "what is that your name again?" and when he replied, "my name is Mmeregini," they would tell him, "you impregnated Igwe's daughter. That's what you did." Evil had lasted for a year and had become a tradition amongst them, but this tradition was the undoing of Merogwu.

It was now five years since Nwabunna and Nancy married, and they had had three additional children in single births; two girls and a boy. He named the girls Ngozika and Nkiruka, after his mother and Mama respectively. He called his fourth son Igwebuenyim, in honor of Igwe Udorji, for his munificence towards his family. Seven children in five years. That made the people to call him a great man, and he was proud of himself and prouder of his wife, who continued to look appealing in his eyes.

"Keep them coming," Oforbuike said of his children. "Children are the strength of a city and wealth its stronghold. Both are weapons of conquest against any enemy. However, what preserves a people is justice." With the assistance of the same man who gifted him with a tract of land, Nwabunna later built a grange and he and his family packed in. He asked Mama to join them, but she refused. She insisted that the greatest honor she could give her late husband was to die on his soil. "Emenike will die in his grave if I ever leave his house," she had said of her late husband. She believed that although death had ended their marriage, it shouldn't end their love. How much she loved her husband, a man she accepted to marry at a trade fair when London still ruled Gnishere. Her beauty attracted him. Her doings kept him till his death in the Inter-kingdom War. But even though he was long dead, she kept her love for him alive. "He always comes around my bed at night," Mama had once told Nwabunna. All of it was possible because she was a good woman. It wasn't every woman that could have held her late husband so dearly in death. There was a certain woman in the same Merogwu. She scooted away with her three children and all of her husband's savings just because he was unconscious in the hospital. The man hadn't died yet but she was already gone. That was why elders used to tell young men to swipe their eyes with seven fingers before they popped the question. "Many are married women, but only a few are wives," they would advise qualified bachelors.

"I'll be paying you visits from time to time," Nwabunna promised Mama who always found hope and courage in her name Nkiruka – what lies ahead is more.

A well trained dog is no mere animal. It's a pet with a personality. Nwabunna understood this, so he was determined to train his children well. He had suffered a lot for lacking parental presence much of his life. He wasn't going to let his children have a taste of such a meal. He was well alive and his wife well around. "Never desire people's pity. It is as good as pee. Your penny is worth more than another man's pearls. Earn it and keep it. Finally, remember that Merogwu is not your land of nativity. Don't be too comfortable here, therefore." These were the words he raised his children with.

Igwebuenyim suffered some circumcision complications which got his body sore. As he was recovering, his older brothers went down with episodes of fever. They laid like woods on a mattress – three of them wore some hand-me-down clothes which Nancy's mother had bought them. The woman who gave birth to them was greatly alarmed. She feared they all were going to die. "They're only getting strong," Nwabunna encouraged his wife. "The fever will make them grow taller. You will see it. So, don't worry your life away."

"Let them grow through nutrients, not through sickness. I'm afraid." Nancy was greatly troubled. Just then, Nkiruka crawled in, crying. Nancy felt her body and found out that an ant had bitten her. So she rubbed 'cooking oil' on her cheek to soothe it. And it did.

Later that day, Nwabunna repaired to Oforbuike's house to join in welcoming his in-law. Lady Unshakable was getting married. Before he left, he asked Nancy to roast him some palm fruits. It was his favorite 'chew-chow.' Mama had warned him that it could predispose him to malaria but he wouldn't hear. Salted and roasted palm fruits were his gluttony, in fact. Lady Unshakable ceased being rough after the market contretemps. The beating fever she developed as a result of it reformed her.

The suitor was Idika, a businessman who dealt in cashew nut export. He just returned to Merogwu from Cameroon and saw Lady Unshakable and loved her at face value. Before he and his company arrived, Oforbuike and his kinsmen, as well as Nwabunna, who had long become a kinsman himself, were already seated. They discussed exhaustively about many things. Idika was a small man with a big air of confidence. He had been to many African countries in the course of his business. Merogwu was a place of cashews. In fact, cashews were their junior indigenes. Visitors were not allowed to leave with its nuts. They ate the flesh and dropped the nuts behind. Oforbuike was worried about something: the compatibility in her heavy-set daughter marrying a manikin. "Are you sure you can cope with my daughter?" he had asked Idika.

"You make me laugh hard, Nna-anyi," Idika had replied. "I love Nonye and everything about her. She's the kind of a woman I need for a wife—somebody that will scare my many relatives away and make them stop asking me for money all the time. She has promised to be responsible and I have enough money to make her happy." When Oforbuike saw his conviction, he gave them his consent and blessings. The marriage proper happened three weeks later.

All Idika wanted was a redoubtable wife who would say his mind in his absence and please his heart in his presence. His father, Mazi Akanonu, was the first man in Merogwu to share his wealth amongst his children while still alive. Also, he was the first man who allotted inheritance to his daughters. Ordinarily, in Merogwu, as well as Orient Gnishere at large, women received nothing from their fathers. They were believed to have shares in their places of marriage only. Akanonu broke that tradition, and unapologetically for that matter. He made a mitosis of his land- related wealth between his two sons. But while Idika multiplied his share, his older brother squandered his. He was the first man that sold an expanse of land without cause and then spent the dosh on no course. Every day he kerb-crawled up and down the social universe and houses of whoredom. After they sapped him arid, he began to work as a bather in one of the brothels. He bathed wenches and other women who were too obese and lazy to do that on their own. Eventually, he became a gigolo to one of his clients, a Russian lady.

While they ate, Idika picked interest in Nwabunna. "You must be the man who doesn't rest," he enquired.

"Yes, I am. I will soon find rest, anyway," Nwabunna replied, holding his horn of palm wine intently.

"Don't mind them. True rest comes from the Creator."

"I don't care what they call me. How can a man rest when his god is restive himself?" This reply enthralled Idika so much. He said in his head, "this man is really smart. I'd love to have him for a business partner."

Just then, Oforbuike's retard of a son emerged from nowhere, slobbering disgustingly. Phlegm everywhere. It was as though the faucet of his runny nose lost its grip that moment. It was flowing like rivulets. Oforbuike was embarrassed. He ordered him to go to his maternal home and never return again. As though he knew the boy was going to be deformed, he named him Onyekere, meaning who created? The young man turned forthwith and returned to the backyard, where his mother and her friends were overseeing viands and comestibles. She was called different kinds of names by her husband's people because of her son's sorry state. When she couldn't have another baby afterwards, they called her a "baby eater" and asked their brother to put her away. He was, however, averse to that idea. So, he told them to remove their eyes from his 'precious' private life. They called him a beatnik and considered him a black head on the skin of their family and an odor in their nose. They further alleged that his wife had kept him in charm.

He was still dealing with his son when Idika asked Nwabunna off for a chinwag. He offered him to join his business and the father of seven was grateful for it. This gesture was a third tangible benefit he was deriving from associating with Oforbuike. First, adaptation in Merugwo. Second, the land gift from Igwe Udorji and the subsequent house on it. Now, a business deal. He couldn't have been luckier. He knew that. Coming close to the man had always blessed his life. They rejoined others and continued with their food. Everybody was in love with the food—a course of pounded yam and cocoyam soup, jazzed-up with achara and ukazi. How Ogubunka was missing out was a mystery. "Are you sure he's alive?" one man asked another. Ogubunka was everybody's kinsman. So, he didn't miss introductions. One Mazi

Ekenta was the one from whom they bought the ukazi. That was his business. He went to forests and plucked the parallel-veneted leaves and supplied them to markets and palaces. And he fared fine with it. A savant in Merogwu, he was called African Mahatma. He had a rich and vast knowledge of a variety of things. His advice was firm and productive.

Before the guests left, Lady Unshakable was handed over to one Nneoha, a chaperone, for grooming, as custom required. Nwabunna wanted to ask his head why Nancy wasn't given to any chaperone. But before he could do that, a probable answer evoked his mind: "It's because you got her pregnant before going to pay her dowry." It wasn't a big deal to him. Groomed by a chaperone or not didn't guarantee a marriage's success after-all. All he had to do, he believed, was take proper care of his family. He kept quiet, and as he lifted his horn of palm wine for a big gulp, Ogubunka appeared from nowhere and hollered him to take it easy. The whole place glowed with excitement hearing his voice. "I said it that if you didn't show up, you must be dead," reckoned the man who had remarked about his absence earlier. "I said you should take it easy, Nwabunna, or Nwa- whatever they call you. If you like you can answer 'Nwabumpa'…You mustn't finish all the drinks here all alone. Remember, nobody can dethrone me as the king of drunks in Merogwu. At least, not a man on the run, not a taboo escapee."

Impeached and irked, Nwabunna took an ollie to Ogubunka and was about to give him a pile driver blow when Ekenta held him back. "Don't mind the stupid man," Ekenta pleaded. "He's only looking for the person in whose hands he will die. He's already dead though. He only wants a free undertaker."

Idika was pleased with Nwabunna's reflex and panache. "I love men who fight, not cowards who clap for crap," he said, reaffirming that Nwabunna would really make a good business partner. And it wasn't a vain hope. He was already making some killing from tilling, and he got a terrific hunger for business blood. That was the second time Ogubunka was tackling him unprompted. He accused him of "tilling" Merogwu girls the other day. Here he was again taunting him for being a fugitive. "Drunks are natural blood stirrers, not nippy kill joys," he spat Ogubunka. "Next time you try me, I kill you."

When Ogubunka regained his movement, he faced the suitor. "I heard that you said you have no problem with Lady Unshakable. She will give you the beating of your existence — she will just beat you the beating a tinker beats pan."

"Shut you up!" Idika scolded him. "A bad-mouthed man like you does not deserve to be in the company of responsible men. Continue going round the whole community for free food. Don't find a way and help your destiny, you hear. You called yourself king of drunks, shame on you." As the guests were beginning to leave, Urudinanwanyi came to give her mother, a good friend of Oforbuike's wife, an important message. Nwabunna took fancy to her body as she sashayed towards the backyard, where the women were. He was beginning to love her deeply. He knew it and it was true. Nwabunna could now see that Urudinanwanyi was no longer the lithe girl she used to be. She had added some flesh. The way she carried her 'backface' area made his maw to drop, he nearly drooled like Oforbuike's mentally retarded son. "This girl can revive a man's love life, including that of an impotent. What does she think she's doing?"

"Remove your eyes from that girl," Nwokedebego hushed Nwabunna from behind, holding his ears in stern warning. "Igwe's son has declared his intention to marry her. In fact, he shall be going to 'drop a drink' on her head this coming Orie market day. Is that clear to you?" Those words got Nwabunna breathless, stock-still, and speech-disabled. He couldn't just believe his ears, so he grabbed a grave gape and a grape gaze.

"But Prince just can't marry Urudinanwayi," a kinsman of Oforbuike's said. "He can. Why not," Nwokedebego pursued.

"She's from Umuudara community. The throne goes there next, so they can't give their daughter in marriage to the current royalty, nor can they marry from the royal Umuda as long as one of their sons remains igwe. That's the custom. Tradition is the foundation of every institution and every people. Or don't you know that?"

"The prince has made up his mind already and Igwe has already consented."

"What! Igwe did what? Tufiakwa!" they said, with a concomitant snap of fingers. "May the gods forbid that our own Igwe, the first denizen of this kingdom, should support something that is against our tradition."

"It is 'impossibus,'" Ekenta declared. That was his way of saying 'impossible.' His late father, poorer than a misery, always told him as a little boy that it was impossible for him to ride charabanc. The bus was the first motor he saw in his lifetime, in 1932. Ekenta was seven then. When little Ekenta saw the bus and asked his old man to buy it, he replied: "It is 'impossibus,' my son." Ever since, it became his everyday word, especially when he was joking.

Nwokedebego was an executive of Merogwu youth council and a close friend to the savage prince. So, Nwabunna knew he couldn't have been kidding. There was babel in Oforbuike's house now, but then his in-laws had gone. Nwabunna didn't quarrel with anyone over that matter. He was still an alien. He never forgot that. He remembered that what a man had to do should be in his heart, not on his lips. He was beginning to feel something forceful for Urudinanwanyi, and he was going to go for her. As for the prince being interested in her too, he chose to allow the dog slug it out with ghosts for the bone. And ghosts are always afraid of life each time they have to contend for a bone with a dog.

CHAPTER FOURTEEN
A Series of Silly Crises

A well fed dog is more confident than a hungry one, which always jumps up at the throw of anything that looks like a bone. Additionally, a well fed dog has learnt that the best way to treat a bone is to lick it dry and drop it. It knows, too, a bone isn't food after all.

Nwabunna had learnt these over the time. He had already established a firm manhood and built a known name in Merogwu, seventeen years since arriving as a fugitive. He became a young yeoman when he built on the land Udorji gave him. He was now planning to become a laird, a real estate owner, having joined Idika in his money-yielding cashew nuts business. A factor that kept him going was confidence. He had always known that the confidence of a dog is the strength of its teeth, not the hardness of the bone it is chewing. He had laid it down in his heart to take in another wife, and the other day in Oforbuike's house, the girl in question was said to have been spoken for by another man, the prince of the land, a man whose father had been kind to him and to his whole household. That was a situation he ordinarily wouldn't have been interested in. He was awfully wary that his conflicting with the prince's interests might cause his father's kindness to go out of kilter. He did know it would, but he wasn't going to give up on Uru. This was the last thing he was going to do.

Something in him told him that the girl wanted him herself; she said it the way she carried herself each time they met. She brought his grandfather to Mama's house a few years back and was unwilling to leave. She saw him at Oforbuike's house the other day and started to sashay. So, saying no to her and staying out of the intention simply because a prince was interested in her too meant cowardice. "How many heads does the Prince have, by-the-way, that he wants to pour gravel into my garri?" He braced himself up. It was at that moment that he remembered his father's name was Akobuaku — wisdom is wealth. So, he chose to capitalize on Ekenta's insistence that tradition forbade the prince to marry Uru. He knew that most chiefs would stand for tradition, because an old man wouldn't stay at home and watch a goat deliver in the tether. Knowing, also, that Oforbuike loved integrity more than jewelry and therefore commanded loyalty and wielded wisdom and influence, he resorted to him. "He will outsmart Igwe and his uninformed son."

When Nwabunna finally made his intentions formal, a series of silly crises ensued. Hence, Merogwu was replete with frantic factions. One supported Igwe and his son. Another sided with tradition, and with Nwabunna invariably. Yet a few other people — the yes men of community — sat on the fence, a collapse-prone wall, which had long absorbed enough water, it could fall flat at any moment.

Most of those on Nwabunna's side didn't really love him. They were only trying to show Igwe Udorji their displeasure at his royal stupidity in giving a fugitive franchisement and making him more comfortable than most indigenes. Others were those who were desperate to vent their resignation on the Igwe for being so barmy that he wanted to bend their esteemed tradition because of a woman. When the matter finally reached Ezemmuo, he ruled that the only thing that could make the prince to marry Urudinanwanyi was for his father to cede reign to the next community in line of succession immediately, thereby making it impossible for the prince to ever succeed his father and complete the two-reign zoning of their province.

"I must marry that girl," the prince dared the oracle. "I'll marry her and still become *igwe* and nothing will happen." He turned and walked out on an onslaught of prominent men, who had collected at the hallowed shrine.

"Hmm!" the Oracle smirked. "A child carried on the back doesn't know that the journey is long. For leaving this shrine in this disrespectful manner, you will return in a disgraceful way." As the people dispersed, they engaged each other in a discussion. "It is his father that caused it," they said of the prince. "We wanted to chase Nwabunna away then, when we confirmed he is the Baruru taboo boy, but Igwe refused."

"My problem is that if there is anyone who may break our tradition it shouldn't be someone from the royal family. Is that girl the only maiden in Merogwu?"

"You're right, Ikem. You see, Igwe is very stupid."

"What! You called Igwe stupid?"

"I'm sorry. I didn't know when it came out of my mouth. Please, let a second ear not hear it."

"My dear, there is nothing I can do because a second ear has heard it already. In fact, four ears have heard it."

"What!" he screamed, turning around to see who the four ears could have been.

"Don't mind me. You have two ears and I have two, so four ears heard it." The other man was relieved. That was how much ordinary people feared an *igwe* then. He knew Udorji would have cooked for him some food he wouldn't have been able to finish.

"You almost made my heart jump out of me. I thought you were going to report me to Igwe."

"How can I? I'm too self-worthy to be a sycophant. You're right to have said he's stupid. In fact, he's extra-stupid. I thought he was His Royal Highness, I never knew he's His Royal Madness actually. I mean, how could he have prospered that alien more than our sons? Imagine Udorji praising a boy that should be stoned to death for being hard-working. Let him not work hard now.

"How many times has he praised our own hard-working sons? And he gave that vagabond our land, and while we were still trying to recover from that shock, he helped build a house for him."

"That is the most '*iberiberic*' thing I've ever seen. Do you see this your *igwe*, he needs …."

"Whose Igwe? He's not my *igwe* please. I am personally *igwe*-less."

"I can't live with this. I am leaving this kingdom as soon as I can. I don't like seeing things that irritate my eyes, except, of course, it will give me some money at the end."

"No, I'm staying behind. I'll stay here and watch him eat this dysentery soup he has made."

The eagle had perched for a shot. There were plots and counter-plots. Nothing could have been more demoralizing than the maturity which Nwabunna showed while the tug of conflict lasted — maturity of taciturnity. Prince was confused. He couldn't quite understand why, although Nwabunna was quiet, a considerable number of Merogwu men backed him. "He has turned our people against us, father," he carped to the Igwe.

"You need not worry, my dear," Udorji assured him. "The girl will definitely choose you over Nwabunna. Women don't reject royalty. They treasure it more than breath," he reassured his tear-away heir.

When Prince finally went to officially inform Onuoha of his contentious intentions towards his daughter, the man called Urudinanwanyi to speak for herself.

"I'm not the one whose hands are being sought in marriage," the girl's father had said.

"My Prince," Urudinanwanyi began, I know you're rich and handsome. I equally know you'll be our next *igwe*, but...."

"But what?" the father interjected.

"Allow her, *Nna-anyi*," Prince implored him.

"... but you have no business doing and you can't stoop low to work. I prefer Nwabunna, who's not ashamed to work hard to earn a living."

"Eat feces there, Uru," Onuoha blasted his daughter. "I said you should eat feces. How can you fault the Prince for having no business? Do you know how much he earns every month for just being the prince of Merogwu Kingdom?" He didn't mean those words. He was only 'mouth- shooting.' He was acting his own character of a script which was aptly written by Oforbuike and edited by Ekenta. Onuoha and his family loved Nwabunna personally, and it was the day

Oforbuike told them of his intentions to take Urudinanwanyi as his second wife that they approved of it.

"So you mean you prefer being a second wife to a man who has no bearing in life to being the next queen?" the prince tried to persuade Uru.

"If you don't marry our prince, I'll kill you!" the father threatened. "I will put pepper in your brain! I'll send you out as a maid to a house of hunger! I will 'dis-daughter' you! I will," he threatened on and on.

"Kill or torture me, I won't marry Uduma," she retorted. The manner in which she mentioned the prince's name got him up on his feet, and he went home. That was the first time someone called him by his name. Everybody had always 'princed' him up-and-down, here and there, now and then. He couldn't come to terms with the fact that a girl called him a spoilt plonk and he did nothing. "If that stupid girl knows what she stands to gain if she marries me, she wouldn't be misbehaving. Well, they say that when you're doing something for a woman, she will be doing something for her besotted." He wanted to betake himself to the shrine, but when he remembered Ezemmuo's words that he would "return in a disgraceful way," he changed his amateur mind and returned to the palace.

His father, Igwe Udorji, was disappointed in Nwabunna. In fact, the exile became his nemesis. "Pigs don't appreciate pearls, so never throw one to them," he said to his son. He wished he had said that to himself seventeen years ago.

"You have to sack him from that house you built for him," Uduma suggested to his father.

"I wish it were possible, my dear."

"Why not! Just send a few guards there."

"It's not as easy as you think. With that land I swore an oath to the gods of my fathers to bless his sons who were born in this kingdom. A man might commit any other sin against the gods, but he dare not break a vow he made to the them."

Some of Nwabunna's associates came to tell him of

Uru's formal rejection of Uduma. They arrived as he was shaving Agurubuike's hair. The boy had dandruff, which had turned his scalp to a graffiti board. He rubbed the sore surface with a mixture of soap-less detergent and wood ash. It was damn painful, so the boy withdrew his head in a reflex, like a serpent upon which liquid fuel was poured. Only goodness could forgive that dandruff. After his birth, the boy also suffered a great deal of pain, no thanks to an opening along his coronal suture. He was taken here-and-there for treatment but it persisted. It was when they were tired of treating him that it healed on its own. Challenges of childbirth. Griddles of growing up. Struggles of survival. It was only the fanfare of those men that quelled the boy's cry.

"You have won hands down finally," they announced. "Let Nancy begin to prepare to welcome her first husband's wife," Ekenta said, looking at the many chattels Nwabunna had got. They were still frolicking when the prince and his henchmen arrived in fury.

"Nwabunna," the prince called out from some metres, "are you sure you can withstand me?" Nwabunna, as well as his party kept mum. "My father said he came to your marriage because of your children. But me, here I am. I came because of you. I ask you once more, are you sure you can handle what I'm bringing your way?" The silence became intense. "I've not lost a fight before and I will never lose one any time, except I choose to gift the other man victory. I'll take his life and give him victory though."

"You've not lost a fight before because you're yet to actually fight one," Nwabunna broke the silence. "I have one word for you, but I don't want your father to call me rude." Uduma was pissed off at that gut, but he chose not to do anything physical.

"Well, I don't hold brief for a thief who deserves grief. I give you three days to convince that girl to marry me. Else, I'll take you to a desert for a dessert of distress."

"It beats my wildest fancy that a toothless dog thinks it can beat a well-toothed one to a fat bone. Uru is my second wife already. I've always known that since the first time I tilled her father's soil. I try to save your father a royal ridicule, but you seem desperate to live in it. It's sad and strange that a royal family wants to destroy a tradition they're supposed to protect." Those statements angered the headstrong prince. He wanted a fight but was disarmed by the presence of Nwabunna's boys, who were standing and looking gung-ho. He felt outnumbered even with his war-ready and taut-chested men. Indeed, "children are the strength of a city," according to Oforbuike's gospel. As the prince turned to leave, he said to Ekenta, "Your repute has come to an end, and you will join the taboo man back to Baruru."

"What the little boy doesn't know is that I have a hand in his father's emergence as *igwe* and can successfully plot his removal. Another thing he doesn't understand is that I know who his real father is…."

"What do you mean, *Nna-anyi?*" Nwabunna and others asked Ekenta.

"He's truly not our prince. You, Nwabunna, are a worthier Merogwu son than that uninformed young man." Everyone couldn't believe his ears, and they covered them with a cusp of their hands. Uduma just pulled a cub by its tail and was going to face its mother's teeth. Ekenta had kept quiet all those while, and now he had been provoked, he was going to stoke the fire with fuel. "This idol has misbehaved. I'll, therefore, show it the wood it was carved from," Ekenta threatened, standing up, and pointing in the direction the prince had taken.

"*Nna-anyi*, please, don't do something rash. Remember the power Igwe has…"

"Which power? I placed him on that throne. The person who actually won and deserved the *igwe*ship was Nkpa but I…don't worry. I'll show this idol the wood it was carved from."

Nancy was so busy in the backyard that she did not know what was going on. She had already begun to prepare for life with a 'husband's wife'. She had had seven children but could still hold her own when it came to body appeal. So, she had nothing to covet or envy Urudinanwanyi for. She was not going to relinquish her husband to a junior wife completely, however. She knew that. So was Nwabunna not going to avoid her bed completely. No matter what he would see in

Uru, he was never going to stop skiing with Nancy. Her waist was one precious gift from the gods. On her own, Urudinanwnayi harbored nothing against Nancy who had been her senior in school. She was an innocent harmless girl who just loved Nwabunna and the deal of his destiny.

The scandal Igwe Udorji had always wished away had finally come his way. The only thing which could stop Ekenta from making a statement that would shake his throne was an apology from the pseudo prince. Uduma got home enraged. His enraptured father was attending to some quorents from a council of *igwes* who had come to Merogwu to inspect an ongoing grant- maintained project sited there. There was excitement everywhere as they congratulated him for attracting such a big project to his kingdom. Every other such project had been hijacked by Umuakaekpe, leaving other kingdoms to wonder whether they were only accompanying them or were a people who also deserved some dividends as well. But, blimey, the human being he made a prince disrupted that proceeding. He was too stupid that he forgot courtesy and lacked temperance.

"I want Ekenta banished immediately!" he requested of his father, who adjusted his buttocks on his throne. And then, he replied to Uduma.

"I can see that you're tired and need some rest, so go and have some food and sleep." The guests were surprised to hear that. Ekenta was a popular figure, well respected amongst elders. They wondered what crimes he had committed that warranted a call for his banishment.

"If you know what that man knows, you will banish yourself first," Udorji continued with Uduma, angry now. "Get out of my sight before the gods finally knock you on your brainless head." Uduma was downright stunned, and he 'pratfell' on a seat.

Udorji was disappointed in himself. It dawned on him he shouldn't have said those words that time, before his cabinet and his guests. When a cat that is big is let out of the bag, it goes for some fishes straight up. In Udorji's case, the cat went for the fish he needed to make some soup with, and it carried it away. The meeting dismissed itself at once, and the attendants dispersed in a scattered pattern.

"What does Ekenta know which no one else knows?" they enquired from each other. And it wasn't something one could surmise. It had to come from the horse's mouth. Udorji was in the doldrums now. He was up for investigation. He was down to ought integrity and was expected to be out of the throne. "When you have a question about the soil, ask the squirrel," one of the guests replied. "Ekenta is the squirrel who knows the ins and outs about the soil in question and it's only wise we wait till we hear from him."

When Nwabunna saw that circumstances had kept Uduma over a barrel, he made some arrangements and married Urudinanwanyi without further ado. She was a girl he was always going to marry.

CHAPTER FIFTEEN
Different Waters in One Pumpkin

A man who alleges that a stranger came to his house and stole his adult dog is the actual thief. The stranger is the real owner of the dog. That was why it followed him without a bark, reluctance, or resistance.

Udorji sent for Ekenta the same day 'the prince' asked him to banish the African mahatma. But Ekenta refused to go with the guards. He rather asked them to tell the *igwe* to send Uduma over for apologies. He was peppering his *ukazi* leaves over a large polythene, which was spread on the ground, with a long stick. He quickly offered them 'bush kola,' a fleshy incandescent hazel fruit with multiple pairs of white pod-like seeds.

His wife was greatly surprised to see palace guards accept and eat something while on an assignment. That was the kind of influence Ekenta had. As they turned to leave, one of them detached some of the *ukazi* leaves for a raw chew. "Tell Igwe that I said he should send that boy in his house to come and beg me…," he repeated, a requisition that got his wife apprehensive, so she warned him to beware of potshard because he had chosen to carry a heavy load without a head pad. Ekenta told her to shut up her mouth and mind her business of idleness. "When you remove a tick from a dog and don't let the dog see it, the dog will think you just pinched it." That was his reply to his shushed wife. He knew the ploy Udorji was putting up, and he was going to outsmart him, in his characteristic 'smartery.' "I can't continue to heal a man of *ibi* while his stomach continues to swell." And certainly, the development had just handed Udorji a big extra-scrotal outgrowth which made sitting down a difficulty.

When he received the guards' reports, he was disappointed, and he went pensive all day, as a result. "Rain has beaten a cow in its eyes!" he exclaimed. He knew he was at Ekenta's elusive mercy and that the fate of his reign rested on the crest of this clemency. The cat was already let out of the bag. And to try putting it back was to have to face its tear-loving paws − some jaw- wrenching endeavor. So Udorji wanted to bribe Ekenta to deny ever making the statement at Nwabunna's house, to call it a tongue's slip. He was downcast when he remembered that the one he said in the palace, in the presence of royalties, could never be denied or withdrawn. His greatest fear of Ekenta was the fact that he was the cat's whiskers: the whole of Merogwu esteemed him highly for his wisdom and for his rich knowledge of and huge regards for their history and heritage.

Now, however, they began to fault his integrity. They reasoned that if he truly loved their heritage or had any integrity at all, he wouldn't have kept quiet over a thing as terrible as the royal robbery and communal mutation. In his head, Ekenta thought that he did it for the "the baby boy." Agreeing to keep the secret was the only thing that was going to keep the boy—foetal Uduma, then—from dying. But since the boy had grown up and one gratitude he got for him was a hard bite of the finger that fed him, he chose to show the idol the wood from which it was carved.

What was the yeast that fermented the bowl of dough? What really happened? What did Ekenta know which no one else knew?" A long story. A long one along a circuitous concentric path. What really happened was that in 1958, Udorji was in his maternal home, Umuakaekpe, on a holiday. He was twenty-two then. One evening, a two-weeks-pregnant couple were going somewhere on foot. Approaching with his grandfather's motorcycle, Udorji accidentally hit the man and he fell down. When his wife confirmed he had pegged out, she quickly turned to a panicky Udorji and told him not to bother. She hated her husband with love and courage and had always looked for a way to walk away from the marriage which, to her, was an entanglement. She never loved him. The marriage was a betrothal thing, when betrothal engagement still existed, when parents and families mutually agreed that their little children would marry each other when they grew up.

It was abolished three years after when a girl betrothed to an heir presumptive of Umuakaekpe reached twenty-two years of age without developing breasts. It was after the prince had taken her in as his wife that he found out that she padded her chest spots all those years.

"Nobody is here," the young woman said to Udorji again. "Nobody saw what just happened. "I'll raise a cry, and when people collect, tell them that a bareback rider hit him and ran away, and he died immediately." Young Udorji was relieved. "But," she continued, "you must marry me as soon as we get away with this."

"But I thought he's your husband," Udorji tried to pity the unfortunate man he just killed.

"Husband kill you there," she snapped at him. "I'm trying to save your life and you're trying to tie a tag of guilt around your neck. If our people find out he died in your hands, they will kill you. Here's Umuakaekpe. Head goes for head, blood for blood and life for life." When Udorji saw her hortatory seriousness, he realized it was in his best interest they act as the innocents. They did and it worked for them. But somehow somebody saw what happened. Yes, a sharp eye saw the smart move of their feet. That eye was Ekenta's. He had seen a cyclist run towards a walking duo but he rushed inside the bush to relieve himself. He was having a terrible stomach trouble which had undone him since morning. And once more he couldn't help stifling it. So he ran inside the bush to save himself. It was when the obligate widow raised an alarm that he came out. When he saw that the motorcycle rider was young Udorji his townsman, he was compelled to go against the court of his conscience by keeping quiet. Ekenta had, meanwhile, gone to Umuakaekpe to join in the struggle for Gnishere's Independence.

Umuakaekpe people were known for basketry, pottery, macramé, and wickerwork. They inherited the name, which meant "children of left-handedness," for being deceitful and crafty. They were known for cheating and maneuver in transactions. When it seemed somebody had gained from a transaction with them, it turned out to be a huge loss. Deals with them passed several renegotiations, in order for other parties to weigh their scales. Also, they were always indecisive and traded trust for 'stomachal' needs.

To make sure Udorji didn't desert her, the willful widow of latter woes took him to a shrine, where they took an oath. That was where he made a vow to the idol that as long as the matter remained concealed, he would always send forty percent of his personal earnings to Umuakaekpe. People who said that the land is not good is the benefit of titled men must have been right. Six days later, Udorji married the beautiful young widow. "She's too young to observe one complete year of mourning," explained the bribed chief priest. "Let her go and find solace in another man's loins." When everything had been resolved, Ekenta went to Udorji and made him know that he saw what actually happened. "Your motorcycle hit him hard and he fell."

"Please my brother let someone else not know about this," Udorji had entreated him. "She's already pregnant from the man I killed. She will kill the baby if she finds out that someone saw what happened. Besides, she was always going to quit that marriage...I mean she never loved that man. Let's just take everything as an act of the gods."

"Hmm!" Ekenta heaved. "Well, for the sake of the child, I'll not say anything."

"Please, don't say anything now. Don't say anything forever. Please." Five months after the event, the previous Igwe of Merogwu, who was completing the turn of his district, took ill, terribly ill that he couldn't manage administrative affairs. So, Merogwu chose to appoint a regent from the next district in line of succession. One Mazi Nkpa was chosen, and throughout a period of seven years of the *igwe*'s sickness, he acted in that capacity. He did well as acting-*igwe*, and when the other man finally died, he contested for the throne but lost to Udorji in a way the people were yet to understand. "The gods have many questions to answer; they have many things to explain to us," Merogwu natives had said, in confusion and helplessness. They didn't just know that what happened was budded between Ekenta and Udorji.

Later, the son of the chief priest within whose earshot Udorji had made the vow unto his victim's wife became the igwe of Umuakaekpe. And when his father told him of it, he pressured newly installed Igwe Udorji into remitting forty-five percent of Merogwu allocation into his kingdom's treasury. That was how he started starving his own subjects.

As old as he was, Uduma didn't know he was neither a Merogwu native nor a prince of theirs. Now he had disturbed bees and was going to be well stung. A spark was dropping from the sky and there was tinder on the soil awaiting it. Udorji could see it coming. He knew he needed to intercept the splint before it landed, or remove the tinder from its spot. A tocsin rang urgency in his head every second: "I either kill Ekenta or share my throne with him. My throne was established on animal blood. I don't mind sustaining it with human blood." He, however, knew that people of his realm would see to the end of the cause of Ekenta's death should something happen to him. And lot never lied in Merogwu.

Clairvoyance was ministering to Ekenta that Igwe Udorji was coming to see him by himself. He relocated to his wife's distant village of Nkanu, without telling his family. He didn't want such a visit. He was keen to see the end of Udorji's rigged reign. No sooner had he left than his first son returned from the city to start his marriage arrangements. "Where is Papa?" he asked his nephew.

"I don't know," the teenager replied. "Maybe he went to Mama's place," he guessed, not knowing he was right.

"Not possible," a voice said from the kitchen. "I mean, how could he have travelled to Nkanu without taking a few clothes with him?"

"That one is nothing now. Have you forgotten that Papa loves wearing one cloth for two weeks?"

"If I slap you people eh," Ekenta's first son heckled the children. "So it's my father you're mocking…alright." All of his siblings were out of the neighborhood at the moment. In the evening, Igwe Udorji came by himself. He was told that Ekenta's whereabouts were unknown.

"When was the last time he went to the forest to pluck *ukazi*?" he enquired.

"Yesterday," Ekenta's wife replied, almost crying, not knowing that her husband was in her father's house having some great moments with her brothers. "So there's no possibility that he went to the forest this evening." Igwe promised the family that if Ekenta didn't return the next day, he would order all Merogwu youths to search the forests for him. "But I assure you that he's safe wherever he is right now, and he will return in peace." He left with a tanka of sympathy on his face, but in his mind, he hoped the worst had happened to Ekenta. "Can it be that evil has befallen him? I'll be a happy ruler if it's true," he relished. Night came and left and Ekenta didn't return. His family was worried.

Igwe had gone home with a high celerity to celebrate Ekenta's supposed death. He didn't know he was dealing with a man who sat down and saw what he couldn't see standing up. Ekenta had gone ahead of Udorji in wit and con. He played politics with white men and tangoed with nationals too, in pre-Independence era, before retiring to the village. It was his slick and quick- and-thick ability that fetched him the forename African Mahatma. His destiny didn't lie in politics. If it did, he would have been an international figure, or at least, a national hero. He could have been wealthy before thirty. He wouldn't have had to be meandering mazes of forests in search of *ukazi*. But he didn't hold it against his god. He preferred the watery soup of 'paupery' to the peppery stew of profiteering. If he had wanted to, he would have joined a cartel which made it big in drug trafficking. But then, he couldn't have lived the long he did; three-quarters of those who took to that business were killed by a firing squad, while others were given lethal injections. He had once outsmarted a Briton who wanted to dupe him. But instead of going away with the money, he later returned it to him.

Uduma was gradually coming to his senses, which heretofore seemed disabled or deactivated. His life was lacking in exuberance. He was greatly troubled by the statement: "If you know what that man knows..."

"What does Ekenta know about me that I don't know," he wondered, as he wandered like a wanton phantom in his room. He went to ask his mother who had been unable to conceive since giving birth to him. "What do you know about what Ekenta knows about me?" he enquired of her.

"Igwe knows as much as I do," she curtly replied.

"But he has refused to tell me anything."

"You're my son but not his…that's what Ekenta knows."

"I'm your son but not his," Uduma parried, unable to understand what was actually happening. "So, it means that I'm not a prince after-all."

"Yes my dear," replied the queen of questionable virtue. "Worse still, you're not a Merogwu man. You're from Umuakaekpe."

This revelation thrust the palace into a madhouse. The spark had finally dropped on the tinder, and a fire which heat scalded both the owner of the house and the rodent he was pursuing took over the whole place. A bush that distastes a basket doesn't have to grow mushroom, they say. But this one had grown mushroom, papyrus, reed, and other things unexpected of it. The royal family chose a girl's love over the throne and were now losing both. And more things.

"Take it easy, Uduma," his mother begged him as he was destroying things randomly. "Doing what we did was Udorji's only way of staying alive and becoming igwe."

"Not at my father's expense. I'll kill who killed my father," he swore, placing the tip of his finger on the ground, touching his tongue with it, and pointing it skyward, which made a sound of '*mhuu!*'

"It was all your father's fault – he ran into Udorji's motorcycle. Your father was a poor useless young man. You wouldn't have been proud of meeting him. It would have been a waste of destiny to hang a promising young Udorji for his sake. So let him rest in peace. All we have to do now is get Ekenta on our side, even if it means you kneeling down to beg him in secret."

He spat on her face for saying that.

"You're a shame to womanhood. A man who never married would have had a better wife than you, even in his bachelorhood. If it were possible for me, I would kill you and offer your blood to the gods. But then, they would not want to perceive a terrible thing like you."

His mother couldn't come to terms with the fact that her own son sprinkled spittle on her face. So she started doing business with tears, streams of tears.

Uduma came out of his room and left the palace, talking to no known person. "If my father had married a prostitute or no wife at all, he would have fared better." He was now outside the palace, and he headed home – yes, he left for Umuakaekpe. He chose not to pick anything from the palace because none actually belonged to him, by his personal principle. Uduma chose to become a legitimate nobody in his homeland over a fake royalty in Merogwu. And he found honor in his father's name and felt peace when he got home.

When he got to Umuakaekpe, he began to enquire about a certain Agwu, a name his ill- mannered mother gave him to be his father's. "I have never heard of him before," the first man he approached answered.

"Oh, Agwu Ikedi!" another replied. "He died over twenty-five years ago. He was a good man, but he married a bad woman, who never truly became a wife until his death. She remarried almost immediately. In fact, before the man could reach his place in the spirit world, his wife had already reached her new lover's house. She sped about that. May his ancestors give peace to his humiliated soul. He didn't leave a survivor behind, so who are you looking for exactly?"

"He left someone behind. Me. And I'm more than a mere survivor. I'm his successor too. I'm back to perpetuate his name and to recover his estate. Just take me to his house."

The man refused. He couldn't quite believe a thing as funny as his being a son to a man who never knew his wife was pregnant. So, Uduma approached a middle-aged woman nearby and went straight to the point. "I am Agwu Ikedi's son. Please take me to his house."

"*Ewoo*, Agwuisi's son!" she screamed. "How? When? Where? Just how are you his son?" She almost asked him why he was or should be believed to be Agwu's son. And that would have been the question of his lifetime. What other reason could there have been other than the fact that the gods of his ancestors chose to bless his father with him. And they gave him a son who, although was nowhere to drop earth into his grave, was determined to see that his barn was not turned to a scrap yard – a son who was worth ten men.

"Take me home first," Uduma pleaded with the woman. When they got to his ancestral home and he told the people there that he was Agwu's son, his father's kinsmen were divided against one another. "But Njide was not pregnant when Agwu died," they argued.

"She told me that she was two weeks pregnant with me when the accident happened and never wanted any of you to inherit her. She covered up Udorji in order to marry him, because he was handsome and came from a rich family in Merogwu. She spared him the death penalty for murder. He saved her from ending up in your arms." They were stunned when they heard all those factual words.

"That woman is evil. I could never like her," one of his uncles said. "Wasn't I saying it? Amadi's daughters? They inherited bitterness from their mother. All of them have ruined their husbands. Dangerous daughters of darkness! They are all beautiful but destructive. Whatever made our father to tie her to our brother, Agwu, must have been an evil fate."

By-and-large, they didn't accept him as one of them. The eldest brother of his father's who had taken over possession of all that belonged to Agwu rejected him. He couldn't imagine how he would return the properties to Uduma. They had buried Agwu in a bush not knowing that he had a child. That was the tradition. People who died without children were interred in bushes. "Nobody is going to have to be shown where their father or mother was buried so as to carry on their remembrance," they believed.

The woman who had taken him to his uncles, having seen their rejection of him, took Uduma to her house. Her husband was late, but they had a daughter together, and she was quite rich. She was simply called Mrs. Odochi. That night Uduma could not sleep. He was disappointed in his uncles for not taking him in. He knew that lying on a jute bag in his real father's house was more rest-giving than sleeping in his eiderdown in Merogwu. What their fears were for was what he couldn't quite understand.

His pensive mood later improved when he remembered Akudo, his Merogwu love interest, and a palace maid. He relived seeing her for-a-lucky-man midriff which always wore a *tiro* pointillism dotting her chest down to her belly button. He had all the opportunity to have her to himself, but wasn't a chancer. He wasn't a smart Nwabunna, who knew how to draw a girl into his room. Of all the palace maids Akudo stood out. Her tresses, her eyeballs, her wonder-of-a- woman areas, and her character all impressed Uduma. And it was no mere concupiscence. He loved her greatly. His royal days were over, as were the privileges of a 'prince.' He had somehow derided Nwabunna for not being ashamed of squatting in an old woman's house, and now here he was under the roof of a woman he barely knew.

CHAPTER SIXTEEN
A Verdict of Deficits

A dog doesn't really need to swallow a bone to prove it is stronger off. All he's got to do is chew the bone hard, lick it dry, and leave the gristle behind. Real meat is muscle. Bone is for courage and fun. The dog has to leave the well-licked bone behind because life is crazy at the turn of events.

Denizens of Umuakaekpe were impressed by Uduma's grit and choice of returning to his homeland. "He truly drank enough breast milk," they acknowledged. "That boy got a heart," others said, all in admiration.

That which was hidden had finally been revealed. Wind had blown and the anus of the fowl had been seen. And it was some dirty stinking thing. Osiri, Igwe of Umuakaekpe, was troubled. He knew that the lucre he was receiving for covering up the atrocity was going to stop. But that wasn't his major fear. Losing his throne, as well as the consequent comedown in the central autarchy, was worse. He feared becoming such a fair game, really. Orient Gnishere, in their entirety, were known for square off against 'king-lords.' No one man, irrespective of who he was or what he had, could push the people over. Those who tried were consigned to a dungeon of no luncheon – oblivion and forgottenness. The people respected their culture and custom and their laws, and they had no corporate tolerance for individual idiosyncrasies. If there was a motto that could best describe their resolve, it was: "one man for all men and all men for one man." 'King- lords' were friends with their people's enemies; they were men who thought they could undo their people for selfish gains; men who fought their own just to share some spoils with an enemy. But they never won or succeeded.

Osiri sent emissaries led by one Nze Arinze, who used to go to Merogwu every month to receive the lucre on his behalf, to Udorji. They were to blame Udorji for ever allowing Uduma to leave his palace. For the Umuakaekpe ruler, that was the only problematical thing therein. Ekenta's testimony meant nothing to him. In Orient Gnishere, one man alone didn't bear witness. Two or more people did, because they believed that a snake seen by one man would always turn to a python. Udorji dismissed the emissaries without a welcome when they arrived, and he told them to say the following words to Osiri, "get ready to vomit all you've eaten, and be ready to eat what I'm about to vomit, too." Such a vomit would surely be a delightfully delicious royal disgust.

As the emissaries were leaving, they saw a demonstration at a distance. A crowd of Merogwu youths had staged a protest against Udorji. So, the messengers hurried and left for where they came from, fearing being mobbed. The conniption came at the heel of the confirmation that Uduma wasn't really their prince and that Udorji had been sponsoring an Umuakaekpe cause with their resources, while they were caused to peel the bark of hardwood with their teeth.

Ekenta was happy where he was. He was happy that, at least, a snake was climbing down a tree the same way it climbed up. The idol had been shown the wood from which it was carved. That too was his joy. So, he returned to Merogwu and resumed his *ukazi* business.

When the emissaries returned and delivered Udorji's message to Osiri, he defecated on the throne. Royal complicity was a serious crime and, therefore, attracted heavy penalties. Arinze was also undone by the scandal. He was no longer going to be receiving a percentage of the underhand money. He was some sour soul, a sad mad man himself. Indeed, the land not being good was benefit of chiefs. Osiri shifted his blame to Uduma. He was galled that he could choose to forfeit all he enjoyed as a "prince" and wondered why he didn't find a wife from amongst the many beautiful maidens of Merogwu. "Why didn't

Udorji poison that idiot of a boy?" he raged. "Why didn't he kill him the same way he killed his father?"

At the other end, Udorji regretted why he had agreed to the conditions the chief priest − Osiri's father − had given him. It was clear to him that the *ezemmuo* was not speaking the mind of the gods. However, manslaughter or murder, he would have been executed for killing Uduma's father, were it exposed then. That was why he had to agree to those concrete conditions.

Uduma's mother came from a family that was known for eye service, face work, and front jobs. They had no real handwork. No sincerity. Ingratiation and labor of laziness were their middle names. Her father was infamous for an extrovert life of gross swank. He always abandoned his family needs to meet those of others, just to earn people's praise and bag a chieftaincy title. What a labor of folly! There was a day his son was very sick. He left the dying boy to attend a machete- dropping ceremony, to mark an old friend's official retirement from civil service. The man was one of a few men of high breeding in Umuakaekpe, who throughout time placed youths from different communities and places on white collar jobs, in the spirit of no-one-should-forsake-his- brother.

On another occasion, Uduma's grandfather preferred to go as far as seventy miles to commiserate with a man he barely knew, but couldn't go to console his own sister when she lost her daughter to an overwhelming flu, despite living barely five-hundred metres apart. As a result of his extra-family stupidity, he was called a useful-outside-and-useless-in-the-house man. That was Uduma's mother's family's life table. Their mother, a clothier, was worse off. She was a woman of abysmal characteristics. Her acts of goodness always resulted in misfortune. One was better off hungry than having her food in his stomach. Her feet transferred heat to the soil upon which she stood, while her air released tenseness into the atmosphere. If she had been a part of any of the World Wars, it wouldn't have ever ended.

Merogwu people became opposed to Umuakaekpe for what their ruler took away from them through Udorji. They carped that "Children of left-handedness" always abused trust, privileges, and goodwill, and therefore needed to be de-allied with. It was a time to defy fear and a time to dare the dread, and they were not going to cover their faces with a basket. They shut down commerce and took their crackers to Udorji's palace, besieging it for seven weeks, and protesting, "you waste our wealth for your personal wakes. You're a punishment for an offence we're yet to commit. *Hanlele*! Step down from the throne."

Some chiefs came to Udorji's rescue, telling the people to stop bringing shame to themselves. "...but at least he's a duly elected *igwe*. Allow the gods to handle this issue their own way. Don't we, as a people, trust the sincerity of their verdict again?"

"Leaving everything in the hands of the gods is why we're lagging every other kingdom in development. These gods have become both too slow to act and too corrupt to care. Our ruler is a murderer, and life is not pleased with him, because he metes out death on our people," the mob charged. "He killed an innocent fellow and took over his guilty wife. Get him and the wicked woman out of this land. He deserves to be banished and the woman should go back to her husband's house, since she has a son for him. That's what custom says, and the gods respect custom. The gods are immortal custodians of our custom. A murderer-ruler and a mother of a false prince can't rule over us. It's shameful."

They were still protesting when one of the palace maids came to the chiefs and said, "someone has to come with me because someone needs some help in there."

"Help!" a voice of another palace maid came out alive. "He has killed her! Help!"

"Who has killed who?"

"Stop asking that kind of question. There is a killing already. That's what's important." As they approached the chamber, a female voice was heard groaning. It was that of the putative queen. The voice sounded like a thud of dud. None of the protesting crowd could gain entrance, thanks to the well-armed palace guards who weren't moved by the distress call. Udorji had staged them about and around the palace to avert invasion, because he knew what his people could do and he expected everything from them. When the chiefs got into the room of doom, they saw Udorji trying to garrote his wife for disclosing those details of their dirty dealings to Uduma, which consequently got him leaving for Umuakaekpe. He wasn't around when she did that. "You want to be a queen yet you can't keep a basic secret. You so easily forgot that kingdoms are built with resources and secured with secrets. You'll join your husband at the other side of life now."

And the woman was close, very close to joining her hated husband when Abundu hit her beater from behind. He was one of the palace guards, and so knew most of his confidential matters. He saved the queen. She was grateful. There couldn't have been a grander way of rewarding her for always giving him opportunities to sleep with her maids. She was his enabler in funny deeds. Abundu had overheard the discussion between Udorji and Osiri the day the latter visited Merogwu. He had said, "it's in your best interest to keep the money coming my way. You don't want to live and have the world find out that the man on Merogwu throne is not Uduma's real father but the murderer of his mother's husband." Abundu heard that. Clearly. Somehow, security men receive information more firsthand than newsmen.

While Udorji was still down, Abundu hit him severally and he sustained severe wounds. Then, he went over to see his enabler in iniquity. She was still breathing. That same time, Udorji managed to get up, and he reached for an object and targeted Abundu's head. But it was intercepted by another palace guard. The guards defended one another with the last drop of their blood. "Lend thy brother thy breath. Allow not a brute to kill thy brother." That was their trust base. The interventionist guard couldn't quite believe the drama which was like a fantasy fight. Still holding the weapon he seized from Udorji, he asked, "What is happening here?"

"He's an evil man," Abundu said, pointing at Udorji, who was truly looking like a hell's angel. "He killed an innocent man by accident. Now, he wants to kill his wife on intention." That's the side of the story everybody knew. None of them endeavored to learn that Udorji was enmeshed into the whole mess. His only actual offence was cowardice. Udorji was bleeding profusely. The queen was breathing uneasily. Both were reeling on the floor. The crowd was seething with rage outside. Guards were still intact at the gates. They made sure none of the protesters, who had besieged off the palace, entered it while the amateur wrestling lasted.

After a while, one of the protesters asked, "but what gain can I have from this protest after abandoning my farms these whole weeks? The Nwabunna we are fighting for is not even here with us."

"We're fighting for our land, not for the rot you just mentioned," another replied. The first man was startled at Nwabunna's abstract yet concrete influence on everything.

"He's saying nothing yet everything is going his way. Even the gods seem to be on his side."

"Leave Nwabunna alone. He who carries nothing on his head doesn't break anything."

"If the stranger hadn't shown interest in that girl, this wouldn't be happening."

"You still call a man who has established himself on the soil a stranger? Be deceiving yourselves."

As the scrimmage was going on in Merogwu, Uduma was enjoying himself in Umuakaekpe. He was advancing in his new and uncharted terrain, 'churchery.'

The woman who had taken him home took him to her church where he was baptized, after confessing his sins and denouncing his 'old life.' Consequent upon his conversion, he was given a forename: Philip. He wanted to take up a job in the local borough, but his faith-father, the man who baptized him, discouraged him, believing that such a job would deny him real time for 'churchery' and evangelism. All he could see was that Philip was 'called of God.'

But Uduma decided to marry before embracing the ministry. He had always felt something for Akudo and she was in his mind till this moment. Strong in character, adequate in beauty, and constant in courtesy, she was a girl he was now going to consider marrying. She resisted all the soft efforts he had made to sleep with her in the palace, and Uduma had thought she was being repulsive then. Now that he had been 'born again,' he realized she was simply a disciplined good girl. As he went to submit his intentions to Bishop Schindler, he thought that the fact he didn't sleep with Akudo would be an advantage towards getting his all-clear, because the church forbade and frowned at, and wouldn't tolerate premarital sex. "Purity of sex is the basis of a holy matrimony," the church indoctrinated and upheld. As a result, intending couples were warned off having designs on or copping out with each other, and mercy was not shown to those who disobeyed. They were ex-communicated or simply pronounced husband and wife without a wedding ceremony. No proper wedding for them. Clerics said that white marriage depicted Jesus' second coming, when He would collect home His holy church, His bride." Therefore, the couple-in-waiting ought to have no designs on each other.

Schindler was happy to hear that his faith-son was planning to marry and he thought it was going to be a sister in the Lord—a girl from amongst his flock, as was required and expected of brothers. He was disappointed in Uduma and wouldn't approve of his intentions for Akudo. "I can now see that your repentance has not truly repented itself," he lashed at the bachelor of faith. "Your salvation is not yet whole or even ready. How can you be going for an unbeliever? Hasn't your Bible told you that you shouldn't be yoked with unbelievers?"

"With due respect, sir...some of our believer-sisters are deceivers," Uduma defended himself.

"What?" Schindler screamed, shocked to hear that.

"Their appearance is terrific, but their character is terrible. The Akudo girl is more responsible and God-fearing than the girls you're indirectly recommending."

"Shut up, boy! How can an unbeliever be more God-fearing than those the blood of Jesus has washed clean? Your heart needs to be worked on. You're not good enough for the Lord's use yet."

"Marriage is not a church service sir. It is a life. I need a responsible girl for a wife."

"My daughter is responsible then. In fact, she is responsibly Godly and behaviorally beautiful. She'll be good for you."

"If she likes let her be 'responsibo-Godly.' I don't like her. I can't marry a girl whose face is rough and rhomboid, like an unfinished Jordanian woodwork."

"What! My own daughter's face rough and rhomboid? Now get out! Get out of my office!"

Uduma got up and left, murmuring like boiling moi-moi, "I can't marry a girl simply because she comes to church all the time. That's religious gullibility and mental manipulation. My mind is made up about Akudo and that's final."

He truly loved that "unbeliever" and this time he wanted her for a wife, not because of her midriff but because of her demeanor. So, it wasn't mere concupiscence. He was still within sight when Bishop Schindler called him back.

"My son, remember the scripture that says, 'no one who puts his hand on the plow and looks back is worthy of service in the kingdom of God. You just can't drop your most holy faith because of an ordinary worldly woman."

"She and she alone is the girl I want and I'm going to marry her, even if it means going out of the way."

"Well, since you prefer a girl who has neither salvation nor education….good luck with that. But know that the church will not join you in matrimony."

"I'll lead her to Christ and I'll send her to school."

When Mrs. Odochi learnt of Schindler's position on the issue, she went to talk to him by herself. She was going to tell him to wed Philip and Akudo.

"Sister Odochi, it's sad that your boy has chosen to go the way of Sampson and Judah and…when we repented in the 50's, we surrendered our everything to God. But these days, these boys keep certain things from God, especially their emotions. These boys will give their lives to God and keep their love for girls. And in Philip's case, let him go ahead and marry an unlearned unbeliever, but I can't wed them."

"Look Bishop. That boy loves the Lord and obeys you. You asked him not to pick a job but rather join the Theology. He did. He goes the whole place telling people about Jesus and His kingdom. He pays his dues and does his obligations with commitment. The church owes her members baptism, wedding, and burial; these are peoples' rights in the church. Don't deny Philip his. He truly loves the Lord, dear Bishop. He does. Just wed them and pray for the girl to repent."

When she saw that the clergyman was not yielding, she wormed her way into a deacon and bribed him with fifty cups of garri and five tubers of yams. "You're the most hardworking deacon in this parish. You deserve to be well taken care of," she flattered him to a bend. It worked. The man influenced the board of venal deacons and they amended the kirk's marriage bye-laws. When Bishop Schindler saw what compromised cowardly coxcombs the deacons had become, he knew the wedding would happen.

"Indeed," he thought, "judgment has to start from God's house because some of the people resident therein are seeds of Satan." He told Philip to go pay the girl's dowry and prepare for the wedding.

The next day, Uduma sent two men to Merogwu to enquire about Akudo's whereabouts; whether she was still in the palace. They were to tell nobody but her why they came. That was seven months since the scandal erupted and five months since the palatial turmoil began. And the men left. He sent for a maid in the palace but didn't care about his mother, a woman he used to take pride in. Wouldn't it have been a complete assignment if he had sent for both? When the men arrived in Merogwu, they learned that over half the maids, who served in the days of Uduma's stay, had left for their homes, following the queen's admission in an infirmary. Akudo was one of them. Her whereabouts was asked for and when the men Uduma sent got there, they were greeted with some sad news, one that was going to sadden Uduma really: his love had become another man's lot already. More saddening and disturbing was the fact that it was a former palace guard that married to her.

The young man was one of those who were opposed to his decision to marry Urudinanwanyi. Udorji had sacked him as a result, and he became a clothier later, and he prospered immensely. He, like Uduma, was impressed by Akudo's attitude. But, unlike Uduma, he was smart enough. "They got married two weeks ago," Akudo's father announced to the errand men. "What are we going to do now?" one of them asked.

"Go home of course," the other replied. "We can't sleep here. The girl is married and nothing can be done about that."

"So what do we tell Mrs. Odochi?"

"We will tell her what they told us; that Akudo is married already. Simple."

"Philip will be sad. I know that. But then feces doesn't smell while still in the body. Every person must face his peculiar fate and deal with his inescapable reality."

Uduma was already leaving for Bible studies when they arrived. He welcomed them and then inclined his ear for their report. He was optimistic. "I know that you saw Akudo and how beautiful she is. Imagine what Bishop is trying to make me miss out on," he lightly said. But when they didn't respond, he deciphered from their countenance that things had gotten funnier. "This one your faces are like feces fried in the fireplace of fate, what really happened?"

"Akudo is married already," they dropped the grenade.

"So I definitely am not going to marry the girl for whose sake the church has lowered its standards," he brooded. "I really have a rough destiny. And only God can help me." If they had told him that Akudo refused to marry him, it would have been less troubling. Again, if it was a man other than that very palace guard in question, it would have been less bitter a memory. He kept losing games to enemy hunters. "I am finally finished," he cried; a real cry. "A man has beaten me to a woman again!" he cried on. "My destiny is really not a good one. In fact, I don't know who has a better destiny between me and Esau."

"God forbid," Mrs. Odochi disagreed with that thought line. "How can you say such a thing, Philip? You're an Israeli of God."

"Leave me as I am, please. How am I an Israeli of God when my father's fate is following me about the whole place?"

In the wake of this report, Mrs. Odochi took Philip to Bishop

Schindler. "He hasn't eaten since yesterday nor has he bathed," she said.

"He does not smell yet, so he can continue to skip his baths," the bishop replied in all seriousness. "Congratulations to him for having not eaten since yesterday. It shows he is coming to his senses. Saul did not eat for three days when he came back to his senses, when he repented. So what exactly can I do for him this time around?"

"This is the second time he's missing out on a woman he loves. So I think he needs deliverance. There might be a slightest chance that a spiritual wife is torturing him."

"Spiritual who?" Uduma screamed.

"It's only a suggestion please."

"Nothing is torturing nobody," Bishop disagreed. "He has always loved the wrong ones. That's his problem. And God has a way of realigning everyone back to his will. That's exactly what the young man is missing. Philip, do you sleep with women in your dreams?"

"*Tufiakwa*, Bishop," Philip said tentatively. "Bishop, I said *tufiakwa*."

"You see it, Sis. Odochi. Like scripture says, everything works together for good unto those who love God. For him to be a successful servant of God, he must not marry a wrong woman. Missing out on the first woman was his only way of coming to his real essence of living. And missing out on this other girl was a confirmation that his wife ought to be a real born-again girl, not a synthetic Christian with a cosmetic faith − an opportunistic believer. There are too many lovely ladies in our church. How he doesn't see them fit for marriage beats my belief."

In his heart Uduma was saying, "worldly women have a terrific worth regardless." And he meant it.

CHAPTER SEVENTEEN
A Day of Fest and Fate

T he beauty of a dog's life is not the number of bones it has eaten nor is it the number of whelps she's begotten. The real beauty of a dog's life is the discipline of keeping its kennel secure, whether or not there is a bone in it.

Nwabunna's children were all growing up at a cracking rate. His home remained peaceful and happy while the scandal destroyed inter-family relationships. He didn't care two hooks about the looks of Merogwu, her drained looks. When the Baruru trouble arose, he found an unusual ford in the river and escaped. Here in Merogwu, while the whole tumultuous turbulence lasted, he stayed put. Reason was this, while his Baruru people were united in the stoning-to-death call, Merogwu natives were divided.

Nwabunna's surroundings were always swept and kept neat by his large family. And size wasn't going to matter anymore. He was earning enough for their upkeep. His triplet sons were in high school already. He asked Adabuasa to wait for a year before she would enroll. The other children were coming behind, too. He was one man who was always going to train his children adequately. "White men ruled over us because when they were planning to launch to the moon, we were busy playing and laughing under moonlight." This assertion of his grandfather's was always going to challenge him to train all his children well. His first sons all did well in school until their fourth college year when Agurubuike, the presumed next of kin, began to struggle with his academics. His grades were so poor and that gave his father some navel-gazing.

However, he chose to be positive about it. "If education is not his destiny line, there are other things he can actually succeed in," he said to Nancy. "What's more important is for him to find something which can feed him well." Turning to Aguru, he said, "You won't have to drift in life like your father did. I was ashamed of myself that at 25 years of age I had no talent, no education, and no business. You're sixteen already and that's your prime." He made the boy join him in his trade, and both were happy about it. Agurubuike smiled at the prospect of taking over the business with time. He was a boy with terrific promise. All he needed was to avoid bad influence as he grew in age and attitude. He was not going to be whipped for failing class work again. He missed his brothers' company and they missed his too. "Educated or not, what matters more in life is for a man to have coins in his pockets," his father continued to counsel him. "It is the most responsible son that is the real heir, not necessarily the first one. So, make it in life early enough so that your father's heart will bless you in his secret place."

Nancy's toddler son enjoyed licking earth to complement breast milk. A day had come and he got bitten by an ant. This made him cry so loud that the ant itself felt threatened. His mother crushed it with a fingertip and rubbed his cheek with it. Vicissitudes of growing up! Parents believed they made their children strong and tough enough to survive. Nwabunna sat under a tree that evening expecting Oforbuike who was beginning to embrace old age on a full scale. Ngozika was at the backyard washing and swilling plates. As she turned, she saw a chubby and clumsy earthworm about five inches from her left foot already. Afraid, she dropped the plates she was carrying, with a speech of screech which got Nsogbubaruru scampering toward her. "What is it, 'Ng Girl?'" he asked.

"It is the small brother of snake," she replied, pointing at the worm of earth, which had already understood its end had finally come.

"Oh! Just an earthworm," he sniffed.

"It is the small brother of snake. It has come to eat into my leg." They looked and saw more earthworms advancing as fast. The worms were being attacked by soldier ants, which already inflicted most of them with wounds, sticking on their soft bodies with their hooks. They gave the worms some kindness by treating them with salt and watched them shrivel to death. Then, Nsogbubaruru, joined by Onwubundu, lodged an offensive against the ant-soldiers, which were not relenting in their pincer movement, with charcoal fuel, with which they were roasting cashew nuts. That was an effective way of killing soldier ants – heat – fire.

Meanwhile, Nancy was roasting corn and pear for her husband, while Uru was cooking some soup with Nkiruka. She was yet to conceive, and while she wasn't concerned, Nwabunna was. Her mother was said to have accused Nancy of tying her daughter's womb up with charms. Her father, Onuoha, however, agreed to differ. "Stop being unnecessarily bitter, woman," he once countered his wife. "A woman's womb is not always as receptive as her palms. When the time comes, our daughter will give us grandchildren. You have always forgotten that your own mother had her first child nineteen years down her marriage, and you had our first child six years after we got married." Other people even bickered that it was Uduma who had tied Uru's womb up, for her refusal to marry him. But when they heard that he had repented and given his life to Jesus Christ, they changed their stance. That was because those who repented in those days confessed their sins and forsook them. And during Uduma's baptism, he didn't mention ever tying up any woman's womb.

Oforbuike arrived just when Nwabunna was served his food. "Your legs are beautiful!" he was told. "I'm always a lucky someone. It's only that my god is taking a longer time to release my blessings."

As they ate together, Oforbuike observed that Nwabunna's children were really growing up speedily. He saw their auspices. He saw their promises. He saw the resources they were and the great things they would achieve together.

"Your barn will never be empty and never will your name be lost," said the guest, still admiring the grace of growth of his host's children.

"The Creator is merciful," Nwabunna replied. "He will not allow me to lack what they will eat."

As they ate, Oforbuike wished in his heart that he had been as lucky with womb's fruits – that his wife gave birth to normal children. It was quite unbelievable that he wouldn't take in another wife. His relatives were disappointed in him for choosing to settle with a retard for a son and a mesomorph for a daughter.

Nwabunna wasn't carried away by his goodwill. Not at all. He simply believed that whatever ate should grow. He was, however, determined to train all of his children in education or craft, depending on their individual talent line. He wasn't going to appreciate a situation whereby a child of his loin would be twenty years or more without having charted a purpose path, or a situation wherein they, especially his sons, would be confused or frustrated as to what to do in order to earn an assured living. His savings were always intact. That was one thing he remained grateful to Mama for. He had since transferred it to his children, a trait they well absorbed and manifested. Each had a saving box or two, and when it could no longer contain coins, the content was used to buy and run livestock and poultry for commercial purposes.

Oforbuike had actually come to collect some medicine which Nwabunna had bought for him in Yaoundé, which language he had a smattering of, compared to Idika, who could chew French like cane sugar. The medicine was said to have restorative effect on persistent idiopathic facial pain sufferers. He was getting old by the day and knew that his name and gate would soon be forgotten and closed down respectively. He had even tried to get a wife for his son on four occasions, but it didn't work. First three girls said no. The fourth agreed only for the retard to reject her. Wonders! The herb was macerated in saline to extract its chemical, before its decant was drunk.

Much later, in the early hours of the next day, Urudinanwanyi went out to pick snails. She went alone – no company – and she didn't tell anybody. Last time out, she had a bumper pick. But this particular night, she wasn't successful at first. After covering past seven hundred meters, all she could find was three snails. She was beginning to go home when luck met her. Luck smiled on her and it was a gracious wide smile. She came across a mass of crud but quickly turned away her eyes. It was gunge, a latex-like substance. Somehow, she looked at it again and observed that a snake, a pantagruelian snake had just sloughed and could be near enough. It was no ordinary scene. And her heart dropped down to her abdomen and displaced her stomach to the left. And she took to her heels, her torch falling on the ground in the process. The unease with which she panted when she got home got Nwabunna troubled. He had earlier gone to her room to make love to her, but found nobody. He was so desperate now to see her conceive that he intensified their meeting lately. So he was outside when Uru returned home in overwhelming trepidation. "Who's after you, Uru?" he asked her. She couldn't complete a word, breathing scantily. But he inferred rightly that she was returning from snail picking. He was disappointed. Each time she had gone to pick snails she informed him. Why she went unannounced this time was what he didn't know. He didn't say any more words. That was him; he did it taciturn whenever he wanted to show his disapproval or dissatisfaction. It was when he remembered the torch which Uru had gone out with, twenty minutes since she returned, that he had something to say. Told that it didn't come home, he wasn't going to wait till it was fully dawn, because that torch cost him some coins, and that was some money then.

As they went for the torch, he let out the anger that was long smoldering in his heart, like the heat of an autoclave. "Look woman," he began, as firmly as a leader of a terrorist group demanding for the release of his captured men. "I'm not sure that I married you for you to be giving me a headache all the time. Give me children, you refuse. Allow me to enjoy the peace the gods have given me, you refuse. What kind of a wife are you? Come and show me where you left my torch please. Or have you given it to your father? I know he doesn't have any."

A miasma was beginning to drop, some cold vapor which taught their nerves some manners. "You should have come with your cutlass. The snake might still be there."

"Big or small, I'll smash it with my gun."

As they approached the purlieus, the Uru woman stopped and was only directing her husband around. It wasn't long and Nwabunna saw a huge snake and a precious substance beside it. He stood still. The snake never moved.

"This must be gold," he reasoned. Whether the snake vomited it wasn't a concern. All he was thinking about was taking out the snake and picking up the precious piece. He simply knew that his god had remembered him. He wanted to open fire at it but knew that it would attract attention, something he didn't want to happen. He looked at his panicky and run-ready wife and beckoned her to come. As she insinuated, he mustered gut and hit the reptile with the butt of his gun. It didn't move. That was when he knew it was dead already. Then, he picked the precious thing. "Take this," he said to Uru, handing the gold to her. He packed the snake into the for-snail bucket. And they went home.

They got home by 3:23am. Nancy and her children were sleeping beautifully. He kept the snake in the kitchen and took Uru into his room. "Nobody hears about this from your mouth. Promise me that."

"Nobody will," Uru replied.

"The gods have blessed us today. And we are grateful to them. I'm grateful to you, my beautiful wife." He held her hand and she began to cry. "What is it, Uru?"

"You...the way you scold me lately like little children because I'm yet to give you children."

"I'm sorry...Your god has vindicated you. See what great fortune you've brought me. I'll never treat you like that again."

"If you will not, swear it to me." He did and they made love finally. It was true he was yet to see Uru's children, but he was beginning to see her many *urus* – gracious virtues and blessings which Nancy, who had given him seven children and was latterly pregnant, didn't have.

When the sun was fully risen, Nwabunna sent for Julius of Nazareth. "Tell him to come as fast as his feet can walk, and make sure you return before this spittle dries up," he instructed his first son.

"Or...don't worry," he recalled Agurubuike, who was to go on a business trip with him. Eventually, he sent Nsogbubaruru. Julius was cooking meat by himself when the boy arrived, while his wife was purling wool.

"This one Nwabunna is calling you, do you have any business with him," she asked her meat-loving husband.

"No," he replied by-the-by. "I'm as surprised…I'll go see him, however. Words don't turn bad in the stomach."

Idika arrived that time his son left. Nwabunna showed him the snake, and he was amazed. "What a fortune!" he marveled.

"I've already sent for Julius."

"For what?"

"For him to come and carry the meat. You know it is what he eats."

"Are you this daft, my friend? Don't you realize that this can fetch you real riches? If we take it to leather-makers, they will flay the skin and process it into fine products."

"What do I tell Julius when he arrives?"

"You can tell him anything. You can tell him that you have missed his stupidity for some time now and just want to have some of it."

"That's quite ridiculous."

"Life itself is ridiculous. So it's no strange thing to invite someone over just to tell them that you have missed them." They were still taking the mickey when Julius arrived. He was offered a seat and kola. After some while, he demanded to know why he had been invited.

"You summoned me, my son."

"Yes, *Nna-anyi*, I did."

"Leave '*Nna-anyi.*' Just call me Julius-of-Nazareth, something meaty will come out of your kitchen or backyard." And they all laughed.

"Well, I called you to enquire about your daughter, Chidalu," Nwabunna lied. "A friend told me to help him ask real questions about her. He wants to marry and thinks your daughter will be good for his loving."

"You should have come to my house then. I shouldn't have been the one to find you."

"You're right, *Nna-anyi*. You're really right. Truth is that business doesn't allow someone to think aright anymore."

"And you don't normally think aright, except when you want to beat a man to a woman's hands in marriage." He took his leave, as did Idika. But before the latter left, he and Nwabunna agreed to call off their business trip that day. They were not going to wait for the snake to start decomposing. This development, cancellation of the business trip, didn't please Agurubuike. His father was happy with his friend's exposure and knowledge. He, however, didn't tell him anything about the gold. A clever guy he was.

No sooner had his visitors left than Nwabunna got some news, a sad one really – Mama was dead. He wept. Just seven months since he got her a house helper and just three weeks since he and his family visited her with foods and goods. She was neither sick nor bed-prone, not even for half of once. Her death brought him some concussion. She was the rock of his ruck days. So, the man cried like a boy. He tried to stifle the tears but couldn't. So, he went into the room he once slept in, same room wherein he got Nancy pregnant, slowly, soberly to weep.

He was still weeping when another terrible news came. And the worst had just happened – Mazi Ikenga had just popped his clogs too. And he sorrowed some more. "Maybe it's time to give death specification – time to tell death whom to take and whom to spare. My grandfather dead? I'm finally finished! The world has seen my nakedness." What a day that was for him. A day of terrific fest and terrible fate.

Arrangements were made and Mama was interred. Oforbuike was around to console sorrowful Nwabunna, who was the chief mourner of the childless old woman.

"Take heart, Nwabunna," a villager commiserated with him. "The Creator foreknew that life would consist of sweet and bitter experiences, so he gave us different taste buds."

Thereafter, he sent Oforbuike to Baruru for his grandfather's funeral, giving him a wreath to lay on his grave on his behalf. It was said that it is those who dropped earth into the grave of a deceased that were his or her true family. Nwabunna was not going to do that because of his circumstances, but he was Ikenga's family, no doubt.

When Oforbuike returned the next day, he was smiling. So Nwabunna wondered what positive thing could have come out of the demise of his grandfather, a man who, for his money, washed his hands neat only to crack palm kernel for fowls. Once more, he rued the fact that the Super Kingdom abandoned a man who categorically fought for Gnishere's Independence – no veteran's welfare package, whatsoever. All he got was enmity and treachery.

"This one you're smiling, *Nna-anyi*," he asked Oforbuike. "You're welcome though."

"The burial went well," Oforbuike replied. "Your grandfather was a hero, although unsung, under-loved, and under-appreciated. What's the better news is that your people asked after you."

"Really? ...like they missed me?"

"I tell you something. It's good you start considering a possibility of going back home."

"They will kill me...my children may go...they have committed no crimes...but not me."

"Now that Ikenga is dead, somebody needs to stay in his house, lest it becomes a refuse site. What do you think, my son?"

"You're right. I still love my birth land. I love Baruru more than Merogwu. But I can't risk my life. I'm staying here. Make my money here and become whatever I can become. All in this place.

"Let's not worry about that now. I have something more important to tell you. And I do it in confidence. I picked gold in the early hours of yesterday."

CHAPTER EIGHTEEN

The Conspiracy; Returning to Baruru

A dog which refuses to bark at a stranger hoping to have a bone from them should remember that its own flesh can make a delicious meat in the stranger's mouth. Dogs bark at strangers at sight. If the stranger has a bone for them, it falls down in dread of the dog. If, on the other hand, they got none for the 'barking-one', they bog off. Certain strangers visit dogs with no bones intentionally. They come for dog meat instead. Bark till such people back off is what a wise dog does.

Oforbuike was still to believe his ears. He was awestruck. Nwabunna trusted him to keep any damn secret. His word was his worth. He got home but couldn't go to sleep that night. Too many thoughts aboiled his heart. He was trying to imagine how the gods of Baruru could be appeased — how they could be made to welcome back their son, whom they had blessed lately.

In his house Idika paid his friend a visit of condolence. Meanwhile, Nwabunna didn't tell him anything about the gold itself all along. He was a man who rarely trusted people. For him, trust itself wasn't trustable. "Trust is a weakness which will someday be exploited. Secrets are an opening into a strong man's heart." That was what he once told his sons.

News got to them that the queen was dead. She had been down with stroke for eleven months, stroke she developed after the royal riot. She died in a local infirmary. Immediately, Nwabunna remembered her son, Uduma, the prince manqué. He remembered how he beat him to Uru's love. The queen's death didn't move him, given how she covered up the atrocity behind her former husband's unfortunate death, marrying his killer afterwards. "Best way to forgive a wicked man is to punish him," he goaded her. "Poor mother of an unlucky son, wicked wife of an innocent husband, and complicit colleague of a criminal ruler," he mocked her. Udorji buried her within the palace despite agitations by Umuakaekpe to hand her corpse to them. They wanted to feed birds with it. They even dragged Udorji to a central assize court, but influence was peddled, like it was when the denizens of Merogwu called for his removal.

They were still talking when Julius of Nazareth came. Seeing him from inside, Nwabunna sent Mama's namesake to go ask him what he was looking for. The visitor felt insulted. But a man who ate anything he was given, including goo meat, what wouldn't he have to tolerate?

"Tell your father that I'm looking for him," he told the girl. When he saw that he wasn't well welcomed, he didn't bother going to the door. Then, Nwabunna came out, greeted him from afar and made a mien to tell him to be snappy. "I came to know whether that friend of yours is still interested in my daughter," Julius said.

"He's since married," Nwabunna curtly said.

"You should have told me since. You just kept my eyes at the gate and my ears in the pathway."

"Is there anything else I can help you out with? I'm engaged inside."

"I'm disappointed in you, Nwabu or whatever they call you. You couldn't convince your friend to marry my daughter."

"Try and be a good boy, old man. Next time you go to someone's house, don't let them know you're this stupid." And he walked out on the dead-meat-loving man. Idika was laughing deeply inside. "He said you kept his eyes at the gate …hahahahaha!"

"See me, see trouble! When did I become a love manager and marriage arranger?"

"Don't mind that man. He's actually looking for dead meat and free snuff."

"Don't mind him. All the animals he's been eating have begun to haunt him. I'll soon keep his nose from the air."

"No, you will kill him. I'm not on that with you."

"Let me kill him now. In fact, he's dead already. This thing he is living, is it life?"

"Please, allow him to carry his ugly world and god and go away."

When all these had passed, Igwe Udorji began to plot harm against Nwabunna. But he knew he no longer had the goodwill of his people whom he would be needing to effectually fight Nwabunna. So, first of every-other-thing, he moved to reconcile with his unhappy subjects, from titled men to the hoi polloi. And he called for a general gathering.

"Good people of Merogwu," he started off his address. "We all know the story in its twists and truths."

"And it is a sordid sorry story of sour sabotage and mistrust," protested a man from the back. He was Akujobi, a careless, jobless, shelter-less, and wifeless village man. He was well schooled but only loafed about the whole place, always claiming, in all seriousness, that because Queen Elizabeth II visited Gnishere without paying him a courtesy call, he would never see anything positive about the colonial rule. People gossiped that his uncle used his destiny for money rituals. Akujobi was living his latter life between the village square and river banks. His words were unacceptable to Udorji, but there was nothing he could do. He was seeking to win back the people so had to be tolerant.

"Calm down Akujobi," a titled man pleaded with him, "so that Igwe may tell us why we're here. I should be in my barn, but here I am." After Igwe Udorji harrumphed, he continued. "It has rained and ceased. The sun has risen and set. But here we are, still living. I have thought through everything. I have recounted our history and victories, our struggles and successes over the times. I have retraced my steps and all I have come to ask of you is forgiveness — forgiveness for my mishandling of our resources; forgiveness for the events that happened in the palace, involving my late wife; forgiveness for everything else. We need to move on together — as a people, as a family, and as Merogwu Kingdom. We can't let what happened a few months ago mark the end. Merogwu has come to be a people and a place to reckon with, more than any other kingdom in Orient Gnishere. Let this not be the end of all of that. That is why I summoned you, and I'm honored that you came and that you have understanding. Thank you Meruogwu!"

After a hiatus, a titled man stood up to speak. "Our people *mamanu!*" he greeted, and others responded "*Iyaaaah!*"

"Igwe," he continued, "May you live long. I think that you're lucky to be alive, Igwe.

Honestly, to have survived all what happened in the palace, it means the gods are with you."

"Which gods?" some displeasured voices attacked him from all sides. One could tell they

were protesting, believing that Udorji had bribed him earlier to speak in his favor.

"Wait first, people of Meruogwu. Hear me out first." When the voices quieted, he continued. "Igwe, you see, when a king who forbids his subjects from farting defecates, his hand is no longer worthy of holding the scepter."

This statement went down well with others who were heard saying: "It's now you're talking. You were joking the other time. You can now raise your voice to the pitch of *ogene.*"

"Igwe," the man continued, "if you must continue ruling over us, if we are to pledge our loyalty to you again, then you have to agree to our terms, because it is immoral to expect absolute loyalty from a people you have put in abject poverty."

People were stunned to hear that marvel. "What terms?" was all they were heard saying. They knew he had a strong argument but most of them didn't know that the red cap men, as well as most illustrious sons of the land, had drafted some conditions already for Udorji to assent to. And then he asked them, "What are the terms? I hope you people are not in with some impossible demands."

"They are not impossible. Nothing is impossible in life. By-the-way, another kingdom has been eating our due all along. And since that was possible, none of the things we have in our documents should be impossible." Udorji was mad in his mind hearing that. It is said that when an animal learns to run smartly, a hunter will learn how to shoot smartly too. Smartness is what gets the better of smartness. Udorji didn't know what to do, so he tried to fob them off to have an exclusive mini meeting, but they rejected it, insisting that, "prawn is not eaten in secret and deliberations are best made amongst brethren."

The conditions included that Igwe Udorji should:

- Appoint a traditional prime minister from amongst them.
- Re-channel the slush fund given to Umuakaekpe to infrastructure.
- Appoint clan heads as permanent members of his cabinet.
- Allow the traditional prime minister to oversee monthly allocation from the central government.
- Let the treasury be open to a quarterly audit.

After reviewing those conditions, Udorji collapsed on his seat and said, "a direct coup would have been better...I mean...you want to strip my reign of all majesty and power." But when they were not going to be compromised, he assented to those demands.

He was more interested in victimizing Nwabunna. That was what mattered more to him, and he was going to do it. For him, once he had achieved that, by turning the people against him, those conditions would be reversed and nullified.

The people were happy with the developments and hailed the brains behind the bask. "Henceforth," the spokesperson asseverated, "strangers shall no longer enjoy our wealth while our own people, especially youths, wilt away in frustration." There was a raucous hurly-burly of excitement and contentment now.

"Now that Uduma and his mother, two great parasites, have left us," Udorji began to introduce his real objective proper, "strangers should never be allowed to take advantage of us again." A man came to his side from behind, and he took the words from Igwe's mouth. He said, "there now remains one stranger, a terrible one really, who has prospered greatly at the expense of our locals."

"And who can that possibly be?" Igwe asked in pretense.

"Who else if not Nwabunna, the defiant devil?"

"Have you seen it my people," Igwe asked. "What do we do now?"

"Send him out of our sacred land of course," the people pursued.

"He's an accursed tabooist after-all," said another man. They agreed that it was because of that helot that their daughters had become harlots, that since he became the first person to impregnate a girl before marrying her, in Meruogwu, boys began to sleep with girls anyhow.

"Igwe," petitioned Julius tentatively, "you needed to see the way Nwabunna treated me in his house the other day."

"What!" another man screamed. "That boy? I knew it. I knew that he would be this ungrateful."

"Exactly how did he treat you?" Yet another man asked Julius of Nazareth. "He slammed his door on me and asked me to leave his house."

"Which house?" Igwe asked, distraught and disappointed. "The one I built him with Meruogwu money and on Meruogwu land?"

"As if that wasn't enough, Igwe, he called me a 'boy', too."

"*Ewoooo!*" the people screamed in disgust.

"But what did you go to his house to do, by-the-way?" one of them asked Julius of Nazareth.

"Just talk about what he did to me, not what I went there to do." The air was heated.

Nwabunna was in trouble. Those who had sided with him before this time were now against him. But did they truly love him? They were only angry that Udorji was giving out their rightful resources to Umuakaekpe... Now he had stopped doing that, they thought it was wise to switch their allegiance, to turn against Nwabunna, a man who had prospered greatly in their land, while most of them remained poor. The crowd was about to cook for one man. They had finished eating what he cooked for them. Udorji was happy to have found in *ukeala* what he was looking for in *ukeelu*.

But to effectively launch any offensive against Nwabunna, they knew that his relationship with the likes of Oforbuike, Ekenta, and Idika needed to be strained, most especially that of Oforbuike, a man who had become everything to him. How he loved Nwabunna that he was about giving him his father's outhouse which had been willed to his late older brother, who died without a child or wife.

Udorji took it upon himself to do the job. He started with Idika whom he served sweetbread and palm wine, that day in his palace. "Imagine a man you once helped is now richer and braver and more prominent than you in your own land. If things are not checked, he will soon peel the earth from under your feet – he will take over your customers and your business, which you labored so much to build, will collapse. All because of some ungrateful stranger." After he succeeded in turning Idika against Nwabunna, Udorji went over to Ekenta. "You're famously acclaimed as the wisest man in Africa," he said to Ekenta. "How can you be Africa's mahatma and a boy you know the day he was born is turning our kingdom to a wasteland. I will make you the traditional prime minister if you help us send him packing." Ekenta did not believe his ears. He was beside himself with shock, and so he shouted: "Prime mini-what!"

"You heard me clean. You're the traditional prime minister. Stop meandering our forests to pluck *ukazi*. It is shameful that the best benefit you can achieve with your rare wisdom is *ukazi*, wandering in forests like a ghost. I need that wisdom in my administration, not in our forests."

"I hereby vow to do anything I can to kick out that boy, even to kill him. I wouldn't even mind carrying him on my head back to his people and watch them stone him to death."

"Our ancestors will be proud of everyone who will help rid our land of the injustice which Nwabunna represents."

When Udorji got to Oforbuike, he knew it wouldn't be easy to persuade him. But he believed that every man had a space in his heart for compromise, irrespective of how principled they are. "The

woman who took him in is dead. It's time for you to give him out...."
Oforbuike refused, saying to Udorji, "you can entice a little boy with a
lollipop, but you cannot intimidate an old man with death." And when
Udorji had seen his resolute integrity, he bogged off. Oforbuike sent
for Nwabunna immediately.

"My son, you may not survive this one, for even Idika, my
son-in-law, has sold you out. In fact, he has personal problems with
you now."

"What exactly do you mean, *Nna-anyi?*" asked a surprised
Nwabunna.

"It's time for you to leave Merogwu. Hurry now to the tanner.
Tell him to pay you for the snake skin in full or give you all the skin.
If he gives you the skin, keep it with a different tanner, at a different
location. Keep the gold safe. Hide it like you've been a thief all your
life."

Nwabunna was about leaving when Idika arrived. The latter
passed without saying a greeting to, or shaking the former's hand.
That told Nwabunna that a snake was in hay indeed. Without further
ado, Idika told his father in-law that he would divorce his daughter if
he didn't disassociate himself from Nwabunna, and that he had till the
next day to do that. And he floundered away like a messenger of fury.
Nwabunna didn't hear this. He was gone already. But clairvoyance
told him that Oforbuike would budge to pressure and would tell
them of the gold. And Oforbuike did. "My daughter is not getting a
divorce," he preferred. "She's not coming back anything. Instead, let
Nwabunna go the way of betrayal." Later that day, Oforbuike visited
Idika, who was sitting in his living room, seething with spleen, envy
and malice against Nwabunna. He had the best building in Merogwu,
bar Nwabunna's.

"Do you know of the gold?" he asked his son-in-law?

"Which gold, Father-in-law?" Idika replied.

"Nwabunna picked gold. It's in his house. He picked it together
with the snake."

"He could – you see – keep things from me. But I tell him

virtually everything about my business." They left at once to tell Igwe Udorji.

Meanwhile, back in his house, Nwabunna picked the gold mass, wrapped it with a fabric, and hid it in his son's napkin. Nancy had just had her eighth child — a boy again. Nwabunna hid the gold in the boy's napkin and none of his wives knew of it. He was concerned that since they were Merogwu daughters, they might somehow be compelled by blood to divulge it. "They think they are smart," he laughed hysterically in his head, "let them come and take it. I will show them that a boy who grew up in a community of casket makers, pall bearers and undertakers cannot be a chick; he's a cheetah."

If there was a man he wouldn't have believed, ordinarily, would ever betray him, it was Oforbuike. That same day, a mob spearheaded by Oforbuike himself stormed Nwabunna's premises, with a chant that very well toned disapproval, displeasure, and disgust under it.

"Igwe has asked us to come and have Merogwu property back...from you."

"Which property exactly," asked a poised Nwabunna, never looking disturbed by the heat wave.

"The mass of gold of course!" vaunted a pissed-off Idika, on whose face rage, hate, and terror were portrayed.

"I don't have such a thing in my house. I never picked any gold."

"He's lying of course!" the like-bees war mongers shouted.

"Well, if you find it, take it. The whole place is all yours to search."

"It is hidden in a pouch under his bed," Oforbuike revealed with a wry smile, not knowing that Nwabunna had long removed it. He was not a snake one could kill with a blunt machete. After ransacking his whole house and finding nothing, after poking suspected soil spots, including mounds and finding not the gold, the mob dispersed and repaired themselves to their respective homes.

"I told you people that I got no gold but you wouldn't believe me."

"Stop lying boy!" Oforbuike blurted.

"I made you a father to me and now you're raising allegations against me."

"You overstayed your welcome already. I can cope without you. I was fine with my sick son when you came. Now you're leaving, I'll be fine without you. I will adapt well. An old woman will always heat up her soup whether her guest stays or leaves. In your case, the guest must leave and the old woman's soup will last long, and will not lose its taste."

It was now that Julius of Nazareth was realizing the real reason Nwabunna had summoned him the other day. He was happy Nwabunna was leaving, but he wished that Idika had not talked him out of giving him the snake meat. "What a great pepper soup that would have made," the human omnivore regretted.

It is said that where a dog goes and has its mouth dripping with oil is where it will go to and have its mouth bleeding profusely. The same Merogwu that gave Nwabunna a life's new lease made him restless. And this was going to be his life's most tumultuous moment and its outcome, he knew, would determine his manhood and soul state. Last time his life was under a threat, he was alone. But now, he had a family to defend and fend for, a family he couldn't leave behind or abandon. His saving grace was his wives — the two responsible women he had married. That they chose to live in peace and love was a blessing and solace for him. They stuck to their husband, daring fate and pressure in its eyes.

Udorji tried to turn Uru against her husband, but her father resisted him. The ruler had told Onuoha to withdraw his daughter from "that crackpot", that a richer man would definitely come and marry her. "She's still young and beautiful, and she hasn't had a child for that opportunist of a stranger."

"Igweeee!" Onuoha saluted. "You will continue to live long o, but, Uru, my daughter, will continue to live with Nwabunna, her husband." Onuoha was never going to be his wife who firmly believed their daughter's womb had been 'tied' by her husband's wife, Nancy. "Nancy has used her grandfather's juju on my daughter's womb," she had always alleged and protested to her husband. But Urudinanwanyi had always believed she was fated to marry Nwabunna, and being his second wife and being childless mattered kitsch to her. She loved him a great deal, and that was some trophy for him. There was no time she envied Nancy or coveted her children. She even found joy in baby-sitting Nancy's last baby, like a nanny who received big penny for her services, and like a charwoman, she swept and kept their large family house all the time. Peace was all she kept for herself and love was all she gave the other woman and her children. What a woman she was. In her Nwabunna had a wife and a sister, a mother and a mould. She was a woman of terrific emotional utility. She agreed, just like Nancy did, to leave Merogwu with Nwabunna.

When the people of Nsogbubaruru heard that Nwabunna picked some gold ore which when processed would yield a large fortune, and that Meruogwu had served him with eviction threats, most of the locals began to soft pedal on the taboo he had committed. Most of them even began to presume that since the gods had allowed him to live for such a long time since the incident, it meant they had forgiven him, and that it was, therefore, unnecessary for mortals to hold onto the matter. "The gods cannot reject their own permanently," one of the Baruru natives believed, "especially since he's shown sincere remorse and repentance."

Nwabunna was greatly surprised to see Okwubungbo in his Merogwu house the next day. He had come to convince him to return home, because the gods had seemingly forgiven him. He was the same man who had busted him on the forbidden act, as well as the man who reported him to late Igwe Dimanochie. All he wanted now was a fair share of his wealth, not whether Nwabunna would be welcomed back home, not whether the gods would spare him.

Meanwhile, Uduma had obtained a Diploma in Theology and was already married with a daughter. He settled down with a girl he had converted through personal evangelism. He won her soul for Christ but kept her body for himself. Such a smart preacher-guy. Bishop Schindler was furious. He was opposed to their marriage, too. He had tried out every religious chicanery he knew to get Uduma to marry his daughter Uloaku, but he failed.

"My own faith-life doesn't reach where my love-life is," he had defied the Bishop's disapproval.

"Look, Philip," Bishop Schindler had said, "If you marry an unbeliever, who has just coated herself with artificial repentance, you won't fare fine as a minister."

"Bishop Sir, family state—not what you're interested in—determines a minister's strength. One needs a peaceful home to have a fruitful ministry. And peace begins with love. I marry whom I love, not the one the church wants...." Although Schindler joined them in matrimony eventually, he didn't wish the marriage well, deep down. But his countenance didn't bother the couple, especially Uduma, who was later transferred to Baruru, and that was the bishop's making. He didn't want to be seeing Uduma's wife, who was chosen to his daughter's disfavor, around. And as for Uduma, Bishop wanted him to go to where he would suffer in ministry, and because Baruru was known to be a place of stubborn Christians with shallow faith, he transferred him there.

Schindler was formerly a businessman before he was "called of the Lord." His native name was Okennam Oleka. He was ordained a bishop of Heaven-is-Watching-the-Earth Church of Africa, the first Christian group that came to Gnishere in 1929, after he had been a 'middle reverend' for eleven years. He was originally going to boycott Uduma's wedding, but for criticism and threat of petition from board of deacons — compromised, corrupt, and complicit deacons. They tackled Bishop Schindler headlong, charging him with hypocrisy and selfishness. "You accuse us of taking bribe from Sister Odochi, the guardian and god-mother of Philip. Now, you're asking Philip to marry your daughter, so that you will have easier access to her money indirectly. You see, we all are interested in mammon. So, keep your morals to yourself when it comes to money matters."

"You're wrong," Bishop defended himself. "I want him to marry my daughter because she's faith-sound, prayerful, and she knows God's word, and she loves Jesus. I think, honestly, that if a pastor's daughter marries a pastor, their family and ministry will be fruitful and successful."

"It's not true, Bishop. Your daughter doesn't love Jesus anything. And as for you, you love money more than Judas. In fact, we suspect that you are the one who told Judas to sell his Master, the Lord Jesus. If spirituality was truly your interest, why did you reject the brother-usher who came to marry Uloaku, your daughter? If you don't wed Philip and Priscilla, we will petition you to the Council of Bishops." That was the situation in which Schindler decided to preside over the wedding.

After Nwabunna and his family had been evicted, after he had returned to Baruru, under strict supervision of Merogwu vigilante, who monitored his every move during the packing, to see if the gold would come out, the chiefs began to bicker with one another, each regretting the role he had just played in sacking that innocent family. This followed a dawning of information by a goldsmith that Nwabunna had actually wanted to establish industries in Merogwu with proceeds from the gold and snake skin. They were pained learning that it could have made them richer as a people. Yet, some other people were happy with his departure. They believed that it was better for him to leave with the gold ore than stay behind and continue to walk into opportunities ahead of them. A sheep once said that what it saw and kept quiet a dog saw it and started making a noise. But keeping quiet didn't make the sheep wise nor did barking make the dog stupid. As for

Nwabunna, Merogwu had barked at him and he just backed away. He seemed to have agreed that he had eaten too much of their bones and had given them little or nothing back.

CHAPTER NINETEEN
Coup De Grace

A dog on a haunt for a prey doesn't forget its kennel. It returns home irrespective of whether or not it gets a game. Hunting is the sport. Returning home alive is the medal. And when a dog goes hunting with clenched teeth, it returns with a sizeable game. Thus, its kennel becomes a kingdom and it rules it so proudly.

Nwabunna was back home now. Everywhere was calm; nobody was seen picking up stones and pelting him with them. Nobody was threatening him with death or grave. Through Okwubungbo he had already covered up many mouths with money. He left a boy with dandruff, but returned a man with wealth. He came back with two wives and eight children. The only thing he left behind was the buildings he had in Merogwu which were later claimed by Igwe Udorji, the benefactor of the land he built them on. Other properties he sold off before leaving.

He was happy to see his people once more, after twenty-one years. Most of his coevals were no longer around. Everyone and everywhere had changed in his eyes. Everything seemed new. But one thing remained constant: the fact that he did something that made life undesirable to others.

He quickly built a chateau for his household and they moved in from the apartment Ikenga built with frog money. His uncle's family members were more-or-less indifferent about his return.

He paid Igwe Ezemsinachi homage. He knew that it's only when the fireplace was cool that a dog could comfortably sleep in it.

And because he got the money, he thought it possible to stop the people from heating it by giving them food always till he would die of natural causes. He knew that there were fires to be doused despite the fact that everywhere appeared calm. One thing he didn't know, however, was that the fire of the gods didn't produce heat sometimes. It felt cold until its target had been burnt completely. He promised Igwe Ezemsinachi and his cabinet that he would build several manufacturing industries in Baruru and that he would always donate twenty- five percent of his royalty to the kingdom's purse for infrastructural development across Baruru. There were thrills and applauses from every perimeter of the palace. Igwe was elated. Red-cap men were excited. Even attendant guards, who were within earshot, were grateful. One of them was saying in his head that once the industries were completed, he would resign from his duties at the palace. Finally, Nwabunna yet again apologized for putting the people of Baruru through the throes of pain, hunger, and death, stressing that he was never proud of it. He bought Igwe Ezemsinachi a tear-rubber jeep to change his Mercedes jalopy, a rattletrap he inherited from his late father. This made Igwe's head swell. They say that when you give a child something that is bigger than his eyes, he will ask for whom you want it given to, except, of course, he has greedy big eyes.

In his euphoria, Igwe ordered one of his valets to go tell Ezemmuo to communicate to the gods that he, IgweEzemsinachi, Mmiri Na-ede Ala II of Baruru land, had forgiven Nwabunna and that he should, as a result, never be seen as one who committed a crime thenceforth.

Before Nwabunna and his team of hagiographers left the palace, he gave Igwe some overweight bag of money, wishing him a long and enduring reign on the throne. Igwe told him to join any church of his choice. "That will make the people to believe you're now a changed person," he argued. "And once they start calling you 'Brother Born-again,' then no condemnation will ever come your way again." The people around were taken aback that such counsel had to come from the mouth of a man who was supposed to stand for truth, justice, and culture. And, as if he read their minds, Igwe quickly asked Nwabunna to be committed to the things of tradition, too, observing that the people of Baruru were divided into traditional adherents and devout church people lately.

Okwubungbo was more interested in the cash than he was in the integrity of the man who tipped it. He wished in his heart that a moiety of the money could be his. Why did he tattle Nwabunna to the authorities when he committed the taboo? Why did he go to Merogwu to talk him into coming back home? It was for money's sake. Money — not morals —was the lining of his heart. He so much loved money he could die to enjoy it.

Nwabunna joined the Heaven-is-Watching-the-Earth Church of Africa much later. Urudinanwanyi took in that night, and Nwabunna, as well as Nancy, was jubilant. "The gods," he rejoiced, "have shown that they accepted their son's apologies and have, therefore, welcomed him with blessings."

As time lived, Nsogbubaruru and Onwubundu got admitted to read Civil Engineering and Business Management respectively. The family was still celebrating that breakthrough when the tanner brought Nwabunna royalty arrears from sales of the processed snake skin. According to the tanner, there was something mysterious about the snake skin — it was inexhaustible, renewable. This made him produce leather products for exports continually. Nwabunna was only going to continue prospering. The tanner couldn't agree less that it was his god that just chose to bless him. Maybe to compensate him for the pathetic heroics of his father during the Inter-kingdom War. But Akobuaku wasn't the only victim of the war, so what exactly made Nwabunna that lucky?

He built the church a magnificent cathedral, which looked like a Jacobean synagogue, the majesty of which fetched the church prestige. And they conferred on him a title as "Baba Solomon of our Time." He, similarly, built an ultra-tech skill acquisition centre for his people, in memory of his late grandfather, Mazi Uche Ikenga. The structure had a menhir with IKENGA IN OUR HEARTS EVER embossed on it. This gesture made people love him some more.

Merogwu were more bitter than bitrex when they learnt of Nwabunna's impacts on Nsogbubaruru. They regretted that those dividends would have been happening in their land and for their own people. Some of them began to suspect that his eviction was motivated by someone's personal interests. Their youths cursed themselves for participating in it, for doing themselves some disservice unknowingly. Nwabunna deserved plaudits for his smartness in keeping the gold from them, and for taking the snake skin to a Merogwu man who couldn't betray confidence. Oforbuike didn't know that napkin was a safer pouch and a child's body a safer stow than an under- bed for a man who was determined to succeed in life. Although he turned against him and led a mob to his house to recover the gold, Nwabunna was grateful to Oforbuike. He and Mama were the fulcrum of fortune in his life in loco parentis. He knew that. And he was eternally indebted to them. He prayed in his heart that, if he ever had to meet Oforbuike again, he would not let go of him; that he would make him welcome in Baruru.

Now, it was seven years since his return. Baruru was having a renaissance — an upsurge in commerce, uplift in living standard, and urbanization. Other sons and daughters of the kingdom, including those in diaspora, joined in the renaissance. They brought their wealth home and invested in their birth land, in their people and in the soul of their soil. People from other kingdoms began to migrate to Baruru to settle, to transact, and to marry. There was a sort of economic revolution and fortune rush.

"Do you still want to stone him to death?" a man asked his friend jokingly. They had been amongst those who were determined, if not desperate, to kill Nwabunna then. They were much younger at that time. "How can I be interested in stoning a savior?" he joshed his friend, with rare liveliness. "I can't kill a savior, and today is not Good Friday."

"The gods must have been deceiving us all along, making us destroy and avoid things that make life beautiful."

"Truth is, whenever you accept anything to be superior to you, it begins to control your fate. To wriggle out of it, you have to disbelieve all you have believed in."

"Nwabunna has my goodwill any day. May an arrow pierce

the head of anyone who still holds a stone against him. Let the gods stone him by themselves if they think he deserves to die."

They were still talking when two young men walked passed them. Samuel and his friend.

"So you people can't greet your elders, right?" they charged them.

"We're sorry, Mazi Azudiuto," the two young men apologized. "We're so sorry. We just forgot that people still expect to be greeted."

"You're forgiven," Azudiuto said on his companion's behalf. "Tell your uncle to wait for me by 4 pm," he said to Samuel. "I'll come around to teach him a lesson on the chess board."

"Which of my uncles?" Samuel asked, with a not-too-happy face. "How many brothers did your late father have?"

"Just one, Mazi Azudiuto."

"And you are asking which of your uncles... they told your grandfather to have more children but he refused. He was imitating White people, who hid their real lives back home, came to Africa, and deceived us."

"How can a man say that two children were enough for him," Azudiuto's friend joined in. "Two children enough for farming, warring, and trading. And allocation is shared based on population. My boy, your grandfather didn't try at all."

"Don't mind him. He's long gone and forgotten."

"My grandfather is not forgotten at all," Sam disagreed. "He lives on in me. I'm named after him, and I'll carry his legacies on."

"It's ok. Just tell your father's brother that I will come around this evening."

"With due respect, Mazi Azudiuto, I won't deliver your message."

"Why?"

"My uncle has refused to help me, and I've decided to avoid him."

"What exactly do you mean, young man?"

"I mean that you uncles of these-a-days have failed us."

"Will you shut yourself up! You should be ashamed of your terrible guts. How many nephews of his did your father help when he was alive? And you, are you not an uncle of three already? How have you helped your sisters' children? I pity your miserable existence. Your uncle has refused to help you and you have decided to avoid him. Look at you. The Nwabunna we're celebrating today, who helped him? Was it not jobs that he resorted to in Merogwu, where he had neither uncle nor anyone? Continue deceiving yourself, did you hear? Continue avoiding your uncle until you avoid your destiny. Don't go and enroll for skill acquisition. Keep roaming the whole place. Keep avoiding your uncle. Mr. Avoider. Will you get out of my sight! Now! In fact, give me back my message."

Samuel left immediately, embarrassed but not ashamed. He was happy to have told them his mind without mincing any words. They called it a practical joke, but he knew he wasn't talking moonshine. For him, it might not have been wise to have depended on and disparaged his uncle, but he was right — he believed — about the rich leaving the poor in the lurch, which had become a trend and tradition in Baruru. People saw others dying and closed their eyes on them. They said 'well done' to a badly struggling poor man, urging him to suffer some more, that his breakthrough would come in the next phase of suffering, even though he was already gasping for breath. The only thing that made the rich help a poor man was if they were sleeping with the poor man's wife, mother, sister, or his daughter, and the poor man kept quiet. Outside such amoral gains, a poor man would only be allowed to grab a bottle of drink in a gathering. That was all he could get from the fist of rich men who preferred to make donations to fellow rich men.

Moreover, a rich man preferred to give a poor man an item rather than giving him cash to buy it. They believed that nobody was indebted to help anybody in life and hence, noblesse oblige was nonsense to them. Like how a skunk fends off predators with bad smell, those rich men kept beggars at bay with stinginess. They wanted no leeches around. It was this reality of free drinks being the only thing a man could benefit from his wealthy brother that Samuel protested against. For him, an uncle was anyone who was better off and could help another who was needy. It wasn't just a man of consanguineal relationship.

After the Inter-kingdom War, people embraced all manners of evil; from deceit to 'diabolics.' People would go to their farms and return with *achere*, or leg ulcers. Things kept getting funnier with time and never seemed to improve half bit, even with intense evangelism and multiplicity of religious groups. Long and far-gone were the days when friendliness, goodness, kindness, and justice were the base of society. Funniest of all things was the fact that these evil men had affiliation with those religious groups. Nothing could have been funnier than that — a leg in religion, another in wickedness. And those wicked souls enjoyed seeing the weedy and weary around. It gave them some immoral rapture.

"Wealth that is not useful to our people is wet rot," admonished Pastor Chetachi one Sunday morning. And that was his last sermon for that congregation, because he was transferred out two days later, following a decision by a local board of deacons, who feared that his adjuring the rich to be obliged to helping those who were down with dire needs would "spoil market" for them. "He wants to chase away those who raise funds for the church. Even the Lord Jesus said that the poor will always be in our midst. Why does he, a mere man, want us to have no poor people around? He must leave."

Within the week a new cleric was sent to replace him. And it was Pastor Philip Uduma Agwu, the prince manqué of Merogwu, the man who had wanted to marry Urudinanwayi, Nwabunna's second wife who just put to bed her first children. Yes, it was Uduma, who was at the centre of the controversy which tore Merogwu to shreds, one of the results of which was the conspiracy that led to Nwabunna's forced exit.

It was a moment of surprise when he saw Nwabunna and other prominent men at the altar on his first day as a priest in Baruru. His displeasure was complicated, but he chose to control his emotion, so that he wouldn't give the congregants a negative impression on his first priestly outing in their midst. And because Baruru was a land of stubborn Christians, the stipends of priests like Philip depended on appraisals. Three weeks later, Urudinanwanyi and her family came to dedicate her daughters, the twin girls her god had blessed her with, after many years of nothing sleeping in her womb. She named them Ndidi and Onyinye, symbolic of the fact that it was in patience that she waited on her god and kept faith with her husband, and now she had been blessed with womb's fruits – two precious gifts really.

When people in Merogwu heard that Urudinanwanyi had twins, they called Nwabunna a multiple-birth-seed-oriented man, in spite of themselves. "That man is a bad boy," their youths alleged in vain talk. "He's a bad boy with a good seed stream."

It was time for Pastor Philip to bless the children and everybody could see some unease in him. It was an unease of envy. "I could have been the father of these beautiful girls, most probably," he glibbed, receiving them from two deaconesses, who had brought them to the altar. "And their mother should have been my wife," he continued, daring Nwabunna. Such a moot wool- gathering that made a man a small fry.

After the church service, Philip narrated everything to his wife, who had pestered him for the reason behind those comments and moments earlier that day, in their manse. She rebuked him for harboring malice against Nwabunna for so long and for lusting after Uru, because Uduma had said of her, "…and I still love Uru so much."

"That is not love but some irresponsible feeling," his wife countered. "She's married and you are too. So, any such admiration or feeling is immoral. You're a servant of God. You should uphold a high moral standard. I should be enough for you, Philip. I should be everything you desire in a woman, and I'm so beautiful and precious." Philip was astonished that this lady whom Bishop Schindler had called an "unbeliever" was so versed in the Word of God. He was proud of himself for not allowing another man to impose his short daughter on him simply because she wore long skirts and covered her hair every church-day. How much he did not like that long-skirt-wearing short girl that he didn't give her a chance or thought at all.

A reception followed the dedication, meanwhile, and it was well attended, with Uru's family visiting from Merogwu. They were wholly wowed by the magnificence of Nwabunna's condominium. Igwe Ezemsinachi, who since Nwabunna bought him a posh car had become a panjandrum without a self-awareness of it, apparently, was the guest of honor. One John Bondman, who came on behalf of the central government, was the special guest of honor. That was how prominent and tall Nwabunna had grown since returning. His gold fortune shed his cold scars and people's stigma against him.

A rich cultural music was giving the pomp a real pump which made the dumb to dump their alms bowls and started clapping for the singer who was some octaves better than a songbird. He sang so beautifully well that the occasion's chair cheered him with sheer crazy gladness. He was altogether excellent with his terpsichorean girls, who made men stand up by taking down their waists with some between-breath-and-death dance moves.

"Children are a precious gift from the Creator," Igwe Ezemsinachi remarked. "And the conception of these girls upon Nwabunna's return to our land clearly shows that Birthmother is glad to welcome him home." Continuing, he said, "I already told Ezemmuo to tell the gods to assume he never committed any taboo. Too, I told criers of our town to go round the kingdom and ask everybody to be at peace with him. Why would anyone harbor evil against a man who loves his people and does good things for them? Look at the many transformations he's brought to us." He equally used that opportunity to invite everybody to crystal anniversary celebration of his reign. And he was applauded with energy and enthusiasm. High noon of his speech was a proclamation that he would honor Nwabunna with a chieftaincy title as "Ukwu Gba Aka Gaa Mba Buru Aku Lota lof Nsogbubaruru," in recognition of how he had left destitute and returned with huge chrematistic substance, with which he was eradicating poverty and reducing underclass numbers in their land, through widespread industrialization and elaborate skill acquisition schemes. Again, the crowd cheered, especially those from Merogwu.

Finally, Ezemsinachi went over to Urudinanwanyi to have a carriage of her babies. He gave them gifts and received some pop and splash of powder and some balls of *nzu*, both of which were a usual ritual of kola in the homes of newly-born babies, in Nsogbubaruru.

They signified a baby's joy, goodness, and goodwill. *Nzu* was, however, to be eaten in small amounts, believed to dry up blood in the body. "Our people usually say that one doesn't see a baby's teeth without something in his hand," he had said while dropping some cash in Uru's hand.

"You will live long Igwe," Uru hailed him, as he pattered to his car to leave, rubbing the powder round his neck and on his chin, receiving a perfect and apt applause from the impressed crowd, yet again.

The ceremony was over and people returned to their homes. Uru's people went back to Merogwu, but her mother stayed back for *omugwo*. She was happy. She was blessed, especially having seen that Nancy never 'tied' her daughter's womb up, as she had alleged. Nwabunna was overwhelmed by Igwe's kind words. More esteem was the nomination for a special chieftaincy title, and most esteem was the fact that Baruru people had fallen in peace with him and now approved of his innocence, save, of course, a few, who knew within them that the gods were not happy after-all. They knew he was still in the bad books of the gods. They were disturbed that a man who did something that was explicitly forbidden by the deity that protected and fought for their foremost father, Ututu, was now absorbed, absolved, and beloved by their ruler, who should have stood for justice, to the contrary, without atonement, sacrifice, or ransom; without hearing from the deity he disobeyed, and without formal words of forgiveness from those who lost their loved ones to the disaster.

One of such people was Obibulo. And true to that name, his heart was his home. He was a thoughtful and careful man who sought for wisdom, justice, and love in everything he did. He celebrated Nwabunna's life, but refused to celebrate his defiance against the gods and his con of covering the mouths and sense of sound judgment of other people with money. Although a titled man, he refused to share in the huge sum of money which Nwabunna had given to the council of red-cap men the day he paid Igwe Ezemsinachi homage. For him, "one who eats from the pot of a dishonorable man provides answers in support of his questionable character." Obibulo withdrew himself from the anniversary committee, consequently, despite it being his obligation as a titled man.

When Ezemmuo heard about Igwe's speech, he was disappointed in him. He laughed scornfully. That was the third time Ezemsinachi was saying something scurrilous against the pantheon of Baruru. He knew the ruler's arrogance had reached its limits. He poked his staff into the soil, incanting, "when did mortals begin to give orders to the gods? And what does a child intend to achieve by striking the mouth of his father? It has to be a catastrophe." After singing satirically, he smirked, and he vented, "the gods that I serve and represent, you have heard Igwe Ezemsinachi. A child who ignores what killed his father dies in like manner. And a man who accuses the sun of being too harsh and the moon of being too mild will never see a blip of the rainbow. He has given you an instruction. Give him a situation."

Obibulo heard those words from some distance. He was coming to the shrine to enquire of Ezemmuo about the gods' take on Nwabunna's bromance with Ezemsinachi. He stood still when he deciphered a tanka of raw wrath in the voice of the traditional priest. What troubled him most was the oracle asking the gods to make Igwe to understand that "when a pregnant woman hugs a man with a jug of hot water too closely, the baby in her womb gets cold." He went no further. He turned and went home immediately. He just got a reply even though he was yet to ask his question. From that day, he restrained his legs from going to the palace, preferring having his title stripped to having his name associated with iniquity, indignity, calamity, and uncertainty. He had never been a milksop all of his life. His colleagues confirmed his latter disinterest in and resignation from palatial engagements when he absented from an emergency meeting three days to the anniversary.

Over there in Merogwu, Idika was doing badly in his business. He was in a swamp of losses and sales slump. Helpless, asked for advice from his father-in-law who was fast becoming frail in health. Oforbuike told him to go seek help from Nwabunna's hand, since Udorji, who turned him against Nwabunna, had refused to help him as he promised. And Udorji hadn't the help to be sincere. Neck deep in needs, he needed some help for himself.

In spite of himself, Idika decided to resort to Nwabunna in Baruru. But before he went, he wanted to separate from Lady Unshakable. This was a fancy way of divorcing her on the grounds of contributing nothing gainful to his life. "Are you not the one who said that you only needed a woman who would be fighting your enemies?" his father reminded him of his statements back then. There had been a day a man came quarrelling with Idika in his house over an unsettled transaction. With a click of his fingers, he asked the man to leave his house before he would unleash his wife on him. "Unleash her now," the belligerent guest dared him. "Unleash your wife on me, since she has become a dog." Lady Unshakable would have been better off if she were a dog; she was a wolfhound. She was a harridan who kept her husband's relatives at bay, as though they were his heart's harm. But she was his harm herself. She made sure they never received any monetary help from their son and brother. Now that his finances were gone, she came to her senses. But it was late already. It was about time she left, therefore. "I warned you not to marry a woman that had nothing of her own, but you didn't listen. You wanted a defender, and you picked Lady Unshakable. Now, you and your business have been shaken and you have become a beggar! Lady Unshakable has dealt with you. Go and bring in Lady Unmovable."

He put the separation decision on hold till he returned from Baruru, eventually, reasoning that marital crisis was one tall wall a man whose life was already awash with financial challenges should not want to climb.

He arrived as Nwabunna was about driving out to attend the anniversary, where he was to receive a meritorious chieftaincy title, a thing that got his ego bloated. Idika was humiliated by the magnificence and majesty of his former friend's house. "Come with me or wait till I return, Mr. Idika. Just choose one please."

"I, I, I'll wait…no, I'll go with you," he stammered scantily. He joined the driver at the front seat, as Nwabunna and his *lolo*-to-be — Nancy, of course — sat at the back of the jeep, relaxed. Uru declined to attend the occasion. She was still nursing her babies intensively, and there was no *lolo* for her. Meanwhile, the joy she derived from her joy bundles surpassed the honor of a traditional title. She was well married yet kept her bonhomie character intact.

Idika made himself a bodyguard that day. When they got to the venue, he hurried out of the car, opened the door for Nwabunna, and genuflected. This got the car owner angry. He expected some courtesy from him, yes, but not that stark servitude. So, he corrected Idika, "come, my man. I don't want that again. You bow to the gods and to the Igwe, not to me."

The ceremony was over and everybody dispersed. Back home, Nwabunna gave Idika some space to sleep over, so that in the morning he would know why he visited. It was night already. But it turned out to be a morning of mourning for Baruru people. "Igwe Ezemsinachi is dead," the sad news greeted them. What a terrible cock-a-doodle-doo that was, and it had them dabbed back from sleep. "A cloudless rain has fallen and it has soaked both our salt and garri," Nwabunna said to Idika. "Our kingdom has been smitten with a rod and our backbone smashed." Idika said nothing. He moped all through and rebuked his god in his heart for allowing such a thing to happen at a time he came to Baruru for some succor.

Nwabunna could not hear his purpose of visit any more as people trooped in and out of his house, mournful and devastated. "What saddens me more," Nwabunna lamented, "is that Igwe was full of life throughout yesterday." The people were beaten by the mystery behind his death, they were bitten by the knowledge that he had no children, and they were bitter that he passed on like his father did. But a few were not surprised, nor were they sad.

Obibulo neither mourned nor rejoiced. He called in his oldest son and counseled with him. "Never befriend a man who offended the gods of our land. Secondly, holding brief for a thief that deserves grief is like exposing yourself to flame in a scene of inflammable fluids. Don't try it ever. Finally, always take care of your farm and your barn and your children. That is where honor and integrity lie."

The council of red-cap men converged at the shrine to enquire into the actual cause of their ruler's death. "How did we offend the gods?" they asked Ezemmuo. "Is it the sins of our children, ours, or those of our ancestors that have brought this calamity upon us that Igwe had to die after celebrating the fifteenth anniversary of his reign?"

Ezemmuo laughed at their saccharine sincerity. Then he smirked and shook his head and said, "kings rule over men and the gods rule over kings. The gods choose kings and determine their days. The only answer I have for you today is this: the gods preserve the throne of the king who acknowledges their power, and they end the reign of another king who despises them for any reason. You may leave now. Go and choose your next *igwe*."

Ezemsinachi was buried befittingly. Ten cows, fifty-seven goats, countless number of fowls and yam tubers; a fusillade of one hundred gun shots, and masquerade parades.

Reign slot moved over to another division, and it was Akoli, Nwabunna's very division. They were to produce the next *igwe*. At once, Okwubungbo began to hobnob Nwabunna's house, persuading him to declare interest for *igwe*ship. That was the last thing in his mind. "You're the most prominent man around," he persuaded him. "Go for it. You should be Baruru's next ruler."

"The day your triplet sons were named in Merogwu, an *igwe* attended," recounted Idika. "The day your twin daughters were dedicated, another *igwe* came around. Doesn't that tell you something?"

Nwabunna accepted their informal nomination after-all. He got the better of his cousin and five other men. His money made the journey a trolley's walk to an attorney's alley.

Idika received words that his father-in-law was ailing badly and had to leave. He had wanted to stay back for Nwabunna's installation, but he just had to go. Nwabunna gave him a large sum of money and thanked him hugely for his counsel and company. Euphoria of victory put him in a good mind mode. "I'm not a man who remembers wrongs done to him," he had said. "Our people usually say that what a man does for his fellow man is 'take and keep it for me'." He acknowledged that Idika saved him from drudgery and introduced him to his business, and that he owed him." And Idika returned to Merogwu.

When Obibulo saw that Nwabunna had won the election, he laughed half-heartedly. He knew that praise was always going to make a puppy jump itself to lameness and that the death that was to kill a

whelp wouldn't let it perceive feces. It was his bounden duty to attend
his coronation, as a red-cap man, but he was unwilling. So, he made
up an alibi and another one. He asked his son to fix his traditional
marriage on the same date as Nwabunna's already slated installation.
Secondly, he excused himself on the ground that he had thrush and
frostbite, which left him with urinary incontinence and sore lips and
needed, therefore, some intensive care from a herbalist. Nwabunna
was on his tod as long as Obibulo was concerned. He vowed not to
ever dine with a man who was yet to pay his fine to the gods.

On the eve of the ceremony, with every arrangement down, some merriment was going on in his residence. As the revelry continued, and as some prominent people, most of whom he had peddled their influence, were upstairs congratulating the *igwe*-elect, a most terrifying thing happened. Nwabunna was a man who loved and kept afro hair always. And it was good on him. As they gloried together, a mass of concrete detached from the deck and landed on his head. It did not just hit him hard, it stuck on his bonce with some burning sensation. He slumped into unconsciousness. He was taken to Central Cottage Hospital, Baruru, for emergency treatment. Medics there stabilized him but couldn't help him any better than that.

So, his children chose to fly him abroad. Why not? He got the money. But that was not without some controversies amongst them. "We're taking him to Germany," his first son wanted.

"No," Onwubundu differed, "Ghana is where we're going. It is nearer. Accra has better hospitals than Gnishere."

"Why not Germany?"

"Because, although ill-health dreads German physicians, German germs are more powerful than Ghanaian germs."

"Germany or Ghana or anywhere else… let's start going already," Adabuasa protested. "Papa's condition is pretty critical." They flew their father to London eventually where a series of scans revealed that the concrete badly damaged his brain.

When Ezemmuo heard about what happened, he was neither surprised nor confused. He was only disappointed in his children, that instead of seeking the gods' help, they stupidly resorted to hospitals.

"A man has to stretch his hand against the gods to incur their wrath, but the gods don't need to stretch theirs to punish his guts. They just expand the pit under his feet." That was the oracle gleeing at Nwabunna.

Several procedures of surgeries couldn't save Nwabunna. He died. And when a gong announced his passing back home, sad was the happiest reality in the land amongst his admirers. However, most other people knew the gods just got themselves a sort of solace after about three decades since being offended. So, there were both Songs of Solomon and Lamentations of Jeremiah. But the thoughts of his triplet sons were not jeremiad at all. Each was more interested in the throne than in his father's tragic demise. So, from right there in London, they began to quarrel over who deserved to inherit Nwabunna's mandate. Their silly squabble beside their father's lifeless body made English medicos wonder when some coons would learn to behave themselves in a land where they needed dompas. "You kids gotta get outta here!" one Dr. Corbyn Brainsfield, a neurosurgeon, rebuked them.

Nsogbubaruru even pushed a janitor into an asphodel tree close by a patio, thinking that "problem is useful," which was the meaning of his name, was obtainable in a Whiteman's place. He was lucky to have gotten away with it.

They deposited their father's corpse in a morgue and flew home separately to lay claims on the throne. Their desperation finally disserved them when Agurubuike, the presumptive first son and apparent heir to the throne, took the matter to court. Consequently, council of *igwe*-makers, which comprised the first sons of every upper clan, disqualified them three for taking a matter of sacred sanctity as the throne of Nsogbubaruru to court, despite being the ones who rigged it for their father. You see it? Well-trained dogs are pets with a personality. Strayed ones are a stranger' spoils. Even their late father could not help being disappointed with how feral the puppies he thought he trained so well became.

The mantle moved to the next division in line of succession. And, zoom, Obibulo was chosen by lot to be the next *igwe*. But he passed it to his first son, Nnadi because of old age and its associated ailments. The young *igwe*, who was recently married, was a man of finesse, adventures, and high-brow inclinations. He loved flowers, war dance, and finger foods. Although he wasn't born yet when London ruled Gnishere, he claimed he learnt only a thing from the colonial masters: skullduggery. "I learnt the intelligence in insincerity from the white men, but I don't live by it," he had once remarked. For him, making children and subduing his enemies were ways of discovering the essence of life. He believed that fear of the gods, good food, and observation were secrets of wisdom.

During his coronation, his father said these words to him, and lo, it was the last time he was going to have to counsel with him. "People will well forget the wealth a man once had, but they will always remember what name he bore. So, be a good man first of all. It will make people to call you '*igwe*' with a good conscience." People were amazed. In a very long while, they had forgotten everything about good conscience. What mattered most to them was apparent success. Everybody was interested in rake-offs from smash-and-grabs, bumper plunders, and you-name-it. "Well," the people responded, "If his reign will restore good conscience in us, the gods be praised." None of them would deny the fact that things had been getting funnier prettily for some time, especially from the manner in which their rulers were dying. "A certain *igwe* celebrated his reign and died. Another was about beginning his own reign when he died. And now, another has been told to rule to awaken good conscience in us." That was the pabulum of the coronation.

Ezemmuo stood to live, and he said the following to Nnadi, who looked so great in his regalia and crown, which was decorated with feathers from a cock that had slept in the shrine for seven preceding market days: "My son, hear you my words, which, of course, are those of the gods, this day. The gods have never been and will never be mates with mere mortals. Do not despise them, therefore. If your scepter delivers justice to the people, you will not need an oracle to tell you the mind of the gods. They will be pleased to reveal it to you directly, and they will bless you." He removed his staff from the soil it had poked, and he left, singing some satires for Nwabunna. "He refused to take a stone from men. Now, he's taken concrete from the gods."

In the small hours of the next day, both Obibulo and Ezemmuo died, and were aged 83 and 78 respectively. The former died in his barn, the latter in the shrine, and Nwabunna died abroad.

Now, nothing is funny anymore.

APPENDIX

Abacha: cassava shreds
Achara: elephant grass
Agada: wooden bed
Agu nwanyi: a stubborn, troublesome woman; a harridan
Akpanjo: a bag of ugliness; someone that is pretty ugly
Ashebi: bridal train
Aturu: sheep
Boy-boy: a male servant
Chai: exclamation of disappointment
Dibia: native doctor
Ediabali: porcupine
Efulefu: a foolish, worthless person
Ego obi nwanyi: a portion of a woman's bride price
Egusi: melon
Ekere: slit drum
Ewoo: exclaimed surprise, disbelief, disappointment

Ezemmuo: chief priest, oracle

Ezigbo dim: my good husband

Fufu: foo-foo

Iberiberic: foolish

Igwe: a king's equivalent; a ruler over an autonomous community

Iju ase: an inquiry about a lady a man wants to marry; an inquiry into something strange

Isee: affirmative response to prayers or good wishes

Iwa akwa: an adult initiation ceremony; a rite of passage to adulthood

Iyaah: affirmative response

Jijijiji: shaking violently

Juju: charms, magical powers

Kanda: cow skin

Kpai-kpai-kpai: a knock on the door

Lolo: a female chief; a chief's wife

Mazi: mister

Mbasa: bonger fish

Mummy water: marmaid

Ngwugwu: package, parcel

Nna-anyi: our father

Nze: a high chief

Nzu: calabash chalk

Obinwa: empathy for one's child

Ochieze: insincere laughter

Ofor: staff, goodwill, prayer.

Oga: master

Ogene: metal bell

Ogiri: locust beans; fermented oil seed paste

Oka: maize

Omugwo: postpartum care

Ori: shea butter

Pami: palm wine

Papa ejima: a father of multiple births

Shasha: galore

Tiro: some sort of make-up; local cosmetic

Tufiakwa: expression of disapproval, angst

Udu: a plosive instrument

Ugba: African oil bean
Ugiri: wild mango
Uha: pterocarpus mildraedil
Ukazi: Gnetum Africanum
Ukeelu and ukeala: when you find in ukeala what you have been looking for in ukeelu, it means you have come by it rather easily; like a grail becoming a cinch
Ukwu anu: leg of an animal
Umuada: women native to a place
Umunna: kinsmen
Uru: flesh, benefit
Utukuru: some edible worms
Yeye: fake, unserious

ACKNOWLEDGMENTS

Primarily, I recognize the Department of Medical Rehabilitation, College of Medicine, University of Nigeria Enugu Campus, Class of 2020, with whom I shared many memory-worthy moments those three years. For, of course, that was where and when my writing journey began.

Additionally, I love to greet all my students at Midlands International Schools Ohiya, whom I taught Physics and Mathematics for seventeen months. Your mischiefs and innocence, goodwill and generosity, expressions and reservations, questions and contributions, suggestions and counsel blessed my imagination.

Finally, may I register my respect for and gratitude to Mrs. Chioma Abazie and Miss Ehisianya Nduka, who taught me Literature-in-English and English Language respectively at high school. The information and love they gave, plus the vision and belief they built in me, have made the world my oyster.

Yet, I can't end without being grateful to The Almighty for restoring my mother to full musculoskeletal form and function after fracturing her femur and ankle, damaging the nerve that supplies her fibula, and dislocating her shoulder joint on February 20, 2024, in a car crash, and for His other mercies towards my family. Glory to His name. Amen.

ABOUT RIZE PRESS

RIZE publishes great stories and great writing across genres written by People of Color and other underrepresented groups. Our team consists of:

Lisa Diane Kastner, Founder and Executive Editor
Joelle Mitchell, Licensing and Strategy Lead
Cody Sisco, Acquisition Editor, RIZE
Benjamin White, Acquisition Editor, Running Wild
Peter A. Wright, Acquisition Editor, Running Wild
Resa Alboher, Editor
Angela Andrews, Editor
Sandra Bush, Editor
Ashley Crantas, Editor
Rebecca Dimyan, Editor
Abigail Efird, Editor
Aimee Hardy, Editor
Henry L. Herz, Editor
Cecilia Kennedy, Editor
Barbara Lockwood, Editor
AE Williams, Editor
Scott Schultz, Editor
Rod Gilley, Editor
Kelly Ottiano, Editor
Carolyn Banks, Editor

Evangeline Estropia, Product Manager
Kimberly Ligutan, Product Manager
Pulp Art Studios, Cover Design
Standout Books, Interior Design
Polgarus Studios, Interior Design

Learn more about us and our stories at
www.runningwildpublishing.com

Loved these stories and want more?

Follow us at www.runningwildpublishing.com/rize,
www.facebook.com/runningwildpress, on Twitter @lisadkastner
@RunWildBooks @RwpRIZE

www.ingramcontent.com/pod-product-compliance
Lightning Source LLC
Chambersburg PA
CBHW051132020726
47501CB00005B/1474